The Legend of
Acorn Hollow

Also by Maureen Klovers:

The Secret Poison Garden (Rita Calabrese Mystery Series, #1)

A Secret in Thyme (Rita Calabrese Mystery Series, #2)

Murder in the Moonshine (Rita Calabrese Mystery Series, #3)

Of Masques and Murder (Rita Calabrese Mystery Series, #4)

Murder Under the Tuscan Sun (Rita Calabrese Mystery Series, #5)

Hagar's Last Dance (Jeanne Pelletier Mystery Series, #1)

Graveside Reunion (Jeanne Pelletier Mystery Series, #2)

In the Shadow of the Volcano: One Ex-Intelligence Official's Journey through Slums, Prisons, and Leper Colonies to the Heart of Latin America (memoir)

The Legend of
Acorn Hollow

Maureen Klovers

The Legend of Acorn Hollow is a work of fiction. Names, characters, places, and incidents are either the product of the author's imagination or are used fictitiously. Any resemblance to actual persons, living or dead, or to actual events is purely coincidental.

Cover design by Ken Leeder

For my dad, the world's most fun grandpa, who is young at heart...and yet the centenarian black widow's biggest fan!

GLOSSARY

(Note: Only terms that are not immediately obvious from the text are included here. Approximate pronunciation shown in parentheses. It.=Italian, Sp.=Spanish, and Fr.=French.)

Acqua passata (ak-wa pa-SA-ta) – It. Passed water (i.e. water under the bridge).

Aspetta (as-PAY-ta) – It. Wait! This is the informal version of the command, used for family and friends.

Bellissime (bell-EES-ee-may) – It. Beautiful (plural, for a group of women).

Capisci (ca-PEE-she) – It. You (informal) understand.

Caro/cara (CAR-o, CAR-a) – It. Dear (for a man if ending in -o, for a woman if ending in -a). A term of endearment.

Certo/certo che non! (CHAIR-toe, CHAIR-toe kay non) – It. Certainly/of course, certainly not!

C'est pas possible! (Say PA po-SEE-blay)—Fr. It's not possible/I can't believe it!

Che peccato! (Kay Pay-CA-to)—It. What a shame! (Literallly, what a sin!)

Che pensate voi? (Kay pen-SA-tay voy)—It. What do you (plural) think?

Chocolat chaud (SHOW-co la show)—Fr. Hot chocolate.

Ci vediamo nella mattina (Chee ved-ee-AM-o nel-la ma-TEEN-a)—It. We will see each other in the morning (i.e. see you in the morning.)

Dai! (DIE!) —It. Come on!

Esatto (Ay-ZA-to)—It. Exactly!

Figlio (FEEL-yo)—It. Son.

Ha ragione (Ah ra-JONE-ay)—It. Is right (literally, has reason).

Locrio de pollo (Lo-cree-oh day PO-yo)—Sp. A Dominican chicken and rice dish.

Nonna (NO-na)/nonno (NO-no) – It. Grandma/Grandpa.

Peut être (Poo-ET)—Fr. Maybe.

Précisément (PRAY-seez-mon)—Fr. Exactly!

Stonzo (STRONTZ-o) – It. A not very nice word for a not very nice man.

Ta fille (Ta FEEL)—Fr. Your daughter.

Togliti le scarpe (TOL-yee-tee lay SCAR-pay)—It. Take off your shoes.

Vedova (VE-doh-va) -It. Widow.

Zio/zia (tsee-o, tsee-a) – It. Uncle/aunt.

ACKNOWLEDGMENTS

This book was inspired by a visit to Washington Irving's charming wisteria-draped home, Sunnyside, in New York's Hudson Valley, and the incomparable storyteller Jonathan Kruk, who brought Irving's tale to life and left my husband and me spellbound. So thanks must go, first and foremost, to Jonathan Kruk and my marvelous in-laws, Jeri and Kevin Gormley, who watched our daughter while we gallivanted around Sleepy Hollow.

Ken Leeder in the U.K. created several beautiful cover concepts for me, and the wonderful members of the Cozy Up with Kathy and the Cozy Mystery Village Facebook groups helped me pick the winning design.

I also had fabulous manuscript editors: my mother, Mary Klovers; my sister, Christelle Klovers; and my fellow author, Eileen Haavik McIntire, creator of *The 90s Club* cozy mystery series. My dad, Kris Klovers, drew on his legal expertise to assist with issues related to wills and powers of attorney.

My husband, Kevin Gormley, also served as an early reader, as well as a sous-chef, taste tester, and food photographer while I perfected the recipes for this book. The recipe for apple crisp is a long-standing favorite of ours, and Kevin is a whiz with the pastry blender!

Even with all of this help, mistakes have undoubtedly crept into this book, and any and all mistakes are my own.

More generally, I would like to thank those friends and readers who have gone above and beyond to promote my books. At the top of this list is my friend Fran Mahoney, who never misses an opportunity to hawk my books to his various book clubs. I would also be remiss if I did not thank my mother-in-law, who sends my books to friends far and near, and my own mother, who tried to get my first "novel," *The Two Greasos*, written at age six, into the Whitefish Bay Library. While she was not successful then, I'm proud to say that most of my Rita Calabrese books are now on the shelves at my hometown library! I would also like to thank Rita boosters Kathy Kaminski, Nicole Dawson Vickers, Julie Cline, and Barbara Brown; Heather Doyle Harrison, who generously invited me for an author takeover of the Cozy Mystery Party Facebook group; the Cozy Mystery Review Crew for many lovely reviews; and fellow mystery authors Libby Klein and Rosalie Spielman.

It takes a village!

Chapter One

For the citizens of Acorn Hollow, it was an article of faith that the Sleepy Hollow in Washington Irving's tale was, in fact, their own bucolic hamlet. They took ghoulish delight in showing visitors the crumbling, oxblood-red, one-room schoolhouse where greedy Ichabod Crane had been a little-loved schoolmaster; the Van Tassel farm, where Ichabod had vied with Brom Bones for the hand of the beautiful Katrina; and the graceful stone arch bridge where Ichabod had encountered the headless horseman and met his demise. Every year, they spent the entire month of October reveling in this connection. They hosted tours of the graveyard surrounding the white-steepled old Dutch church, raced horses with headless horsemen down Main Street, and re-enacted *The Legend of Sleepy Hollow*.

And every year the commemoration dominated the front page of the area's only newspaper, the *Morris County Gazette*, which was why star local reporter Rita Calabrese was now staring at a jumble of mossy cobbles at the base of the old stone bridge and straining to hear her source over the sound of rushing water.

"Right there," Emma Schmalzgruben was saying, pointing a pale, gnarled, veiny finger, "just at the water's edge. That's where the smashed pumpkin was found when Ichabod Crane disappeared. His horse Gunpowder was wandering in the brambles just beyond."

They were seated in the widow's golf cart, the only vehicle she was legally allowed to drive. Rita squinted through her bifocals and thumbed through the dog-eared volume of Irving's short stories that lay open on her lap. "I don't see any brambles. And Irving didn't say anything about them."

Emma shot Rita a piercing look. "There were brambles," she insisted, pursing her lips until they were all but invisible, "and they were still here when I was a girl, before the Van Tassels let the farm go and these woods sprang up."

She said this in an accusatory tone, as if it were the trees' fault that the Van Tassel farm was nothing more than a few foundations and a faded memory.

Rita cast a dubious glance at the offending trees, whose trunks shot up at least six stories high. But she supposed it was possible that there had once been brambles there, since the widow Schmalzgruben was the oldest person in Acorn Hollow, a repository of the town's living memory. She was so old that she had buried three husbands, boasted of having voted for Herbert Hoover, and claimed, as a little girl, to have taken part in temperance marches—and more than a few axe-wielding raids on saloons.

"I knew the Van Tassels growing up," the widow said. She jutted her chin out defiantly as if daring Rita to contradict her. "The family matriarch was still living when I was a girl, and *her* great-grandmother was the Katrina Van Tassel whose story inspired Washington Irving. So the real Katrina told the real story to her great-granddaughter, and her great-granddaughter to me."

The widow then fell silent, and Rita knew that she was in for a long wait. Being the mother of three grown children was excellent preparation for a career as a journalist. The trick with any interrogation—whether of a four-year-old caught with his hand in the cookie jar, a teen surprised while sneaking through the window at three a.m., or a recalcitrant interviewee—was to say as little as possible, until the culprit (or source) just couldn't help him or herself and blurted out a confession.

"Irving got it largely right," the widow at last grudgingly admitted, "especially about poor Ichabod's appearance. He did have the most awful snipe nose and a big head and scrawny neck that really did look just like a weathercock. But Irving took some artistic license. Most significantly, of course, the location. Irving got his inspiration for the tale during a stay right here in Acorn Hollow, but he set the story in Sleepy Hollow, down near Tarrytown. I can't imagine why. Perhaps out of some misplaced concern for the privacy of those involved. But then, if it was privacy he was after, surely he'd have changed the names. But he didn't, because there was a real Ichabod Crane right here in Acorn Hollow. And as for those who say the character was based on that attention-seeking impostor of a schoolteacher Jesse Merwin in Kinderhook—

Kinderhook, of all places!—well, I've got a bridge I'd like to sell them."

The widow's dark eyes were flashing, and she shook her head indignantly so that her snow-white bun bobbed violently up and down. This was the widow at her most severe, although her aspect, truth be told, was always rather severe. She nearly always wore a black, long-sleeved, ankle-length dress and black button-up boots, the sort of widow's weeds that were last in style when the Titanic sank. She always accessorized with something red, which had sparked more than a few unkind comparisons to a black widow spider. The fact that she was rumored to have killed at least a couple of her three husbands did not help, nor did her habit of perching on their gleaming white marble tombs and reading the newspaper aloud as if they were just enjoying a leisurely Sunday morning at home.

"And," the widow went on, eyes blazing, "the headless horseman was not even a Hessian. Some say that the inspiration was a Hessian soldier whose head was blasted off at the Battle of White Plains, which is nine miles from Tarrytown. But everyone knows it was a local boy from a good Dutch family whose head was blown off at the Battle of Saratoga Springs before his headless corpse was brought back here for burial. His mother was so distraught at him being buried without a head that, at the last minute, she thrust the family's prized pumpkin into the coffin, carved up with his facial features. And that's why he rides about with a jack-o-lantern on his head."

"I never thought it made any sense for a Hessian to ride about with a pumpkin on his head."

"Exactly!" The widow thumped the hard plastic seat of her golf cart. "But that's the problem nowadays—no one ever thinks. They're lemmings!"

"Mmmm, so true," Rita murmured sympathetically, hoping to forestall the widow's oft-repeated rant against modern, "newfangled" ways. After all, Rita was on a deadline, and she still need to glean some new nugget of information—the more sensational, the better—about the two more recent cold-case disappearances linked to the headless horseman.

Rita jutted her chin in the direction of the riverbank. "So this is the exact spot where mobster Joey Gambone disappeared in 1936, right? And your nephew Bobby Bruickhuisen in 1962?"

"Who can say?" The widow's bony shoulders shot up. "No eyewitness can place them at this exact spot. All that can be said for certain is that, in both cases, they were last seen headed in this direction, and this is where their vehicles were found. Joey Gambone's Ford, one of those flat-topped models with the big sideboard—the same model driven by Dillinger and Bonnie and Clyde—was flipped over in the river, marooned on some rocks. The smashed pumpkin was right behind it, there, at the water's edge. And twenty-six years later, Bobby's motorbike and the smashed pumpkin were found at almost that very same spot, though Bobby's motorbike was on the riverbank."

Rita followed the widow's finger with her gaze. "They didn't put Bobby's motorbike in the river," Rita murmured, "because then it might actually be swept downstream. They wanted it to be found."

"That's always been my theory. But as to why, I've never figured that out. Why call attention to your crime and risk getting caught?"

"As a warning to others, or to throw the police off the track."

The widow frowned. "Well, in that case it worked. More than fifty years later, they still haven't got one good solid lead."

Rita looked back at the riverbank and, for a moment, she felt as though she were transported back in time. She pictured the birch tree, shorter and spindlier than it was now, but with leaves in equally fantastic autumnal splendor, keeping vigil over the motorbike, forlorn and abandoned, the water lapping at its back wheel. Her heart broke for Bobby's mother. She knew that if any of her children disappeared, she would go to the ends of the earth to find them.

"So what do you think happened to each of them?"

"Ichabod?" The widow started ticking them off on her gnarled, veiny fingers. "Brom Bones either killed him or scared him off. That's why Katrina never married Brom—she always suspected him of murder. She married a poor cooper instead, had thirteen children, and then died in childbirth—or so they say." The widow laughed. "For my money, I'd say she died of fright, just thinking of adding one more to her brood."

Rita nodded sympathetically.

"Joey Gambone? Killed by his wife probably. He was two-timing her and she was not a woman to be trifled with. My mother always told me to scurry across the street if I saw her coming. And Bobby? They never found hide nor hair of him. Whoever killed him was thorough—and cruel. My sister followed him to the grave not six months later without having been able to bury her son."

They watched in silence as a torrent of red and gold leaves shot over the rapids and flowed swiftly towards the stream's confluence with the Hudson. Out of the corner of her eye, Rita saw the widow's dark eyes filled with tears. Since the widow was childless, she and her nephew had been especially close. But just as soon as the tears appeared, the widow blinked them back. That was the widow—always stoic, always in control.

Rita attempted a joke to lighten the mood. "So, you don't believe a headless horseman was behind all of this?"

But the widow did not even crack a smile. "The living have far better motives for murder than the dead." Then the widow slapped her knee, so bony that Rita could make out its sharp contours through her long black dress. "Although I can think of more than a few people I'd like to haunt after I'm dead!"

With a disconcertingly gleeful cackle, the widow revved up her golf cart and they eased back onto the road. Rita looked over her shoulder and cast one last look at the hauntingly beautiful spot where three men had met their demise—or at least where someone wanted the townspeople to *think* they had met their demise.

"Speaking of death," the widow said suddenly, "I was hoping to ask a favor."

"A favor?"

Rita was puzzled. She was already the executor of the widow's will and had her healthcare power of attorney. She could not imagine what more the widow could need. Plus, Rita had the sneaking suspicion that, somehow, the widow would manage to outlive them all.

"I would like you to cater my funeral," the widow said. "Next Friday."

Chapter Two

If the widow had asked her to cater any other event, Rita would not have been that surprised. Rita, after all, was a nineteen-time champion of the St. Vincent's pasta-making competition, the seven-time winner of the Acorn Hollow pie-making contest, and generally regarded as the best home cook in Morris County, if not the entire Hudson Valley. She was renowned for her Italian desserts—creamy, cocoa-dusted tiramisu, chocolate-drenched peanut butter biscotti, and overstuffed, sinfully delicious cannoli. Rita's lasagna was second to none, and something people actually looked forward to when recovering from surgery. And no one could match her inventiveness for putting garden produce to good use— her vine-ripened San Marzano tomatoes, nurtured in her imported volcanic soil, became gazpacho and bruschetta; Italian eggplants the color of purple velvet were transformed into caponata, *pasta alla norma*, and eggplant parm.

But she had never been asked to cater a funeral—and certainly not for a person still very much living and breathing.

"Friday?" Rita said weakly. "How do you know you'll be, er, that is—"

"Oh, no!" the widow exclaimed, showing her crooked little yellow teeth. "It's not that kind of funeral. It's not a party where everyone sits around glumly, making polite chit-chat in the presence of a waxy, rouged-up dead body. Where's the fun in that?"

Rita begged to differ. She rather enjoyed funerals. They were essentially family reunions, but with better food. And when she was working, there was no better place to gather information for a murder investigation.

"Oh, I don't know," Rita said. "Funerals for Sal's relatives can be, well, if not fun, at least entertaining."

Rita winced remembering how one funeral for a relative of her husband had actually involved men in dark suits swarming in and sticking pins in the body, just to make sure he was really dead. Sal was the white sheep of a rather dark family tree, and Rita lived in fear that their youngest son Vinnie would one day migrate to its shady recesses.

"No, no!" the widow cried with a dismissive wave of the hand. "I want this to be a delightful little soiree, and I want to be there in the flesh, so to speak, to enjoy it. I want to hear all the lovely little things—all lies, but lovely nonetheless—that people say about me."

"Ah, so it's a celebration of life party."

"You could call it that, I suppose. But I prefer to call it a funeral. The name gives it such a lovely sense of occasion. Plus, I think it will boost attendance."

The widow steered the golf cart onto Main Street, and they crawled along at five miles an hour, holding up traffic. "I leave the menu up to you," the widow shouted over the honking horns in that rich, plummy voice that always put Rita in mind of a society matron from the thirties, someone fabulously rich and clad in furs who would endow an orphanage or two. "The refreshments should be very fresh, very seasonal. And don't skimp on the good stuff. Full fat, full sugar, full everything. If I'm going to die, I want to die happy."

"But you're not going to die," Rita pointed out. "Not for years, anyway."

"Oh, don't be too sure of that. My ticker may be good, but someone could always try to ease me out of this world a bit early."

"But surely you're not insinuating that someone wants to murd—"

"Heavens to Betsy!" the widow suddenly exclaimed, glancing at her watch. "I'm going to be late for rehearsal."

Rita frowned, confused. She could only think of one rehearsal going on in town right now, and she couldn't see how the widow could be involved. "Of *The Legend of Acorn Hollow?*"

"Of course." The widow looked very pleased with herself. "I parlayed my role as town historian into a job as the historical consultant for the Acorn Hollow Players." She winked at Rita. "I haven't been this popular since the Eisenhower Administration."

Rita sat in the back of the darkened auditorium, trying to wrap her mind around the idea that she was going to cater a funeral for the very much alive woman sitting beside her. But the widow seemed to have forgotten all about her strange request; she was enjoying the rehearsal of *The Legend of Acorn Hollow*, which purported to tell the story of the three unsolved disappearances linked to the headless horseman.

The first act was a faithfully rendered word-for-word performance of the original *The Legend of Sleepy Hollow*, performed by the town's only semi-professional storyteller, Sylvester Schmidt, who doubled as the high school drama teacher and the director of the Acorn Hollow Players.

When Sylvester's performance ended, Rita, the widow, and the actors waiting in the wings applauded enthusiastically. Then the black velvet curtain came down.

When it rose again, they had leapt forward in time at least a century. Orlando Rinaldi, the town's most eligible sixty-year-old bachelor, was dressed in a pinstripe suit, a fedora, and spats. Rita's identical twin sister, Rose, was wearing a slinky silk outfit—more of a slip, really—and standing on her tiptoes.

And they were locked in a passionate embrace. They may have been playing their assigned roles, as 1930s mobster Joey Gambone and his moll, Viviana, but there was no fooling Rita. For her sister, at least, the passion was anything but feigned. Rose had had designs on Orlando ever since his divorce seventeen years ago, and it was no accident that she'd been cast alongside him. Rose hadn't acted a day in her life—on stage at least, said a snarky and hastily silenced voice in Rita's head—but Rose was the county's top-selling real estate agent and she'd promised Sylvester a steep discount on her commission if he cast her opposite Orlando.

Rose was used to getting whatever she wanted because she nearly always did—except, so far, when it came to Orlando.

Squirming in her seat, Rita couldn't tell if she was more discomfited by her sister's ardor, or by the comparison the audience was bound to make between Rita and her much more glamorous twin, whose charms were on ample display. It was hard to believe that Rose was pushing seventy, with her toned limbs and gravity-defying, just barely concealed cleavage. Sure, they were both short, with swarthy complexions, bright dark eyes, and strong Italian features, but Rose was the picture of the successful businesswoman, chic in sleeveless sheath dresses, chunky gold jewelry, and teetering leopard-print heels, with expertly highlighted blond hair.

Time had been far less kind to Rita—for which she roundly, and loudly, blamed her family. Her eldest son, Marco, had been a joy (not least because he was a *mamma*'s boy through and through), but it seemed as if she had sprouted a new wrinkle and a new gray hair for every day she had spent under the same roof with her two younger children—headstrong, unlucky-in-love Gina and Rita's late-in-life problem child Vinnie. All that running to the principal's office on account of Vinnie had given her plantar fasciitis, which had condemned her to a lifetime of dowdy flats. Endless cooking for her family had made her rather *grossa*, which made chic form-fitting dresses out of the question. And all the time she spent cleaning up their messes—literally and figuratively—left very little time for personal grooming, which was why she seemed to always have a silver stripe down the part of her bushy black hair.

Rita breathed a sigh of relief when Orlando finally broke off their kiss and pushed her sister away. Then they began arguing about whether he would leave his wife for her.

"Your sister's really something," the widow murmured and then laughed. "If I didn't know better, I'd think she wasn't acting."

"You don't miss much, do you?"

"People think that once you get old, you lose your faculties. But they forget that every year you get more experience reading people and situations, dealing with disappointment, handling conflict. You get better at living."

"Tell that to my kids. They don't seem to think that sixty-eight years of living has taught me anything."

The widow laughed.

Joey Gambone's wife, played by recently widowed Penny Albanese, now entered stage right for the dramatic showdown between wife and mistress.

Rita could almost feel the waves of heat coming off her sister as she squared off against Penny. She wished her sister weren't quite so obvious. She didn't like the idea of people laughing at her sister behind her back, plus she rather suspected that Rose's sheer obviousness was a turn-off for Orlando. Judging from his greedy, grasping ex-wife and his recently murdered fiancée (whose killer was only caught, Rita thought with a touch of pride, because of her investigation), Orlando preferred high-maintenance, not terribly independent women who at least initially played hard to get. Orlando was a bit old-fashioned, almost chivalrous, while Rose was shockingly modern, like a Millennial trapped inside an exquisitely preserved middle-aged body.

The fight ended with both women storming off. When the curtain rose on the next scene, the mobster was driving his Ford on the lonely road out of town. The set design was ingenious. The boxy black vehicle with its snout-shaped hood slowly made its way up a ramp and over a platform made to look like the old stone bridge. The steeple of the old Dutch church glowed a ghostly white in the background and, like a radio show of old, the sound effects underscored the drama: church bells tolled as the hour struck midnight, Joey's Ford backfired as it struggled up the incline, owls hooted, crickets chirped, and the stream rushed past boulders.

"Vinnie is such a brilliant set designer," the widow whispered.

"My Vinnie?"

"Yes, of course—your Vinnie."

This was news to Rita. She knew her son was working on the set, in addition to having a role in the third act. And she knew, of course, that he was studying mechanical design at the local community college. But she had no idea that he was this creative—at least, for anything other than a prank.

"I guess he's motivated," the widow said. "Love will do that to a man."

Rita stared at the widow, open-mouthed. "*Love?*" she squeaked.

But the widow would say no more.

Suddenly, the clip-clop of horses' hooves pounding on pavement drowned out the nocturnal sounds of

Acorn Hollow. A mechanical horse appeared from stage right, in slow but steady pursuit of the Ford. Astride the horse was a billowing black cape that flowed out as though there were an invisible torso underneath. And bobbing just above the collar was a jack-o'-lantern, illuminated from within to reveal a grotesque grin and hollow, gaping eyes.

The effect was mesmerizing, spellbinding. Rita felt her chest puff up with pride, and the swelling only increased when there was a sudden puff of smoke and the Ford seemed to vanish into thin air. The stage suddenly went black. A split second later, the lights came up to reveal the Ford suddenly down below, tossed against a few rocks and brambles, with a smashed pumpkin beside it.

"Now," a disembodied voice announced loudly, "we invite the audience to vote. Who killed Joey Gambone?"

Rita and the widow played along with the actors' attempt to make the show interactive, Rita raising her hand for the mistress and the widow choosing the wife.

But the real question in Rita's mind was not who killed Joey Gambone, but how she had missed her son's transformation into a very accomplished magician and artist.

Chapter Three

Just as the lights were dimming for the third act—the dramatization of Bobby Bruickhuisen's 1962 disappearance—Rose slid into the seat beside Rita.

"Well?" she said. "What did you think?"

"*Troppo ovvia*," Rita said in a low voice between gritted teeth. She had switched to their native Italian in a bid to keep their conversation from the widow who, despite all appearances to the contrary, had excellent hearing.

"Well, of course I'm obvious. What is this—sixth grade? I want Orlando to realize I'm interested so he'll ask me out already."

"Trust me, he knows," Rita said. "Hard as it may be to believe, there are a handful of men on earth who are just going to escape your net."

"Not Orlando. Not this time."

"Lord help him," the widow deadpanned.

"Oh, hush," Rose muttered.

Stifling her laughter as best she could, Rita tried to concentrate on the third act. Her son Vinnie had been cast as Vito, a local bad boy and loyal friend of Kate Van Tassel, who was a descendent of the ill-starred Katrina

Van Tassel. Clad in a black leather jacket, a white T-shirt, and jeans, with a cigarette dangling from his lips, her son reminded her of a young James Dean.

The widow must have been thinking the same thing because she took a sharp intake of breath and said, "I bet his dance card's all filled up."

"Vinnie can't dance to save his life."

"It doesn't matter," the widow said, "when you look like that."

What surprised Rita even more than his appearance was the fact Vinnie could actually act. He looked brooding, dangerous—the antithesis of her sweet but aimless prankster—and, despite having relatively few lines, she found her eye was continuously drawn to him. She was fascinated by his subtly shifting body language as he observed the two rivals for Kate's affections, Bobby and Sandro.

"That was some inspired casting," the widow murmured into Rita's ear. "Vito was stockier than your Vinnie and a few years younger of course, but the mannerisms are just right. Now Jake Johnson"—she pointed at the sandy-haired boy onstage—"looks a bit like my Bobby, especially in profile, and he's student body president, just like my nephew was."

"What about the boy playing Sandro?"

"Tommy DePalma," the widow said, and Rita nodded with a glimmer of recognition. She sang in the St. Vincent's funeral choir with the matriarch of the DePalma clan. When Angela DePalma wasn't belting out "On Eagle's Wings" in a key so high Rita had occasionally feared for the stained-glass windows, she was singing the praises of her grandson Tommy, the star of the Acorn Hollow Squirrels' football team.

With a wink, the widow added, "And in a strange case of art imitating life, I hear Jake and Tommy are both angling after your young protégé."

The widow inclined her head in the direction of the tall, slim, dark-skinned girl at center stage.

"Ana!" Rita had been so mesmerized by Vinnie that she had somehow failed to notice that her teenaged colleague, Ana Rivera, had been cast as Kate Van Tassel. "She's my peer, not my protégé. It's quite humbling—annoying, really—to be occasionally scooped by a seventeen-year-old."

The widow laughed. "How do you think I feel," she asked, "when we have presidents of our country—leaders of the free world—young enough to be my grandson?"

"It's a brave new world."

"So it is—although I'm not sure I want to keep living in it."

Rita cast a sharp glance at the widow, who waved a pale, almost spectral, hand in the darkness.

"Just the idle talk of an old lady, dear. Don't mind me." Rita felt the widow's scaly hand on her arm, then a surprisingly strong squeeze. "There's my younger self's cameo appearance," the widow whispered. "And look who they have playing me—Penny Albanese. She's a mite older than I was at the time and of course I would never show that much décolleté, but I consider it quite a compliment. She's very glamorous, don't you think? And so versatile too, to go from playing the wronged wife of Joey Gambone in Act Two to prim-and-proper me in Act Three."

The widow cast an apologetic glance over at Rose, who returned the look with a supercilious, defiant stare. Rose apparently did not share the widow's enthusiasm for Penny. Rita wondered if their onstage rivalry carried on offstage as well.

"I didn't realize," Rita said, "you were at the party right before Bobby disappeared."

"Of course I was!" the widow hissed over the fireworks erupting on stage, where Ana was re-enacting Kate Van Tassel's tearful confession that she was pregnant but refusing to name the father. "I was not only Bobby's aunt, but Kate's mother's best friend. I attended all the Van Tassel parties, and the cast party for *The Legend of Sleepy Hollow* was no different except, of course, that there were a lot of teenagers there."

"So Kate," Rita said slowly, "played her ancestor Katrina, your nephew Bobby played Ichabod Crane, and Sandro played Brom Bones?"

The widow nodded.

"And just like Ichabod Crane—whom he played— Bobby disappeared...."

Rita felt a sudden chill go down her spine. She did not consider herself to be the least bit superstitious. She enjoyed the headless horseman races and ghost stories as much as the next person, but she regarded them as just that—stories.

And yet, as she snuck a glance onstage at her son— that glowering heartthrob who was at once familiar and yet, suddenly, terrifyingly alien—she suddenly feared for him, and for Jake and Tommy and her dear Ana.

What if there *were* some sort of curse? Not involving the ghost of a Hessian mercenary, but rather the flesh-

and-blood passions that the tale seemed to dredge up, a recurring tragedy with a beautiful young woman at the eye of the storm.

"And what about Vito?" Rita whispered into the widow's ear as she watched her son onstage. Vinnie, Vito. Their names, their physical appearance—it was all too eerily similar. "Did he have a role to play in *The Legend of Sleepy Hollow*?"

"Just as an extra, I think." The widow frowned. "Or maybe he worked on the set—I forget."

"Was he in love with Kate, too?" Rita murmured as she watched Ana cross the stage and whisper something into her son's ear. Then Ana ran off stage, followed by the two boys playing her suitors and then the actors playing her father and brother.

"Oh, yes, Vito was very much in love with her, too. He married her, you know—later. Raised her son as if it were his own. Until well..."

The widow's voice cracked, and in the dim lighting, Rita thought she saw a thin sheen of tears veil the widow's rheumy brown eyes. Then the widow shook her head, as if putting something firmly out of her mind.

"Until what?"

"It doesn't matter now." The widow sighed. "Your Vinnie really captures Vito well. No one can brood quite like Vinnie."

Rita smiled weakly, as if the widow were not telling her anything she hadn't learned the hard way during those horrid teenage years. But the truth was that Vinnie had tried her patience in myriad ways, but brooding was not one of them. He'd commandeered all the high school cafeteria trays for a sledding competition, kidnapped the rival Mount Washington Bulldogs' mascot and paraded him around town in an Acorn Hollow Squirrels' costume, and even suspended the high school football coach's car over the pool. But through it all, through the endless visits to the principal's office, her exasperated pleas, and her husband's incandescent bursts of temper, Vinnie had remained sweet and clueless—infuriatingly so.

The spotlight had now centered on Vinnie, who was staring offstage in the direction that everyone had fled. She knew it must be an optical illusion, but she could swear she could see tears in his big puppy dog brown eyes.

"Emma," Rita said as Vinnie ran off stage after Ana and the other actors, "when you said Vinnie was in love, you didn't mean with Ana, did you?"

The widow turned to regard her with an enigmatic smile but said nothing. Now, there was a snicker from the other direction. It was an earthy, almost bawdy laugh, and it was coming from her twin.

Rita turned on her sister. "Well?" she snapped. "You've been in rehearsals with both of them."

Rose shrugged. "*Forse.*"

"Maybe? That's all you can say?"

"I have seen them talking, and he does drive her home."

"On his motorbike?"

Rita was incredulous. She could not imagine her eminently responsible teenaged colleague getting on that rumbling, rattling deathtrap, period—much less with her son. Ana was a straight-A student. She was disciplined, driven, and poised, hardly the sort who would risk getting entangled with a twenty-two-year-old man-child going nowhere fast.

The stage went black, and in the blackness, an uncomfortable image arose in Rita's mind's eye, unbidden, of just how close Vinnie and Ana would have to be to keep Ana safely on the bike.

"I'm going to have nightmares," she muttered to her sister, sinking lower in her seat, "all because of you."

"As you should," Rose said. "She's a minor."

Rita shuddered. The stage lights flipped on again to reveal a scene eerily reminiscent of the last scene in Act Two—the bridge, the white-steepled church, hooting owls and rushing water.

"How about this?" Rose muttered. "You get me together with Orlando, and I'll keep Ana and Vinnie apart."

"How am I going to do that?"

"Oh, you're resourceful. I'm sure you'll think of something."

Rita couldn't argue with that. If there was one thing being a mother, a reporter, and a sleuth had taught her, it was to be resourceful. And so, before she had time to properly think it through, she muttered, "Deal."

Onstage, there was a sputtering that grew louder. Then a motorbike chugged slowly across the stage. The sandy-haired boy from the prior scene was riding it, and Rita heard the widow gasp beside her.

She knew what was going through the widow's mind: Was this what her nephew Bobby's last moments had really been like?

Now the sound of hoofbeats, muffled at first, grew louder, until it all but drowned out the motorbike. Rita could feel her heartbeat syncing with the pounding on the stage; she could feel the tension in every limb.

This is just a play, she told herself.

But then she reminded herself it was more than that; it was also a re-creation of a real-life tragedy.

The sandy-haired boy playing Bobby looked around frantically and tried desperately to accelerate, but the bike would only plod along. He had reached the bridge when the horse appeared from stage right in hot pursuit. Once again, the cape billowed out majestically behind the shadowy figure, and the jack o'lantern grinned its ominous grin.

Rita felt the widow reach for her, the bony fingers almost clawing into her wrist. But Rita did not cry out or push the widow away. When the motorbike was at the top of the bridge and the headless horseman just below, the stage went black.

There was a startling neigh, as if the horse had reared up, spooked.

Then there was an ominous thud and the lights went up.

Rita had expected to see the motorbike cast down below the bridge, in the spot the widow had pointed out to her, with a smashed pumpkin below.

And that was all there, of course. But beneath the smashed pumpkin was something else—the crumpled figure of Jake Johnson.

For a moment, there was total silence. Was this all part of the act?

But then the widow leapt to her feet and cried out in a quavering voice, "Bobby?" as if the actor were indeed her nephew, just as a clutch of actors rushed in from the wings.

"Jake?" the director called, springing from his seat. "Are you all right?"

And then from above the stage, a plaintive wail echoed through the auditorium. "That wasn't supposed to happen!"

Chapter Four

An hour later, after Jake had been hustled off in an ambulance and Rita had gotten quotes from everyone at the rehearsal, Rita was in her backyard, picking gloriously ripe McIntosh apples while talking to her blue-haired, tongue-ringed, if-it-bleeds-it-leads editor.

"Why do I hear birds chirping?" barked Sam (short for Samantha, although she never liked to admit it).

"Because I'm outside picking apples."

"Apples! Rita, how can you be thinking about apple picking at a time like this? We've got a killer story on our hands: 'The Legend of Acorn Hollow Returns.' We've got an attempted homicide with a pumpkin—can you believe it, a pumpkin!—as a murder weapon."

Rita sighed. She liked her editor's feisty spirit, but sometimes the drama was too much. "I'll get you your story by six, Sam, but you're barking up the wrong tree. It was just an accident. Roxanne got confused about which rope to pull. She opened the wrong trap door, so instead of Jake being whisked away, he was stuck onstage when the pumpkin fell and—splat!—he just happened to be in the way. And he's hardly dying. I heard the EMTs say it was just a minor concussion."

"Sure," Sam said darkly, "and we all know what that's code for—a traumatic brain injury. He'll probably go off the rails and kill himself—or become the next school shooter. They'll call us Colombine-on-the-Hudson."

"Really, Sam—"

"Besides, that's not what Ana says."

The mention of her young colleague brought Rita up short. "Ana?"

Her voice sounded strange, unnatural. Usually, she said her colleague's name with warmth, even grudging admiration. But now irritation, suspicion—even envy—had crept in. Why? Because she was afraid of being scooped yet again? Or because that slip of a girl had captured her son's heart—and just might lead to his ruin?

"Ana Rivera," Sam said, sounding annoyed. "You know, your colleague? The author of our hit 'Teen Talk' column? That Ana. Anyway, she followed Jake to the hospital."

"How?"

"How what?"

"How did she get to the hospital?"

There was an exasperated sigh. "Vinnie's motorbike, I assume, since I could hear him in the background." Rita plucked a plump red apple with a glorious splotch of green and plunked it down in her bucket, imagining it was her sister's head. So much for her Rose's pledge to keep Vinnie and Ana apart.

"Really, Rita," Sam said. "Are you going to blame your son for getting Ana the scoop? You're on the same team, remember?"

"Of course," Rita chirped, watching the sun set over the distant smoky blue ridgeline of the Catskills. Lying between her teeth, she said, "We're all professionals here."

"Mmmmm. Glad to hear it." Sam didn't sound as if she believed Rita for one second. "Anyway, Ana talked to Jake's distraught mother, who of course raced to the hospital, and she said Jake had been receiving threatening messages in the mail. They weren't postmarked, and the mail carrier, when confronted by Mrs. Johnson, denied having delivered them. So, there's a lot more to this story than an accident, I think."

Rita's mouth suddenly went very dry. She dropped her bucket and sank into the grass, her heart hammering so loudly she was sure Sam could hear it.

"Rita? Are you still there?"

"Oh—yes. I'm just taking in the new information."

"Kind of changes everything, doesn't it?"

Sam sounded very pleased with herself. When murder and mayhem were afoot, Sam was like a bloodhound on a scent.

And, normally, so was Rita. She loved a good puzzle and a chance to make sure justice was served, to make their bucolic corner of the world cozy and peaceful once more.

But not when her son Vinnie and the victim were rivals for Ana Rivera's affections.

Not when Vinnie was the set designer.

28

And not when Rita very well knew that Vinnie had frequently made secret deliveries to the Johnsons' home at Rita's request, dropping off her homemade short rib ragú with sweet potato gnocchi, meltingly tender chicken parm, and shattering crisp and achingly sweet overstuffed cannoli.

But now she wondered if Vinnie had also dropped off something else.

"Rita?"

The voice was tinny and faint. Rita had dropped her phone on the ground, and Sam's voice now struggled to be heard over the chirping of birds and the rustling of the breeze through the branches of her apple trees.

Snatching the phone back up, Rita said, "Sorry, Sam. I've got to go. I'm on a deadline, remember?"

Half an hour later, Rita filed her story, and half an hour after that, she was angrily reducing her McIntosh apples into tiny little slivers and spiking them with too much cinnamon. Cooking was therapy, Rita liked to say, and most days, it was. But that also meant that whatever emotion was coursing through her veins made its way into her food—and her family knew it.

"Apple crisp for dessert?" her husband, Sal, said as he wandered into the kitchen and petted their Bernese mountain dogs, who were in their normal position right in front of the refrigerator. Sal sniffed. "With a lot of extra cinnamon today. I'm not complaining—you know I love cinnamon, *cara*—but is anything the matter?"

He said it like "the matta" because that's how Sal was: a little rough around the edges, more street smarts than book smarts.

"It's been a long day," Rita said as she attacked a bowl with a pastry blender. She really put her shoulder into it, cutting the butter into little pieces that studded the flour mixture like tiny gold nuggets.

"First,"—she eyeballed some oatmeal and dumped it in—"I was asked to cater a funeral for the widow."

Sal frowned so deeply that his bushy salt-and-pepper eyebrows almost melded into a single squiggly line. "I didn't know she kicked the bucket."

"She didn't. She's still very much alive and kicking, probably in better shape than you and me."

She shot a look at his gut, which spilled slightly over his waistband, and he self-consciously sucked it in. "Just overdeveloped washboard abs," he grumbled.

Rita rolled her eyes. "But"—she greased the pan with a flick of her wrist, then poured in the apple mixture—"she kept dropping these strange hints that she might want to die, or someone might want to kill her."

"Well, I can see someone might want revenge. I mean, she did kill at least two of her three husbands."

"That's a vicious rumor," Rita sniffed, even though she knew better. That was one secret she kept from Sal—that the widow had come very close to confessing to Rita, although of course, the widow was completely, in Rita's mind, justified. Rita glared at her husband. "The evidence is purely circumstantial."

She cleared her throat severely to forestall any further discussion. "Then," Rita continued, "I went to the rehearsal for *The Legend of Acorn Hollow*—"

"Oh, yeah? How's Vin? Ready for Hollywood?"

"Surprisingly good. Did you know our boy can brood? Because he can, like a young James Dean." She tossed the crumb mixture on top, threw open the over door, slid in the crisp, and slammed it shut with a loud bang. "And apparently, he's a heartthrob too. Can you believe it?"

"Yup. For the last few months, we've been attracting a whole new demographic to the nursery."

Sal owned Acorn Hollow's only nursery, and Vinnie—now in his third year of community college—helped his dad out.

"Lots of young women," Sal with a smile. He brought his fingers to his lips, puckered up, and kissed them. "*Bellissime.* Don't worry, though, *cara*"—he winked—"I've only got eyes for you."

Rita lay a deep purple, sensuously shaped eggplant on the chopping block and brought her sharpest knife down in a swift slicing motion. "Is anyone in particular hanging around?"

Sal thought for a moment. "Come to think of it, yeah—your co-worker. That little spark plug, Ana."

She raised her knife, and it glinted in the late afternoon sunlight that streamed through their picture window. She held the blade gently against the dot above the first "i" on his "Kiss Me—I'm Italian" T-shirt, and he backed away until he was pinned against the countertop. "Promise me, Sal, on your mother's grave, that you'll have a talk with Vinnie. She's a minor, for goodness sake. She's got a bright future ahead of her, and Vinnie, well...."

"What are you saying, *cara*? That our son doesn't have a bright future?"

She backed away and dropped her knife onto the counter with a clatter. "Let's just say the jury's still out on that one. But getting entangled with Ana Rivera will not earn him brownie points with anyone. Remember, I learn a lot in my murder investigations. And here's what I learned from a recent one: Ana's mother owns a firearm, and she's a regular in the shooting club." She picked up her knife again and began slicing the eggplant with surgical precision. "And if Ana were my daughter and some twenty-two-year-old man-child were hanging around?" She held up the knife and made a slicing motion a few inches from her neck.

Sal laughed weakly.

"Have the talk," Rita said. "And remember, I'll be watching—and listening."

Chapter Five

Dinner was an unusually subdued affair, so quiet that they could hear their knives scraping across their plates as they dissected Rita's eggplant parmesan. Rita kept shooting meaningful glances across the table at Sal, then popping out to the kitchen on the pretense of checking on the apple crisp.

But Sal was infuriatingly silent and kept looking from his plate to the ceiling whenever she attempted to catch his eye.

"Is something wrong, Ma?" Vinnie finally asked.

"No—why?"

"You keep screwing up your face and squinting."

"Oh—no!" She sliced her eggplant in half loudly, surgically, while staring straight at Sal. "I'm just trying to figure out why your father is staring at the ceiling instead of his beautiful family."

Sal flushed, the way he always did when he felt guilty. "Just trying to work out what to do about that spot," he mumbled. "It could be water damage."

"I don't see a spot," Vinnie said.

"Oh, it's there all right." Rita swilled the red wine in her glass and glared over the rim at her husband. Two could play this game, but only one could win—and Rita intended it to be her. "My long showers must be to blame."

Without taking her eyes off her husband, Rita reached under the table and texted her sister: "Call me now." Then she took a sip of wine, licked her lips, and said, "I guess I'll have to stay with Rose for a month while you renovate the bathroom."

That did the trick. In five seconds flat, a full range of emotions washed over Sal's face: a first flush of anger, as he realized he was definitively beaten, followed by a flicker of anxiety, his bushy eyebrows frowning with the realization that meant a month of no lasagna, no cannoli, no freshly laundered lavender-scented towels, and no conjugal visits. Then his eyes bulged with sheer terror, and his big, meaty, hairy hand shook as he reached for his water glass.

As if on cue, Rita's operatic ring tone broke the silence. "Oh, look," she said brightly, making a big show of checking the caller ID. "It's Rose! I can ask her if I can stay."

"*Aspetta!*" Sal practically lunged over the table. "I mean, that's not necessary, *cara*. I'll talk to"—he jutted his chin in Vinnie's direction for her benefit—"er, the guy who did the Balistreris' bathroom. They said it was done in three days with very little disruption."

"*Grazie, caro. Perfetto.* Be sure to talk to him—the Balistreris' bathroom guy, that is"—she winked—"tonight."

With an apologetic smile to her now nearly green husband and her befuddled son, Rita waltzed through the swinging door to the kitchen. She pressed one ear to the door and the other to the phone.

"So," her sister barked without so much as a greeting, "are you holding up your end of the bargain? Has Orlando ordered our monogrammed towels yet?"

"It's only been five hours, Rose."

"Huh." Rose's tone was dismissive, cutting. "Well, I haven't been too busy to help *my* sister. I've—"

Just then, Rita heard Vinnie's ring tone from the other side of the door. "Hold on a sec, Rose."

Pressing her ear even closer, Rita heard him say "Ana?" in a tone she'd never heard before. It was the sound of her baby in love—and in trouble.

"How long have you been throwing up?" Vinnie was saying, his voice dripping with concern. "Do you want me to bring you something? I could stop by the pharmacy..."

"*Mamma mia*," Rita groaned, slumping against the countertop. "It's worse than I thought. She's pregnant."

"He told you that?"

"No, but I can hear him talking on the phone. She's throwing up."

"Oh, it's just the stomach flu," Rose said, as if it were nothing more serious than a hangnail. "I was doing my office hours, see, and one of the realtors came down with the flu, so I dug her coffee cup out of the trash, followed Ana and Vinnie to the hospital, and poured a few drops in her water bottle when she was busy interviewing Jake Johnson's parents."

35

Rita found herself impressed and horrified in equal measure. Her sister was a genius, but also a bioweapons terrorist and criminal mastermind. Rita was about to really lay into Rose about her reprehensible behavior, but the mention of Jake was a sobering reminder that Ana was hardly the only danger to her son. There was also the not trivial matter of Jake being targeted and Vinnie being a possible suspect.

"Rose," she said slowly, "you need to switch vehicles with Vinnie."

"What? Why?"

"Because your car will make his 'mojo,' as the kids call it these days, shrivel to the size of pea. Then Ana will stop paying any attention to him, and Vinnie and Jake Johnson will no longer be rivals for Ana."

"And what am I going to say? 'Hey, Vinnie, your ma wants me to kill your mojo'?"

"No!"

"I'm thinking about joining a motorcycle gang?"

Rita sighed. "No. Just—you'll think of something."

"Tsk-tsk, sis. I thought you'd given up meddling for good."

"I have." Rita's tone was defensive and self-righteous in equal measure. "But this falls under exception 4(a)." Rita had drawn up her own handbook with extensive guidelines of when it was appropriate to meddle.

"Possible criminal activity, huh? Well, that sounds like Vinnie."

Rita heard Sal loudly clear his throat in the next room.

"Gotta go," she whispered, then rang off. She raced across the room, opened the freezer, slammed it loudly, grabbed a bowl and spoon, and raced back to the door. She pressed her ear against the door and listened breathlessly, occasionally clattering the spoon in the bowl as if she were busy scooping out gelato to serve their apple crisp *à la mode*.

"*Figlio*," Sal began, then stopped. Rita didn't need to see his face to know that it was splotchy and bright red and he was massaging his temples with those thick, stubby fingers. "Your mother and I, well..." His voice trailed off. He cleared his throat and started again. "In high school, I had this red Pinto."

Now it was Rita's turn to turn red. She did not like where this was going.

"And your mother," Sal said, "was hot. I mean, she was smoking. Kind of like a shorter, Italian version of Kim Kardashian."

"Um, Dad—"

Rita could tell Vinnie was squirming.

"Sorry, Vinnie. What I'm trying to say is, teenage hormones are a very powerful force, but your mother was stronger than that. When we were in the backseat of the Pinto, she always wanted to leave room for the Holy Spirit..."

Rita's eyes bulged out and she started to choke, but luckily the sound was muffled by a clatter and then the sound of breaking glass. Either Sal or Vinnie had spilled their wine, and Rita's money was on Vinnie.

"—and that was a good thing," Sal continued. "Here— use my napkin to sop it up. Because otherwise she would have ended up preggers and we just weren't ready for that."

"Um, Dad, why are you telling me this?"

"Because the Holy Spirit's weaker than he used to be, *figlio*, and girls, well—it's a woman's world nowadays. They just let us live in it—until they don't. *Capisci?*"

"Not really."

There was a thump, and Rita could tell Sal had just slugged their son in the arm. "Just keep your zipper zipped, *figlio*, and if it slithers open, well, just be sure it's with someone your own age."

And then Vinnie said the one thing Rita never expected to hear.

"Um, Dad, I'm a virgin."

Unfortunately, Rita missed Sal's response because at that exact moment she fell to the floor and fainted.

Chapter Six

"Rita?"

"Ma?"

For a moment, their voices were disembodied, far away. Then two faces began to emerge from the gloom, like some sort of Cubist masterpiece—a big maple syrup-brown eye here, a patch of gray stubble (Sal) or wispy moustache (Vinnie) there.

"Virgin?" Rita whispered weakly as everything came crashing back to her.

The blurry faces turned bright red.

"The Virgin!" Rita shouted suddenly, turning red herself. She could not let Vinnie know she had been listening at the door, as that would jeopardize any future intelligence-gathering operation. "I saw the Virgin Mary for a moment," she said. "She was wearing a beautiful blue cape and leading me towards the light..."

She reasoned that she was not wholly lying, as she could just make out the figure of her tiny Virgin Mary statue on the kitchen windowsill. She *was* wearing blue, and the sunlight *was* streaming behind her.

"Rita!" Sal cried. She suddenly felt his strong grip on her hand, pressing against her fingers, almost crushing them. "Ignore her and come back to the darkness. To the kitchen, that is. You can't leave me yet!"

Rita tried to fight the smile that was tugging at the corners of her lips. Surely, her husband couldn't be this obtuse, but she rather feared he was—Sal was a notoriously poor actor, and this was no act. He was genuinely worried she was on death's door.

"Oh, *caro*," she said. Her voice was still weak, and it sounded strange to her ears. Propping herself up on her elbows, she blinked several times, and their anxious faces slowly came into focus. Vinnie was white as a sheet. "I'm not leaving you. I just fainted. I'm dehydrated, I think, and I reached down to pick up a spoon I dropped and stood up too quickly."

Sal helped her sit up. He reached around and brushed his hand against the back of her head. "You've got a bump the size of an egg back there."

"Just a little kitchen mishap," she said, attempting a laugh. "An occupational hazard of being an Italian *mamma*. There—help me get up."

She took their proffered hands and staggered to her feet. Then they helped her up the stairs to her room. "You'd better stay home and rest tomorrow," Sal said as he gently laid her down on their bed.

"Oh, but I can't. The widow's walking me through the disappearances of Joey Gambone and Bobby Bruickhuisen. It's guaranteed to be the front-page story of the *Morris County Gazette*."

Sal looked at their son and clapped him on the back. "Well, maybe Vin should go with you tomorrow."

Rita was about to demur. Thanks to Rose's diabolical machinations, Vinnie could hardly get into trouble with Ana the next day.

But then she thought of Jake Johnson, and the fact that if any more threatening letters arrived in his mailbox, Vinnie would not have an easily verifiable alibi. But if he were with her and the widow, on the other hand....

"*Mille grazie, figlio,*" she said, even though he hadn't actually agreed to anything.

Vinnie dutifully bent down and gave her two *bacci* on the cheek.

"*Ci vediamo nella mattina,*" she murmured.

Sal and Vinnie tiptoed out of the room to let her rest. As she sank back under the covers, she thought of the old adage to keep your friends close and your enemies closer.

To this, she added a silent corollary: keep your children closest of all.

Rita wolfed down her breakfast the next morning in a splendid mood. Sal had done the dishes for a change, the widow was going to help satisfy her editor's lust for murder and mayhem, and Rose called at nine o'clock on the dot to ask Vinnie to borrow his motorbike, under the pretext that she was trying to impress some young(ish) Romeo on a motorbike.

Yes, Rita thought as she dunked her chocolate-drenched peanut butter biscotti in her piping hot latte, all was right with the world.

Whistling one aria after another, Rita walked Luciano and Cesare around the block, then got into her Buick and followed Vinnie to Rose's house so he could leave his motorbike there.

As Vinnie walked back towards Rita's car, a second-story window opened.

"Hey, Rita," her twin shouted with a wink so big and obvious Rita could see it from the street below. "I hope your plan works. Today!"

"What plan?" Vinnie asked as he slid into the passenger seat of Rita's car. Luckily, his back had been turned when his aunt winked.

What plan, indeed. Rita had still not formulated a workable plan to deliver Orlando Rinaldi, Acorn Hollow's most eligible, quasi-age-appropriate bachelor into Rose's arms. (Rose was seven years older than Orlando, but reasoned that since the average American woman lived significantly longer than the average American man, she was actually, in effect, younger. "It's like dog years," Rose had once explained. "Men and women are on two different time scales.")

Rita sighed. She was sure inspiration would hit eventually. "Oh," she said, "Rose means my plan to get the widow to tell the previously untold story of Joey Gambone's 1936 disappearance."

They were passing by the turn-off to the Johnsons' street.

"Do you have a bag of food to deliver to the Johnsons?" Vinnie asked. "I could hop out and leave it on their doorstep."

Rita sat bolt upright and gripped the steering wheel. She pretended to be concentrating on the road but kept glancing at her son out of the corner of her eye. "Why do you say that?"

"Well, I dunno." He kicked desultorily at the floor mat. "I mean, cuz they're poor. You know, because Mr. Johnson lost his job and all." He frowned. "I mean, Ma, you've only been delivering food to them for six months now. Why stop today?"

He was drumming his fingers on his threadbare jeans now. Was that an indication of guilt? Nervousness? Anxiety? Was he suggesting this merely out of Christian charity, or to have an excuse to go up on that porch and discretely leave a message?

Rita wasn't sure she wanted to find out.
Plus, even if her son had nothing to do with the letters, the neighbors might see him and then come to the wrong conclusion.

There was no way she was letting her baby anywhere near the Johnson house.

"I forgot," she said grimly, "what with fainting and all. I'll drop it off tonight on my way to the quilting circle."

She knew Sal and Vinnie were planning to watch the game at that time, so Vinnie's movements would be fully accounted for.

"Do you know Jake well?" Rita asked casually.

"No, not really."

Vinnie's jaw was slightly clenched. Rita could tell there was little love lost there.

"I mean," Vinnie said, "he's in the play with me. He plays Bobby, but he doesn't have to act much. They're pretty similar—straight-A students, kind of goody-two-shoes types."

"I hear," Rita said, "that Jake is going out with Ana." Vinnie turned sharply towards his mother. "Where did you—?" He stopped suddenly, face flushed. "I mean, no, I don't think that's true. I heard she's going with someone else."

"Anyone I know?"

Vinnie shrugged. "Just a rumor I heard."

Rita pulled up in front of the widow's house, a grand old Victorian painted lady, all tarted up in garishly bright lavender and bubblegum-pink, and topped with a gleaming turret.

"Well, he should be careful," she said, "because someone might think that what happened to Jake wasn't an accident."

"It wasn't."

"*What?*"

"Yeah, like I told Detective Benedetto, I checked those ropes myself earlier in the afternoon, and they were fine."

Rita's heart was really pounding now. "You read Ana's story, right?" Rita felt like reaching across the passenger seat and throttling Vinnie. "You know Jake's parents say he was receiving threatening messages?"

"Yeah." Vinnie looked unconcerned, which should have been reassuring. It was not the look of a guilty man, the look of someone afraid the police would connect the dots.

But Rita felt anything but reassured. It was yet another sign of how naïve, how trusting her baby really was.

How easy it would be to manipulate him, to pin the blame on him.

"Vin," she said as they got out of the car and walked up the flagstone path to the widow's front door. "You didn't see anything on the Johnsons' stoop when you delivered the food, did you?"

He shrugged. "One time, I saw one of those messages. I didn't know it at the time, though. But I saw an envelope with no stamp, just Jake's name on it."

"Which day?"

"I dunno, Ma. I think it was the day you had to take Luciano to the vet because he got nipped by Mrs. Tarantino's mutt."

Rita made a mental note to check her credit card statement for the date of the vet bill. She slipped her arm in Vinnie's as they stepped onto the front porch. "You know what the police are going to think, Vin. That Jake's rival for Ana's affection—this mystery man who's seeing Ana—"

He looked at her sharply.

"That is, who's *rumored* to be seeing Ana—that he sent the messages, that he arranged for the accident on the set, with Jake as the intended victim." She tightened her grip on his arm. "If I were him, I'd stay as far away from Jake as possible."

Chapter Seven

They picked up Rocco, Vinnie's best friend and the *Morris County Gazette*'s photographer, on the way to the old Van Tassel farmhouse. Now, as they surveyed the gloomy, dimly-lit interior, with its moth-eaten curtains, creaky floorboards, and steady stream of plaster flakes falling from the ceiling, Rita found it strangely fitting that this melancholy site was the last place Bobby Bruickhuisen was seen alive.

"We're standing in the parlor now," the widow said. "It was once such a beautiful room— wallpaper with a delicate pattern of roses and nosegays, gleaming woodwork. And the people were more beautiful back then too, of course. None of this looking like you just rolled out of bed and wearing ripped jeans on purpose! The girls were in Poodle skirts and cashmere twin sets, their hair in neat little pigtails; their mothers were in sheath dresses—very Jackie O. And the boys in suits and skinny ties—well, except Vito." She shot an accusatory look at Vinnie, as if he were somehow responsible for the sartorial choices of the young man whose role he played.

"The buffet table was pushed against the wall next to the roaring fire." The widow ran her finger over the brickwork on the chimney. "I remember it like it was yesterday. 'Angel' by Elvis Presley was playing on the record player. People were dancing cheek to cheek, trying to forget the Soviets had missiles pointed at us, ready to blow us to smithereens. Not everyone could, of course. You'd hear snatches of conversation where someone would brag about how their fallout shelter was kitted out with one hundred jars of canned pears and a grill and a radio. As if it mattered! But mostly, people talked about the play and what a marvelous job everyone had done. Especially my Bobby!"

The widow clapped her hands. "He was such a handsome boy, really, but somehow he managed to look like that ugly sniped-nose Ichabod Crane on stage. And Sandro—everyone said he was terribly menacing as Brom Bones. People said he reminded them of the villain in *Oklahoma*."

Rocco and Vinnie looked confused. Apparently, that was one musical Rita hadn't made them watch.

The widow laughed. "Just picture a big, dumb, menacing oaf with a creepy stare and violence lurking just below the surface." The widow's eyes took on a faraway look; Rita could tell that, for the widow, it was as if this had occurred yesterday. "I was standing right about here, warming myself by the fire, and congratulating Kate's mother on her daughter's performance. Kate and Bobby were dancing in the corner over there, right about where Rocco is. Vito was sitting by himself by the buffet table, eating one pig in a blanket after another—"

Rita made a face. They really did have the most awful food in the sixties. At least, the non-Italians did.

"—just staring, all moody-like, at Bobby and Kate. Sandro was over there, huddled in the corner with Lydia Van Zandt, who up until then Kate considered her best friend. Those two were thick as thieves. But I always knew Lydia was up to no good. She was—what do young people call it these days? An enefriend?"

"A frenemy?" Vinnie suggested.

"A frenemy." The widow nodded gravely. "She always wanted whatever Kate wanted and Kate—who was too nice for her own good, if you ask me—always let her get it. In first grade, they picked names to decide who would play what role in the church Christmas pageant— and Kate got the role of the Virgin Mary. Lydia was to be a shepherd. But Lydia wanted to be the star of the show, not some smelly back-row shepherd. So she pitched a fit, claimed she was allergic to wool—despite her grandparents owning a sheep farm—and would be traumatized by playing a shepherd and so on and so forth. So Kate just gave her friend the part. Same thing with the eighth-grade spelling bee—Kate won, and Lydia was the runner-up. Lydia convinced Kate to pretend she had the flu so Lydia could go to the state spelling bee. But Lydia"—the widow's thin little fish-lips curled in disgust—"placed sixteenth. Kate would have come in first, mark my words, and brought the trophy home to Acorn Hollow. But we were robbed of glory—robbed!—all because of the selfish machinations of Lydia Van Zandt."

Rita was amazed how much outrage the widow could muster for the ignominious loss of the 1958 New York State Spelling Bee, especially given that she wasn't even

48

related to any of the participants. But she faithfully jotted it all down. Rita never knew when an anecdote would wind its way into her article.

"And then Lydia wanted Sandro, too, huh?" Vinnie said, his eyes lingering on the spot Lydia and Sandro had occupied.

"It was an open secret," the widow said, "that Lydia was angling to have Sandro as her beau. Everyone seemed to know that except Sandro and Kate."

"But what about Bobby?" Rita asked. "He was dating Kate, too."

"No." The widow's beady dark eyes flashed, and she adjusted the blood-red brooch at her throat. "That was a vicious rumor."

"Vicious?" Rita could not imagine why the widow would oppose a relationship between her beloved nephew and her best friend's daughter, on whom she doted. "Why? He was a lovely boy, by all accounts."

"They were friends," the widow sniffed. "Nothing more. After Bobby's disappearance, people tried to spin something salacious out of it, drag Kate's name through the mud. That she was two-timing both of them, that she was even having a relationship with Vito on the side."

Vinnie's ears perked up. In the Acorn Hollow Players' version, Vito's regard for Kate was portrayed as entirely one-sided.

"Kate was dating Sandro," the widow said. "End of story. And vile little Lydia couldn't stand it. The music stopped, and Lydia blurted out, 'Kate's pregnant!' The silence afterwards was deafening; you could have heard a pin drop."

"But why," Rita said slowly, "would she have done that? If Sandro was the father, wouldn't he already know?"

"Oh," the widow demurred, "I didn't say he was the father."

"But you just said she was only with Sandro."

"Well, based on Sandro's reaction, he wasn't the father. He must have known he couldn't be the father. Because he just roared, 'who's the *stronzo* who knocked you up?' Kate wouldn't answer. Personally, I've always suspected she was raped. Otherwise, why not name the father? Why not marry him?"

"Maybe," Rita said, "because she didn't want to. Maybe she'd discovered something about him that made her realize he was unsuitable. Maybe he was married. Maybe her family wouldn't allow it. Maybe she was seventeen and frightened and wanted her freedom. I can think of lots of reasons besides rape."

There was a cry above her, and Rita looked up to see a pair of vultures circling just outside the gaping window; the glass was long gone. A shiver went down her spine. There was something haunted about this place. Vinnie and Rocco noticed it, too, because they suddenly began fidgeting, eager to show the vultures they were very much alive. But the widow didn't take the slightest notice, remaining rooted to the spot.

"Assuming for the moment you're right," Rita said, "who do you suspect of raping her?"

"In these cases, it's often a family member, isn't it? Kate's father perhaps—"

"Surely not!"

Ignoring Rita, the widow said calmly, "Her older brother, Hank—"

Now it was Vinnie and Rocco's turn to shudder. They were no doubt thinking of their own sisters.

"Maybe a farmhand," the widow said with a shrug. "Her father employed quite a lot of them. A passing tramp. Who knows?"

Rita jotted all of this down in her notebook, her head spinning. The rape allegation was pure speculation, not something she could corroborate. Unless....

Rita wondered if, after all this time, Kate herself might be willing to set the record straight. She'd be an old woman with a whole life behind her, not a frightened young teen facing an uncertain future. And rape no longer bore the stigma it once did. "Where's Kate now?"

"Long gone." The widow's voice was brittle, flat. "She and Vito left town in a hurry when the scandal broke, cut ties with everyone and everything. And then a couple of years later, she died in a car accident. Her little boy died too." The widow fiddled with the blood-red brooch affixed to the stiff neck of her black dress. "That's all I heard. It was all very hushed up. No obituary in the paper, nothing. Just a brief article in the *Morris County Gazette* saying she had died."

"I'm sorry," Rita said softly, squeezing Emma's arm. "What a short, tragic life."

"Two short, tragic lives," Vinnie interjected, and Rita looked up in surprise. "I mean," he said, "the kid's too. Whose was he, anyway?"

The widow shrugged her bony shoulders. "Kate wouldn't say."

"But who did he look like?"

"He was blond," the widow said. "Blue-eyed, chubby-cheeked. Really cute. The kind of kid they'd put on a cereal box."

"So not Italian," Vinnie said. "Not Sandro's, not Vito's. Bobby's?"

"Not Bobby's," the widow insisted again. "They were not an item. And anyway, Kate herself was blonde. The child took after her."

Rita moved to the window. Her gaze roamed over the weed-choked lawn to the river beyond it.

"So Kate," Rita said, "burst into tears and ran out this way."

The widow nodded. "Then Bobby. He threw on his leather jacket and a scarf I'd knitted just for him—it was adorable, with a squirrel motif—you know, for the Acorn Hollow Squirrels—and dashed out the door. He was just trying to comfort her, I'm sure, but of course that made everyone think he was the father. Then Sandro leapt up, trembling with rage, shouted '*Stronzo!*,' and dashed after them."

So Sandro had thought Bobby was the father of Kate's baby. That was certainly a motive for murder. Sometimes, Rita thought, the most obvious explanation was the right one.

"Kate's father was out like a shot after them."

"Did you get the sense he was going after his daughter—or after Bobby?"

"At the time, I thought he was going after Kate, either if he was the father, to hush her up, or if he wasn't, to make her tell him who the father was so he could make sure they got hitched." The widow looked amused. "Can you imagine the scandal—a senator's unmarried daughter in the family way? No, it was unthinkable in those days." She cocked her head. "But later, when Bobby disappeared, I wondered if I was wrong. Maybe he'd gone after Bobby to confront him." The widow wagged her chin in the direction of the other corner of the room. "Then her brother ran out—"

"To protect his sister?"

"Protect her, console her, calm his father down—who knows? And then, the last to rush out"—the widow turned towards Vinnie and eyed him keenly—"was Vito."

Vinnie jumped up as if he'd been accused of something. "Hey, I'm not Vito."

"No, but you play him very well."

"And then?" Rita prompted, her pen poised over her notebook.

"And then I went home." The widow's eyes clouded with tears. "And I never saw my Bobby again."

Chapter Eight

Rocco snapped a few dramatic black-and-white photos of the ruined mansion, and then the foursome piled into Rita's Buick, which lurched unsteadily over the uneven terrain; the oak-lined alley to the Van Tassels' estate was now just a parting of the trees, crisscrossed with gnarled roots and jagged rocks. Rita caressed the dashboard, urging her car on.

"*Dai, dai,*" she murmured. Her car, she was sure, understood Italian—the language of Dante, of Verdi, and of Ferraris, too, after all—just as well as her dogs (and much better, regrettably, than her children). "*Solo un po' di piu.*"

There was an ominous rattling over the crunching of tires, a whinge, and a wheeze, and then, from the passengers, a collective sigh of relief as the tires hit the pavement.

They sped off down charming country lanes, through an ever-changing kaleidoscope of amber, russet, and scarlet leaves, wending their way past orchards and wineries. As the landscape grew hiller, an old white clapboard farmhouse came into view. It stood sentinel over a sun-dappled orchard, the trees groaning with the sorts of heirloom varieties never found in any supermarket—the green and red striped Esopus Spitzenburg apples that formed the basis of many a craft cider; the rosy-cheeked Cox's Orange Pippin, with its hints of citrus and mango; and the tart, crunchy, evocatively named Northern Spy.

The widow tapped Rita's shoulder. "Make a right here."

They hurtled down a steep narrow lane, paved but bumpy, then meandered past a few corn fields, another orchard, and a herd of lazy dairy cows before entering a deep, dark wood through which almost no light penetrated.

The widow tapped Rita's shoulder again and indicated a rutted path that Rita didn't think was even a road. "Now left."

They bumped along, deeper and deeper into the forest, until trees branches were scratching the sides of the car. Flocks of startled wild turkeys fled their advance, scattering with an angry screech.

Then, as they came out into a clearing, the widow commanded Rita to stop.

"There," the widow said, tapping the window, "is the Gambone farm."

Rita gaped at the limestone farmhouse, butter-hued and covered in ivy, its roof long since gone. There was a red barn behind it, leaning like the tower of Pisa, a silo, and a picture-perfect stone mill and waterwheel perched over a rushing steam.

"Kind of in the boonies, isn't it?" Rocco said. "I mean, even for a farm."

"Well, that was kind of the point," the widow said. "They were bootleggers—and worse. They needed somewhere discrete to manufacturer moonshine"—she pointed a gnarled, veiny finger at the mill—"and they needed to be close to a navigable tributary of the Hudson to be able to transport their bootlegged liquor by boat under cover of darkness."

Rita squinted and could just make out the silvery sheen of the stream through the trees. She grabbed her notebook, and they clambered out of the car and ambled towards the ruins.

"It was Halloween, 1936." Emma recounted, "The height of the Depression, Prohibition in full swing. The Gambones hosted a big party, and the guest list read like a who's who for the world of organized crime. Arthur Flegenheimer, better known as Dutch Schultz, Dominick Petrilli—his speakeasy was where North Plank Road Tavern is in Newburgh now—Lucky Luciano, progenitor of the Genovese crime family, Meyer Lansky, and Legs Diamond."

"Joey Gambone," the widow said, her eyes narrowing, "was middle of the pack—not a small-timer, but not one of the big wigs. But he was ambitious, with both a good head for the business side of their operations and a knack for handling the police. He knew how to give bribes that were just big enough to get them to look the other way, but not more lavish than what was needed. And he took care not to be too brazen, to give them plausible deniability."

"Was he violent?" Rita asked.

"Oh, of course! You couldn't be in that line of work if you weren't. But his genius lay in controlling it. He used violence selectively to advance the organization, but he never used it unnecessarily. He never wanted to attract undue attention. And, he made a shrewd match—he married the favorite daughter of the crime boss in Albany, then married his sisters and sisters-in-law to other crime bosses in the area."

"It sounds positively medieval," Rita said indignantly.

She could not imagine women being treated as chattel so very recently, and the Italophile in her winced. These people shared with her a history, a culture, a language, and some vestigial DNA.

And they were brutes.

"And then there were rumors," the widow went on, "that he schemed to get many of those men killed. But the evidence never led back to him. They always died in shoot-outs with the police, or at the hand of a petty rival who himself later went to a watery grave. Soon, there were only a handful of rivals left—the most notable being his wife's favorite brother, who was the oldest son in their family and slated to assume the mantle of the family business."

"So you think he was killed by the brother—or another mobster?" Vinnie asked. "That's not how it comes across in the play."

The widow shrugged her bony shoulders, and her blood-red scarf—more ominous than jaunty, Rita thought—bobbed up and down. "Well, his wife, Anita, did catch him in flagrante with his mistress Viviana earlier that same day, and the two women had quite a cat fight. Your sister and Penny Albanese really do it justice."

The widow started heading back to the car. "Everyone who was at the party—supposedly, the last place he was seen—was tight-lipped, of course. The police didn't get much out of them, but they probably didn't try too hard either. All anyone would say is that he left the party in the wee hours of the morning."

"But why would he leave?" Rita called after the widow's retreating figure. "The party was at his house." The widow's black-clad form blurred into the shadows, taking on an almost spectral quality. She knew so much, had seen so much. She was like their living ghost and for a moment, it struck Rita that perhaps this was why the widow was still there haunting, in a sense, Acorn Hollow: she had unfinished business.

"That's never been clear," the widow called over her shoulder. Despite the stiffness of her gait, she was now walking surprisingly briskly for someone of her advanced years. Perhaps she too felt unnerved by the stillness of this lonely place, the claustrophobia of the sheltering, tall trees and the ever-deepening shadows. "They said he was alone, that he often liked to go for drives late at night."

"Was he drunk?"

"I doubt it. He could hold his liquor, and he was shrewd enough never to lose control of his faculties—especially when there was work to be done. And those mobster parties—they weren't all fun, you know. They were work. Kind of like the modern holiday office party. Networking with a side of fun."

So that ruled out the possibility of a drunk-driving crash, although Rita had always supposed that to be a remote possibility. After all, if he'd died in an accident, why would anyone steal the corpse? But there had been no body, no traces of blood.

Rita mentally reviewed the route from the abandoned farmstead to the old stone bridge in Acorn Hollow, past farm fields, through woods, and over rushing streams, past white-steepled churches and moldering graveyards, skirting the edges of colonial-era hamlets so exquisite and quaint they belonged in a snow globe.

Why had Joey Gambone felt the need to drive that route that night? To dispose of a body in the woods, to rendezvous with a "business associate" in a moonlit glade, or perhaps to seek uncomplicated comfort in the arms of one of the sad-eyed beauties who'd once thronged the long-gone bordello at the crossroads? Or had he never left the party? Had some frustrated English teacher-turned-mobster, a thug who liked his murder with a side of poetic irony, driven Joey's car to the graceful stone arch bridge, thus forever linking Joey's disappearance to the sad tale of Ichabod Crane?

The widow slid into the backseat. Rocco and Vinnie buckled their seatbelts, and Rita started the engine. In the rearview mirror, Rita watched the widow reach out and tuck a stray silver tendril back into her severe bun, then adjust the frilly, high-necked collar of her long black dress.

"You want my opinion?" the widow suddenly said. "I think there was an alliance between his wife Anita and her brother. After she found out about Viviana, she wanted revenge. And that dovetailed perfectly with her brother's desire to rid himself of a rival for his father's organization."

The widow suddenly cracked a crooked yellow smile and let out a giggle which turned into a cackle. "Plus my husband Thomas the druggist, husband number one"— she said his name and husband number reverently, to underscore that he was her favorite husband, the one she absolutely, definitely did not murder—"sold rat poison to Anita the day Joey disappeared."

Chapter Nine

Rita was enormously pleased with herself. In the span of just a few hours, she'd typed up her story on the last days of Bobby Bruickhuisen and hatched and set in motion a terrific plan to throw Rose in Orlando Rinaldi's path, thereby keeping her end of the bargain.

"Orlando!" she'd trilled on the phone, shouting to be heard over the din of his winery tasting room. "Guess what I have tickets to? *Aida*! Yes, at the Met next Saturday...Yes, with Sonya Radvanovsky...Of course, you know how Sal feels about the opera."

She said this last bit in a low, solemn voice, the way one might talk about your third cousin who was a little touched in the head and had disgraced the family when he ran off with a thrice-married stripper before going on a bank robbing spree. Sal's almost allergic reaction to any kind of culture was extremely embarrassing to Rita.

And Sal's aversion to culture reached a fever pitch when it came to opera. He claimed that they sang in a register only dogs could hear (to which Rita had retorted, "So you can't hear anything? Well, then enjoy three hours of blissful silence."), that he did not understand why they insisted on all that weeping and wailing and gnashing of teeth when the plot could be summed up in a single phrase (as Sal put it, "love sucks; they die"), and that, quite frankly, he'd enjoyed his last root canal ever so much more.

Sal did not mind in the slightest if she took Orlando to the opera; in fact, he encouraged it. He assumed Orlando's love of opera meant he was secretly gay. She assumed Orlando was straight, and that they had a completely platonic opera-fueled friendship, à la Ruth Bader Ginsburg and Antonin Scalia.

As she had expected, Orlando accepted her invitation with alacrity, "Shall I pick you up at three?" he said. "Perhaps we can grab dinner beforehand on Arthur Avenue."

Arthur Avenue was in The Bronx, and it was home to New York City's *real* Little Italy. The one in Manhattan was just for tourists.

"*Perfetto.*" Rita made a mental note to tell Rose to wear red, just in case she spilled any red sauce down her front. Plus, nothing said va-va-voom like a red dress—not that her sister needed any help in that department.

She rang off, not even feeling guilty that she would stand Orlando up at the last moment, begging off on account of a terrible gastrointestinal illness, and spring Rose on him in her place. Her only regret was that she would miss out on seeing the incomparable Sonya play the role of Aida.

But that seemed a small price to pay for her twin's help protecting Vinnie from himself.

Rita sank blissfully into the well-worn depression on her sofa and propped up her feet. She was immediately enveloped by two huge balls of fur. One of her Bernese mountain dogs, Cesare, was content to just nuzzle against her thighs, but Luciano opened one eyeball and peered intently at her plate of warm apple crisp and the mound of homemade vanilla bean gelato on top.

"*Proibito*," Rita said sternly, pointing her fork at Luciano. She always spoke to her dogs in Italian, and unlike her other children—her human children—they seemed to understand. "You're supposed to be on a diet, remember? We've got to get you back down to a hundred fifty pounds. Plus, the vet says you're lactose intolerant."

Luciano snorted, got back up on his haunches, and very slowly and noisily turned tail, then plopped down so his rump was now facing her.

"Well, serves me right," Rita muttered. "That was pretty much my reaction when Dr. Stein told me to give up dairy and gluten and lose thirty pounds."

She laughed at the absurdity of the situation—both she and her dogs had been given the same target weight, but they were far more likely to achieve it. Because while they had someone monitoring their every morsel, she did not. But this, she decided as her lips closed around a mouthful of cinnamon-y goodness, was really a good thing.

At this time of day, the house was quiet. Sal was working at the nursery he owned, and she had sent Vinnie off with a list of useless errands to keep him busy—and far away from Ana.

And like a good mamma's boy, Vinnie had cheerfully acquiesced, even though that meant the ultimate "drive of shame"—tooling around in Rose's bubblegum-pink Mercedes emblazoned with "#1 Realtor in Morris

County" and her phone number in gold glitter. (Rose was one single lady who never needed to give anyone "her digits"; they were there for all the world to see.) It also featured a larger-than-life portrait of Rose with a blindingly white, almost maniacal grin. Rocco, who worked as an auto mechanic and detailer when he wasn't the *Morris County Gazette* photographer, had done the paint job; when he was done, Vinnie had remarked that it seemed to convey the message, "Hire me or I will eat you." "No dummy," Rocco had replied, "You're supposed to think, 'I want her on my side. She's gonna eat the other guy for lunch.'"

The car's interior was champagne-colored leather and smelled of fresh-baked chocolate chip cookies, not because Rose was a baker, but because of her air freshener, which she regarded as her secret sales weapon. "Chocolate chip cookies remind people of home," she explained, "and that makes them want to buy a house. And that means"—she rubbed her fingers together—"cha-ching."

Rita was sure that if Ana got one look at Vinnie in that souped-up, sparkly Barbiemobile, his sheen of bad-boy mystique would surely be tarnished.

She still had to type up her story on Joey Gambone's disappearance, of course, but Sam had given her an extra day, since they wouldn't run it until Thursday. So Rita turned her attention to the next task at hand: planning the menu for the widow's funeral.

"Something seasonal," Rita murmured, remembering the widow's words, as she flipped through her recipe binder. "Full fat, full sugar, full taste. No skimping on calories."

Luciano looked up hopefully, one ear cocked.

Rita's mind raced over the possibilities, thinking of the apple trees groaning with fruit, the plump wine-colored cranberries just now being skimmed off the bogs, the fat bright orange pumpkins dotting the fields. And in her garden were the last of the season's tomatoes and basil and the first of the season's spinach.

"For the appetizer," she said slowly, "bruschetta, crostini with spinach-artichoke dip rich with full-fat Parmesan cheese—"

Even Cesare sat up at the mention of cheese. That was one of her dogs' favorite words, and they knew it in both English and Italian.

"Pumpkin ravioli in a sage brown butter sauce...."

Luciano and Cesare looked less impressed.

"Oh, you want meat?"

They perked up again.

"Italian meatballs," she said, "in a rich red gravy. With little skewers so it's easy finger food. An enormous antipasti platter piled high with prosciutto, salami, and sopressata, and an array of cheeses from the creamery: burrata with a soft runny center drizzled with balsamic vinegar, manchego with honey and fig jam on the side, and a delicious crumbly pecorino. And, of course, with olives, marinated artichokes, roasted red peppers, and homemade focaccia still warm from the oven." She paused for a moment, her pen hovering over the list. "And Oysters Rockefeller," she decided. "Just the name says decadent, and I can use the spinach from my garden. Fried calamari, too, with a spicy tomato sauce. For the few health nuts—"

Her dogs grunted, unimpressed.

"A tureen of ginger carrot soup. And for dessert, an apple crisp, a cranberry-pecan tart, and a pumpkin cheesecake."

She jotted this all down, then frowned at the list. The desserts were all very seasonal and hardly low-fat, but there was something about fruity desserts that lacked the sufficient level of decadence.

Cesare and Luciano licked their lips and cocked their heads to one side.

"Suggestions, boys? Peanut butter biscotti? Chocolate chip cookies?"

This did not pique their interest.

"Too commonplace? Too hard for all of those dentures?"

Rita hadn't actually asked to see the guest list, but she rather supposed that everyone the widow knew was at least pushing ninety—and those were the young'uns.

"Something soft, mushy, denture-friendly...and delicious? Jello?" She shuddered. That was one American dessert she could never understand. "Pudding?" That was another one she'd never been a fan of, at least if it came out of a box.

Inspiration finally struck. "Tiramisu! Those seniors may stay awake all night"—for Rita did not intend to skimp on the espresso or the velvety deep dark cocoa imported from Italy—"but they won't crack a tooth."

She was about to put down her pen, but Luciano and Cesare still looked at her expectantly.

"Oh, all right," she said with a sigh, but it was a happy one, as Rita rather enjoyed being begged to make her signature dishes. "And my flourless chocolate cake with a layer of homemade sour cherry preserves tucked under the ganache. Now if that doesn't say decadent, I don't know what does."

It was time to start dinner. Rita went into the kitchen and belted out her favorite aria from Puccini's *Madame Butterfly* as she worked.

"*Un bel dì, vedremo, levarsi un fil di fumo,*" she sang as chopped sprigs of rosemary and fresh green leaves of thyme, oregano, and sage into a bowl of flour, then dredged the chicken through the herb-flecked mixture.

"*Vedi? È venuto!,*" she sang triumphantly as she tossed the chicken pieces into a Dutch oven and heard them crackle in the hot oil.

"*Chiamerà Butterfly dalla lontana,*" she belted out as she tossed in the peppers and onions.

She was just plating the chicken, scooping the rich, velvety sauce over the chicken, and garnishing with fresh basil when Vinnie burst in the front door, whistling off-key (some horrible heavy-metal tune, definitely not opera) and kissed her on the cheek.

"Wow, Ma. Looks delicious."

He smelled of chocolate chip cookies like she knew he would.

But what she had not expected was that he would be so chipper after half the town had seen him in the world's most distinctive, most embarrassing "ride."

"You seem happy." She tried to sound neutral, but it came out suspicious, almost accusatory.

"Do I?"

She could tell he was stalling for time.

"Oh." He ran a hand through his spiky black hair, which made her notice that it was *less* spiky than usual, almost as if someone had been running her fingers through his hair, smoothing it out. "Well...I enjoyed running your errands, Ma. It made me appreciate you even more, you know? All those secret deliveries to people in need—it's really inspiring. Sometimes it's better to be the giver than the receiver, you know? All that Sunday school stuff. It made me think. It was fun to duck around the corner and see people come out on their doorsteps and just break into a big grin."

Rita smiled at the memory. Yes, that was one of the things that most brought her joy. She was glad her son had felt it, too.

"And did you, er, run into any of your friends?"

"Oh"—he looked away and pretended to lean down and inhale the herby scent wafting off the chicken—"just, uh, Ana. I happened to pass her and she wanted a ride."

"In Aunt Rose's tacky car?"

Vinnie shrugged. "She liked it. She loves pink, and she loved how it smelled." He turned sheepish. "In fact, it made us so hungry we stopped at the Sunshine Café and got some chocolate chip cookies to go. We figured it was better than eating all the biscotti we were supposed to deliver." A goofy smile crossed his face. "And she thought it was pretty cool that I was—what did she say?—'secure enough in my manhood' to drive a hot pink girly car."

Rita let out a strangled cry. Luciano and Cesare were hovering by her feet in hopes she would accidentally drop a chicken breast, circling like sharks awaiting chum. At this they looked up and shot her a contemptuous look, as if to say, "And you thought you'd worked this out so perfectly. Hah!"

"Ma?" Vinnie looked concerned. "Are you all right?"

"Oh! Er...the basil, I chopped it too finely." She sprinkled a few more leaves on top and then said, as casually as possible, "And how is Jake doing after that unfortunate encounter with the pumpkin?"

"Better, I think. Ana went to the hospital to check on him. She said he'll probably be released tomorrow."

Without having to be asked, Vinnie uncorked a bottle of Sangiovese, poured three glasses, and set them on the dining room table. When he came back through the swinging door to pick up the plates of chicken cacciatore, he suddenly said, "He should be careful, though. We dropped by his house, see, to return a book Ana had borrowed..."

Rita felt the bile rising in her stomach. She had explicitly told Vinnie not to make any deliveries to the Johnsons. She had not counted on the possibility of him picking up a passenger.

"And?"

"And there was one of those notes again."

Despite the steam rising from the chicken, Rita shivered. Someone might have seen her sweet, guileless baby. Someone might connect him with the threatening messages and the mysterious malfunctioning of the set for *The Legend of Acorn Hollow*. The set that Vinnie himself had designed.

"It was written with letters cut out from different magazines. All higgly-piggly, you know? And it said, 'Stay away from Ana unless you want to become part of the legend of Acorn Hollow'."

"How do you know that?"

"I took it out of the envelope." Vinnie shrugged. "I was curious, I guess."

"Vinnie," Rita groaned, "do you realize what you've done?"

"Yeah. Help, Ana. She's writing a story about the threats."

"No, Vin." Rita glared at her son. "You just left fingerprints at a crime scene."

Chapter Ten

She awoke the next morning feeling cross. All
through her morning routine—revving up the espresso
machine, sipping a latte, munching on chocolate-dipped
peanut butter biscotti, walking Luciano and Cesare
around their charming, tree-lined neighborhood—she
was haunted by the knowledge that she'd miscalculated
spectacularly: Rose's car, which she'd imagined to be the
most embarrassing mode of transport possible for a
twenty-two-year-old, had turned out to be, in Vinnie's
words, a "babe magnet," more of a lure than a deterrent.

It had not kept Ana and Vinnie apart.

Worse, it had actually been responsible for bringing
Vinnie to Jake's doorstep, and causing him to muddy the
waters further by putting his fingerprints on one of the
threatening messages.

And she had given up a two-hundred-dollar ticket to
one of her favorite operas for nothing.

If that weren't enough, she had a sneaking suspicion
that her story about Joey Gambone's disappearance was
not up to scratch. Sure, it contained the never-before-
revealed salacious detail about Anita Gambone
purchasing poison. But Rita felt she had failed to

71

capture the eerie beauty of the last place he'd been seen. Nor had she captured the contrast between the hothouse tensions boiling over on that long-ago Halloween and the quiet malevolence that now pervaded the site.

She decided to walk the Gambone farm site once again and to bring along Luciano and Cesare. The day was cool and crisp, the drive was just as beautiful as it had been the day before, and the glade was just as eerie, perhaps more so now that she was alone.

Luciano and Cesare trotted beside her as she paced the property, unsure of exactly what she was looking for.

Until she saw it.

On the edge of the clearing, where the glade disappeared into the woods, two rusted, gun-metal gray doors lay flush with the forty-five degree angle of the side of a low earthen mound. The right-side door featured a long metal handle, which Rita tugged at, but in vain.

Rita swore under her breath in Italian, and Luciano and Cesare shot her a look of reproach.

"Oh, hush," she said irritably. "It doesn't count if it's in Italian. You know that."

Just then, she heard "*Va, Pensiero*" blaring from her pocket. A quick glance at the caller ID made her heart beat faster. "Ana? What's wrong? Is it Vinnie? Is he OK?"

Rita had visions of her baby pinned beneath the overturned wreck of Rose's Barbiemobile, her twin's absurd grin visible beneath the rising waters, or her baby smushed beneath an errant pumpkin in yet another accident on the set, or her baby in an orange jumpsuit behind bars, accused of having sent those horrible notes to Jake Johnson.

"Huh? No, he's fine—at least, I think he is. I mean, he's only my co-star. I'm not his keeper."

Rita breathed a sigh of relief. Her baby was not in trouble, and Ana did not return his affections. Or was that just what Ana wanted her to think?

"I was calling," Ana said, "because Sam thought maybe you'd need some help with the story on Joey Gambone's disappearance. I'm on a big story, see, but it's on hold for a few days."

"Really? What story?"

But Ana was infuriatingly coy. "Uh-uh-uh, Rita. You can read my big scoop with everyone else in the *Morris County Gazette* on Saturday."

Rita clenched her fists, suddenly remembering all the things she didn't like about Ana. At the top of that list was that smug self-confidence, annoying at any age, but absolutely insufferable in one so young. Rita was about to hang up, but then thought better of it. There was no real downside to involving Ana, other than a glancing blow to Rita's pride and the ignominy (not for the first time) of sharing a byline with someone who only had a Cinderella license. Rita would get brownie points from her editor as a "team player" and she'd get a chance to observe Ana up close, to see if her indifference to Vinnie was for real. Plus, she could pump her for information about the incident on the set.

"You know, dear, I could use your help actually. I'm at the old Gambone estate, and I'd like you to explore it with me." She rattled off some directions. "Oh, and Ana...bring a crowbar, would you?"

****

"What even is this?" Ana asked, slightly out of breath, as she wedged the crowbar in the crack and tried again. She was skinny, but surprisingly strong; Rita could make out the outlines of her biceps through her red crewneck sweater.

"An old fallout shelter."

Ana strained against the crowbar and grunted from the exertion. When it did yield, she rested for a moment and eyed Rita though a mass of dark, slightly kinky hair that had fallen over her face. "You called me 'dear' on the phone."

"Did I? What's wrong with that?"

"You usually call me '*cara.*'"

"Well, it's the same thing. *Cara* is just 'dear' in Italian. *Cara*, dear—it's the same thing."

"Not to you. 'Dear' is for acquaintances, '*cara*' means they're part of your inner circle, part of your tribe. When I was an intern, I was 'dear.' Then you saw me as more of an equal and I became '*cara.*' And now I'm back to 'dear' and I want to know why. This isn't because of Vinnie, is it?"

"Vinnie?" Rita decided to play dumb. "You're co-stars in *The Legend of Acorn Hollow*. How could I possibly object to that?"

Ana eyed Rita suspiciously, and Rita could tell Ana was trying to work out whether Acorn Hollow's best investigative reporter—and the world's most involved mother—could really be totally oblivious to the gossip swirling around her son.

"Well, Vinnie and I are friends, too." Ana pushed her shoulder against the crowbar. This time, there was a little anger behind it, and the door budged ever so slightly.

"That's wonderful, dear—er, *cara*. We can all use more friends, and having an intelligent, levelheaded girl like you as a friend—well, let's just say that's a refreshing change from Vinnie's usual crowd." Rita lowered her voice, as if letting Ana in on a secret. "Vinnie means well, but he's always been a bit of a troublemaker. And he always seems to get his friends and girlfriends in trouble, too."

Ana stopped pushing on the crowbar. "Girlfriends?"

"Oh, Vinnie's always had a way with the ladies. Once, at the library, he felt up Mrs. DePalma, the poor woman."

"That doesn't sound like Vinnie." Ana wrinkled her nose. "And Mrs. DePalma is...old."

"Oh, Vinnie's not too particular."

Rita neglected to mention that the event in question had occurred twenty years ago when Mrs. DePalma was in her late thirties and Vinnie was still in diapers. He'd had a fascination with pantyhose and, consequently, a habit of grabbing every pantyhose-clad leg in toddling distance.

"And then there was his Prom date, Eva." Rita shook her head sadly. "A straight-A student headed for the Ivy League. Next thing you know, she gets caught helping Vinnie and some friends kidnap the Mount Washington Bulldogs' mascot, Harvard's rescinded her offer, and she's taking correspondence classes from prison."

Technically, that was all true, but Rita omitted the little detail that the stay in prison had nothing to do with the dognapping and everything to do with a hit-and-run. Vinnie, mercifully, had not been in the car.

Ana's frown deepened.

"And I hear from Sal that there are girls falling all over him at the nursery."

"Vinnie can't help it if he's good-looking—that is, if some people think he's good-looking."

"Of course not. But I just hope he doesn't lead those poor girls on. I mean, I can't see Vinnie settling down anytime soon. He needs to sow his wild oats."

"I'm surprised to hear that from a church lady like you."

"Oh, I didn't say I *approved*. I'm just being realistic. I'm sure he'll settle down someday—maybe in ten, fifteen years—with some nice unambitious girl who's perfectly happy to be stuck in Acorn Hollow."

"Stuck?" Ana let the word linger in the air a moment. "Lots of people love living here. You've lived here your whole life."

"Yes, but I'm from a different era. Nowadays, ambitious, intelligent young women—well, women like you, for instance—leave and go to the big city, rack up impressive degrees and launch a real career. The sky is the limit! Guys like Vinnie—well, they'd just hold a girl like that back."

Ana pushed down, hard, and the door flew open.

They descended into the abyss, the damp, musty smell growing ever stronger. Rita's hands shook as she trained the pale golden orb from her cell phone on the crumbling concrete steps. She tried to ignore the scurrying noises that echoed through the chamber—no wonder Luciano and Cesare were so excited—and the cobwebs that brushed her lips and eyelashes.

"It kind of feels like the entrance to the underworld, doesn't it?" Ana joked, but she didn't fool Rita. Even the normally unflappable Ana was spooked.

They arrived at the bottom of the steps, and Rita swung open the heavy lead door and let go of the leashes. Luciano and Cesare scurried inside, snouts down, tails wagging.

Rita took a tentative step inside, propped the door open with a discarded nearby cinderblock, and shone the beam over the crumbling cement floor and walls, the rusted metal bunk bed frames, shelves upon shelves of canned pineapple, canned corn, and Campbell's soup. A few kerosene lamps were discarded in the corner, and an antiquated radio with a broken antenna lay on the floor. Rita was just reaching for her camera to capture this eerie time capsule when she heard a chorus of frantic yelps and the scritch-scratch of claws on a hard surface. She swung the beam towards the sound.

"*Luciano! Cesare! Smettete di cavare!*"

But they paid Rita no mind at all. Not only did they not stop digging, but their excavations intensified. Flakes of cement and clods of dirt were flying through the air, tails were furiously wagging, snouts were pressed against the patch of damp earthen wall that grew as more and more flakes of cement were brushed away.

She had rarely seen her dogs this delighted, and she wondered what could be lurking behind the wall. A warren of terrified bunnies? An old tin of beef jerky? A jar of peanut butter?

The yelps crescendoed as a chunk of the wall came tumbling down. Rita looked up at the ceiling and prayed it would hold.

Then Luciano struck his snout into the rubble and emerged, like a conquering hero, with a long, slender object between his teeth.

Cesare leapt into the fray. One hundred and eighty pounds of fur and muscle reared up and pounced. But Cesare missed his target, Luciano, and fell back on a cabinet with peeling lime-green paint and sharp metal edges that were now showing through. It wobbled back and forth, the metal cans that lined its shelves crashing against each other, before coming to rest on its side.

Rita gasped. There was a dark hole where the wall should have been, a waist-high crawl space that had been artfully concealed by the cabinet. Not for the first time, her dogs had proved their worth as sleuthing sidekicks.

"Ana, look, it's a—"

But the words died on her lips as she felt Luciano nuzzle against her and press the long, slender object into her hand. She clasped it in her fingers and gently rubbed off a layer of grit. Beneath, it was cold and smooth, hard as ivory.

She heard Ana gasp beside her.

"Is that...human?"

Rita shone the light on it and turned it over carefully. She traced the long, straight ridgeline, then ran her fingers over the bulbous end.

"I think so. A femur, maybe."

Rita and Ana crouched down in the dirt, Luciano and Cesare beside them, panting, ready for action. Rita patted one, then the other. "*Bravi*. You've done well, boys."

Somehow, her dogs seemed to understand that Rita would take it from here. They sat on their haunches, patiently, while Rita and Ana gently scooped out the rubble and peered behind it. In the dim light, Rita could make out the vaguest outline of the human form. She reached into her purse, extracted a make-up brush, and set to work brushing away decades of dirt and grime.

Ana shuddered as an earthworm slithered out to greet them. "I hope you're not going to use that again."

"*Certo che non!* I'm tan enough as it is."

Ana giggled. "You're like MacGyver, Rita."

"Ah, but unlike MacGyver I carry more than a pocket knife and duct tape." Rita brushed away for a few more minutes, until she had uncovered a set of ribs and a portion of the skull. "I'd say we've got a full skeleton."

She took out her camera and started to snap away. "Sam will love this. 'Joey Gambone Found at Last'—and in an abandoned fallout shelter, no less, on his own farm! I'll share the byline with you, of course, and in all fairness, maybe we should credit Luciano and Cesare too. I mean, they did find the body and the secret pass—"

"Uh, Rita? You might want to hold off on writing that headline."

"Well, I mean technically we don't write the headlines. I know that. But I'm sure it will be something—"

"No, I mean it might not even be Joey Gambone. Look." Ana snatched Rita's phone out of her hand and shone the light behind the back of the overturned cabinet. "It's a torn piece of clothing."

Rita moved closer and squinted. She reached into her purse, got out a small plastic bag, and slid it over her hand. Then she reached down and scooped up the swatch of fabric and held it to the light.

"It looks like...."

The words caught in her throat.

"...a scarf with a squirrel pattern?"

Rita nodded. Her voice thick with emotion, she said, "Just like the one Bobby Bruickhuisen was wearing the night he disappeared. The one his Aunt Emma knit for him."

Ana slithered through the opening first. As her pert little denim-clad butt reared up for a moment and then disappeared into the darkness, Rita tried not to imagine Vinnie's hands there. But the harder she tried, the more firmly the image lodged in her mind.

And her conversation with Ana had told her everything Rita needed to know. Ana hadn't said an incriminating word, but her body language spoke volumes: the way she stiffened whenever Rita brought up Vinnie's other paramours, the way she blushed when Rita came too close to the truth.

Ana and her baby were in love.

Rita shooed Luciano and Cesare through the opening, then got down on her hands and knees. The opening was narrow—too narrow, really, for a woman who enjoyed her tiramisu, biscotti, and gelato just a little too much. Rita sucked in her stomach, the way she always did in photos, and lowered one hip.

"Rita!" she heard ahead of her. "Are you coming?"

"Yes." Rita gritted her teeth. "Remember, dear, I have child-bearing hips, not slither-through-a-hole-in-the-wall hips." She blew a lock of hair off her face. "Obviously, the Gambone women had no idea how to cook. Otherwise, their men would never have fit through this hole."

Rita exhaled sharply and held her breath while sucking in her gut. Then she rocked forward and felt herself slide past a few inches of earth. But then, gasping for breath, her lungs filled again with the suffocatingly wet, heavy air, and she felt herself hemmed in once more.

She had a sudden image of the Morris County Sheriff's Office hoisting her remains onto a whale sling to bring them to the surface, where the waiting medical examiner would declare her demise "death by tiramisu." "If only she'd listened to her physician and lost thirty pounds," he'd say, "she would never have been in this predicament."

Luciano and Cesare must have had a similar premonition, because they too got into the act now, tugging at her sweater.

"This legend gets stranger and stranger, doesn't it?" Rita lurched forward with a grunt. "I mean, first Ichabod Crane disappears—"

"That was just a story, Rita."

"Not according to the widow." Rita groaned and inched forward again. A torn piece of sweater was now in Luciano's mouth. "Then Joey Gambone disappears in

1936 and was last seen right here, on this farm. Then Bobby Bruickhuisen, who played Ichabod Crane, disappears in 1962. He's last seen on the Van Tassel farm, but for some reason it turns out he was murdered here—or murdered elsewhere and taken here. And now Jake Johnson, the boy playing Bobby Bruickhuisen, is receiving threats and having a pumpkin fall on his head. And all of these incidents over a woman."

On the word "woman," Rita made one final push and squeezed through the opening, emerging into a larger, more cavernous space.

"A woman?" Ana's voice was louder now, as if she'd turned back towards Rita.

Rita shone the beam of light off the walls and ceiling. They were lined with concrete, and the tunnel was now plenty wide enough to accommodate her girth and high enough for her to easily stand. The air was cooler and drier, too. Rita felt as though she had stepped into another world.

"Yes—a woman. Katrina Van Tassel in the case of Ichabod Crane, Anita Gambone and Viviana Rossi in the case of Joey Gambone, Kate Van Tassel in the disappearance of Bobby Bruickhuisen, and..."

"And?"

"And you."

"Me?"

"Come now, Ana. Like any good reporter, you must have heard the rumor by now. Jake Johnson is being threatened—and having pumpkins mysteriously fall on his head—all because someone's jealous he's dating you."

"But I'm not dating Jake."

"Does he know that?"

Ana snorted. "Well, if he doesn't, he should. We're debate team partners, co-stars in *The Legend of Acorn Hollow*, and friends. But that's it."

"But you could see how someone might get the wrong idea."

"Stopping for a burger on the way home from a debate tournament," Ana said firmly, "is not a date."

They were walking briskly now; Luciano and Cesare were trotting on ahead. It seemed as if the tunnel would never end.

Rita said, "Ana, you should know that your suitors are at the top of Detective Benedetto's suspect list."

Ana stopped dead in her tracks, causing Rita to bump into her. "Did he tell you that?"

"No, but he didn't need to. That's how he thinks. Trust me. And trust me when I say that if one of your suitors' fingerprints should turn up on those incriminating messages, well—it won't look good for him."

Ana turned a paler shade of brown. "That's, um"— she wrung her hands and looked as though she were about to be sick—"oh, no, he thought he was helping me with my big story. What have I done?"

"Your big story's about the attacks on Jake Johnson?"

Ana nodded glumly, too chastened to try and deny it. So that was her big scoop. More of the same story she had been covering all along. All Ana's smug youthful self-confidence had suddenly drained away, and she looked like a frightened wisp of a teenaged girl.

"And this boy who's helping you?"

"I—I can't say. But I feel terrible. If I had known..."

Rita reached out and squeezed Ana's hand. "It's not your fault, *cara*." She felt the old, familiar rush of affection return. "What's done is done. *Acqua passata*. But you must keep Jake and this other boy apart and do nothing to feed the rumor mills that you're together. And you must tell Detective Benedetto that this boy— this other suitor of yours—was helping with the story and if there are any of his fingerprints on the messages to Jake Johnson, that is why. *Capisci?*"

"Yes." Rita couldn't see Ana's face, but she could hear a smile in her voice. "And now I'm back to *cara*."

They walked in companionable silence for several minutes, marveling at the endless, zig-zagging tunnel. A sudden chorus of frantic barking ahead brought them up short.

Ana and Rita broke into a run. The beam of light bobbed up and down, illuminating two giant fur balls pounding against a concrete wall.

"It just...ends," Ana whispered.

Rita shone her light upwards and pointed at a grate in the ceiling. "No, it doesn't. Here—get on my shoulders."

Rita reached into her purse and handed Ana a screwdriver. Ana deftly unscrewed a few bolts, sending the grate crashing down to the concrete floor.

Rita could feel a blast of warmer air, as though the chamber above had central heat. She could also hear a man's low voice, then a woman's. Could this be the secret lair of Joey Gambone's modern-day descendants? Were heinous crimes being plotted just above their heads—arson, bribery schemes, even hits on rival mobsters?

Ana's head disappeared through the grate. Rita felt the weight lift off her shoulders, then glimpsed Ana's slim legs vaulting up through the gap in the ceiling.

Rita heard the man sputter, "What the—?"

And then she heard Ana's voice, bewildered but not unpleasant. "Oh—it's you."

"You—who?" Rita hissed. She did not realize her teenaged colleague (and son's secret girlfriend) was on friendly terms with organized crime.

Ana poked her head back through the shaft. "It's Orlando...and Penny." There was something odd about her voice, as if there was something she wasn't telling Rita, or at least couldn't tell her now. "We're at Rinalidis' Winery."

Chapter Eleven

Orlando paced back and forth by the fireplace in his cozy, oak-paneled study. "So you're telling me," he said, "that there is a half-mile-long tunnel that leads from an abandoned fallout shelter on the old Gambone estate to right under my study?"

"*Esatto.*"

Rita was warming her hands by the roaring fire and enjoying a glass of Rinaldis' prize-winning red wine. Luciano and Cesare were curled up beside her, and Ana was tucking into the cheese plate so thoughtfully provided by Orlando. Penny was seated in an armchair, sipping a glass of wine and frantically trying to re-arrange her disheveled platinum-blonde hair.

Rita watched out of the corner of her eye as Penny hastily buttoned the top button of her sky-blue silk blouse. Now Rita understood the odd tone in Ana's voice earlier. She had surprised Orlando and Penny at a most inopportune time—perhaps the way Anita Gambone had surprised her husband and Viviana all those years ago. But in a supreme twist of irony, they had caught Orlando with the woman who played Joey Gambone's wife, not his mistress.

"You didn't know about the tunnel?" Rita asked.

"Not at all. I always just assumed that grate was over the wine cellar." Orlando rubbed a hand over his head, as smooth and hard as a billiard ball, and furrowed his thick, dark brows. "The grate was there when I bought the place sixteen years ago. We replaced the HVAC a few years back, but there was no need to replace the air ducts, so we just left them alone."

"You bought it from the Bertinellis, right? After the old man died? Teri wanted to hold onto the farm, but her sister wanted to cash out her share of the inheritance."

"That's right." He frowned. "Little did I know Teri would be a thorn in my side ever since."

Teri and Orlando were forever clashing over his plans to expand the winery—and bring ever more visitors down their shared country lane.

"But before the Bertinellis owned it...." He crossed over to his enormous solid oak desk and opened a drawer. "How old did you say the tunnel was?"

Rita thought of the scrap of blue fabric in her purse. "It was built by at least 1962, I'd say. But it's probably older than that—used by bootleggers, I'd say. Maybe Joey Gambone himself."

Orlando chuckled. "Now that would be ironic, wouldn't it? If the guy I'm playing in *The Legend of Acorn Hollow* turns out to have used my farm for his little bootlegging operation."

He started rummaging through the drawers, yellowed papers falling to the floor like snow.

Ana eyed Orlando and then Penny over a raisin crisp topped with manchego cheese and a drizzle of fig jam.

"We're sorry," she said, her voice dripping with insinuation, "to have barged in like this."

"Barged?" Orlando stopped rummaging abruptly, his hand resting on a sheaf of onionskin-thin papers. "Oh, no, we—we were just rehearsing."

"Ah." Ana nodded sagaciously. "Working on your chemistry."

Orlando looked helplessly at Penny, who crossed her arms over her ample chest and shot him a frosty look.

"Er, yes," he said, "I suppose that's a good word for it. Getting into character—isn't that what they call it?"

"But Anita and Joey didn't have chemistry," Rita said, her tone nearly as icy as the look on Penny's face. For some reason, she found herself indignant on her twin's behalf. "They were just an old married couple, and he was two-timing her with Viviana who, I'm told, my sister does an excellent job channeling. All that fire, all that passion. Don't you think so, Orlando?"

Orlando choked midway through a sip of red wine and emitted an unflattering sound somewhere between a groan and a yelp of surprise.

Rita calmly took a last sip of wine and placed her empty goblet on the coffee table. "You should have invited Rose to your little rehearsal. To get the love triangle just right."

"Yeah," Ana said, "and maybe you should schedule some time for just the two of you—Orlando and Rose, that is—to work on your chemistry."

Penny flushed to the roots of her dyed platinum-blonde hair. Orlando leaned on his desk, looking as though he might be sick. He shuffled through a few more papers.

"Ah!" he suddenly exclaimed. His voice was unnaturally loud, although whether because he had finally found what he was looking for or because he had a reason to change the subject, Rita could not tell. "I knew I had the title search somewhere. The Bertinellis purchased this in 1982 from Alexander Van Zandt, who purchased this in 1971 from Guido Montelusa, who inherited this from Guido's father, Silvio Montelusa in 1935...." He looked up expectantly. "Do these names mean anything to you?"

"Alexander is Lydia Van Zandt's father, and Lydia was the one who spread the rumor that Kate was pregnant. Guido was Sandro Montelusa's father, and Sandro, who was dating Kate, was a suspect in Bobby Bruickhuisen's disappearance." Rita decided not to tell them about the scarf fragment. "Well," she said brightly, springing to her feet, "It's time for Ana and me to go. *Mille grazie per tutto.*"

"Shall I drive you to your car?" Orlando said.

Rita peered at the grate and tried to imagine lowering herself back down into the tunnel. At the end of the descent, she very much doubted her dignity would be intact—or many of her bones. "That's very kind of you, Orlando."

Penny shot them more daggers, but Rita just smiled sweetly in her direction.

Orlando drove them back to their car. "Creepy place," he said with an uneasy chuckle as Rita clambered out and slid behind the wheel of her Buick. Ana opened the back door, and the dogs leapt in. With a honk and a friendly wave, Orlando sped off.

Rita made a quick call to Detective Benedetto to report the skeleton in the fallout shelter. "Good work," he said, "though the chief will not be pleased."

"Why? It's not like he needs to do anything. You'll call forensics and confirm it's Bobby, I'll solve the case, and then he'll try to swoop in and get the credit."

"That's probably how it will go down, all right." Detective Benedetto laughed and rang off.

Ana turned to Rita and said, "So, are you going to tell your sister that Orlando and Penny are an item, or shall I?"

Rita did not know which task she relished less: telling the widow she had found Bobby's remains lodged in a fallout shelter on the Gambone farm, or telling Rose that she had no chance with Orlando.

"*Che pensate voi?*" she asked her passengers in the backseat. "Rose?"

Luciano growled. Rose tolerated Rita's dogs, but that was about it.

"*O la vedova?*"

Four ears perked up, and she heard the thwack-thwack-thwack of merrily wagging tails on upholstered seats. Rita knew the reaction had little to do with the widow and everything to do with the widow's main haunt: the cemetery. Luciano and Cesare loved romping among the headstones, searching for bunnies and squirrels, lolling about in the sunshine, and rolling on the grass. She was nevertheless glad that someone else had made the decision for her.

Rita drove back down sun-dappled country lanes, past white-steepled churches, rolling hills, apple orchards, and herds of dairy cows. Soon, they were back in Acorn Hollow. She dropped off Ana, then eased onto the gravel roads that wound through the cemetery. At the top of a familiar grassy knoll, beneath the shade of an old hickory tree, they came to a stop.

Rita and the dogs clambered out. Rita mumbled a quick prayer over her mother's grave, unscrewed the flask that hung from Luciano's neck, and splashed a few drops of limoncello on the ground. Then, with a look of grim determination, she marched towards the tiny black figure perched on a marble slab, half-hidden by a wall of newsprint.

"Oh, Rita!"

The widow's rich, plummy voice floated over the rows of headstones, carried by the wind. The newspaper rustled in the breeze, then lowered to reveal a pale, almost ghostly, image.

"You've given us"—by 'us,' the widow meant she and her three deceased husbands—"so much reading pleasure today. Your story on Bobby's disappearance was excellent. You really wrote so beautifully, so movingly about my nephew. Thomas here"—she patted the marble slab upon which she was seated—"was particularly touched. They were close, you know. Thaddeus, of course"—she squinted at the adjacent slab—"doesn't come out that well in the story but, well, you've got to let the chips fall where they may."

The widow sighed and shook her head. "And of course, Leonard isn't much of an intellectual or a historian, so he was a bit bored with the piece. But I read him the Sports section and 'Teen Talk'—Leonard was a teacher, you know, so he's always fascinated by the goings-on at the high school. Oh! And I read him 'Ask a Dude.' Did you read 'Ask a Dude' today?"

"Not yet," Rita demurred, hiding a smile. One of the few secrets she kept from the widow was that she knew the identity of Acorn Hollow's anonymous male advice columnist. Rita settled into the cool marble surface and motioned for Luciano and Cesare to lay down on the grass. She patted each dog on the head affectionately and tossed them a treat.

" 'Dear Dude,' " the widow read, pushing her spectacles up the bridge of her long, bony nose, " 'I'm in love with a boy who's a little older than me. His mother's the domineering grizzly mamma type, one of those women who's a terrific friend but a terrible enemy. She also happens to be my co-worker and, until now, we've gotten along well. I'd even say we're friends...or at least I thought we were. Lately, she's been cold and distant. I was going to tell her about us, but now I'm not so sure. My boyfriend doesn't want to tell her, either. What should I do? Yours truly, Scared of the Grizzly Mamma' "

The widow wiggled her wispy eyebrows in Rita's direction. "Sound familiar?"

"No," Rita said in her haughtiest voice. "I can't think of anyone I know who's a domineering grizzly mamma."

"Is that so?"

"And even if I could—which I can't—it doesn't seem like much of a dilemma to me. If the girl hopes for any kind of future with this boy, she's going to have to stand up to his mother some time. You can't survive in an Italian family if you don't."

"She never said the family was Italian."

"Oh, well—it's obvious, isn't it? Anyway, what did The Dude have to say in reply?"

"Ah." The widow's eyes twinkled. "The Dude was particularly perceptive today. 'Dear Scared, I've survived sixty-eight years as the son, son-in-law, and husband of a formidable grizzly mamma. Trust me, you do not want to get between them and their baby cub—it could get ugly. So, you have two choices: back away slowly, like any good Girl Scout would, so as not to startle her, or get on her side, make her realize you, too, are protecting her baby cub from the big, bad world; you are an ally and a worthy successor. You, too, will be a grizzly mamma someday to her three perfect, Italian-speaking, Mass-attending, *nonna*-worshiping grandchildren. You, too, will make a killer cannoli.' "

Rita frowned. Sal wouldn't stay anonymous long if he persisted in sharing overly personal details.

" 'I wish you luck because you're going to need it. The Dude.' " The widow looked up sharply. "Well? What do you think?"

Rita shrugged. "Not bad advice," she muttered with grudging admiration. Then she cleared her throat to get back to the business at hand. "I have news, Emma."

Rita's hands shook as she reached into her purse, took out her phone, and scrolled to the photo. She hesitated for a moment, cradling it in her lap, delaying the moment when she would have to tell the widow of her nephew's fate. Would the widow be pleased to have closure, or crushed to have the last spark of hope die?

The widow had said that Bobby was dead, but did she truly believe that or was it a matter of hardening her heart?

"Well?" the widow said sharply. Her pale bony fingers fluttered up to her throat and brushed the memento mori fastened there. It was one of those Victorian lockets with the hair of a deceased loved one twisted into a grotesquely beautiful image. This one was of a black widow spider, and it was woven, Rita knew, out of the raven-haired locks of the widow's long-deceased younger sister, the one that the widow's second husband was rumored to have killed.

No, Rita decided, the widow would want to know. She was accustomed to living intimately with death, to celebrating it, even wearing it. But she was not accustomed to uncertainty.

Rita turned her phone around slowly and placed it in the widow's lap.

Emma let out a little strangled cry, then looked up at Rita. Her eyes were bright and shiny, hard as flint. "It's Bobby's, isn't it? The scarf I knit for him."

The momentary surprise was gone. Her tone was one of grim determination.

"And just a foot or two away," Rita said, "we found a body—well, a skeleton."

Rita shuddered, but the widow did not look perturbed in the least. Perhaps that's what happened when you spent your days in a cemetery communing with the dead. When you outlived everyone you'd grown up with and nearly all of the next generation too. And when you'd taken a life—or two—as well.

The widow squinted up at her. "And you found this—where?"

Rita told her about the fallout shelter, the tunnel, and the tunnel's surprising endpoint.

"Rinaldis' Winery," the widow repeated softly. "The old Montelusa estate."

Her dark eyes roamed the hillside, then over to a grassy knoll where a stone angel watched over a cluster of dark gray headstones silhouetted against the bright blue sky. From her own wanderings in the cemetery, Rita knew that was the Montelusa plot. The widow's gaze then flitted further on, to the dark spiky rail, its gate creaking in the wind, that enclosed the Gambone plot.

Emma frowned and finally turned her gaze to the Bruickhuisen plot, far tidier and more modern, but with a conspicuously empty six-foot-long strip down its center. It was the space they had left for Bobby.

"Anita Gambone's maiden name was Montelusa," the widow murmured thoughtfully.

"So her brother owned what is now the Rinaldi estate."

The widow nodded. "Guido. Rich as Croesseus, as the Italians used to say back then. All ill-gotten gains, of course, from his father, Silvio, who ran all kinds of rackets in Kingston and Albany. This was Silvio's country retreat; I guess it made him feel less dirty, like some sort of gentleman. But Guido was supposedly on the up-and-up and had left that lifestyle all behind. He let Anita's and his other brother, Pietro, take over the family empire. Guido was a legitimate businessman. He was the one who planted the vineyards and started the winery—after Prohibition ended, of course. Plus, he grew fruits and vegetables and sold them through a cousin in Brooklyn. You know how Italians dominated the produce markets in those days." Suddenly, the widow's eyebrows shot up. "You know, Penny Albanese's a Montelusa, too, on her mother's side."

Rita's mouth fell open. Penny hadn't said a thing when Orlando mentioned that Guido Montelusa had once owned the winery.

"Who knows?" the widow chuckled. "Maybe this clandestine little fling with Orlando is just an elaborate scheme to get the winery back in the family."

Rita could hardly believe her ears. "You know about that?"

"Oh, everyone knows about that, dear."

Rita reddened, loth to admit that, until today, she hadn't had a clue. She glanced back at the Gambone plot and then the Bruikhuisen plot. "And what about the other end of the tunnel—the Gambone estate? Who lived there in 1962?"

"No one. By the time Bobby was in high school, it had fallen into ruin. Anita moved to a little bungalow in Acorn Hollow. She said the farm was too much upkeep after Joey disappeared. She tried to sell it, but after what had happened, no one wanted to buy it. Everyone thought it was haunted."

Rita frowned. There had to be a very small circle of people who knew of the existence of the tunnel—and one of those people had buried Bobby there. Probably killed him, too.

"It all comes back to Sandro, doesn't it?" Rita said. "He had a strong motive to kill Bobby, and he lived above one end of the tunnel. He must have known about it—probably played in it as a kid, that kind of thing."

The widow pursed her lips. "I don't know if he had it in him, though. He was a gentle soul."

"Still, if it was a crime of passion, an accident maybe even..." Rita shook her head. "There's another thing that's been bothering me...when a young girl winds up pregnant and the paternity is in question, it's almost always the girl who winds up dead."

The widow nodded thoughtfully. "Why Bobby, you mean? Why not Kate?"

"Exactly. Even if Bobby was the father of Kate's child..."

"—which he wasn't—"

"...what's the point of doing away with him? Killing him wouldn't change the fact that Kate was pregnant with someone else's child. It wouldn't make her love the murderer. Usually, when jealousy is the motive, the murderer's attitude is 'if I can't have her, no one will.' So, what if we're looking at this all wrong? What if the murderer wanted to kill Bobby all along, for reasons having nothing to do with Kate, but he's worried about getting caught. Then, when Kate's pregnancy is revealed and people jump to the conclusion the baby is Bobby's, the murderer sees the perfect opportunity. Bobby's out looking for Kate, while Kate's dad and brother and Vito and Sandro are out looking for Bobby. If the murderer can just find Bobby before anyone else does, he can make it look like the work of a jealous cuckolded lover or maybe an enraged father or brother."

The widow picked up the thread now. Her eyes took on a faraway misty look; in her mind's eye, she was picturing the murderer stalking through the deep dark woods, lying in wait by the old stone bridge. "He puts some obstacle in the road—a log, maybe, something Bobby doesn't see until it's too late. His motorbike flips over, Bobby falls to the ground, and the killer bashes him on the head with a rock."

Rita thought of the cobbles lining the stream bed beneath the old stone bridge and winced. Then, as now, there was no shortage of improvised murder weapons. All it would take was one perfectly timed blow to exactly the right spot.

"But," the widow continued, "it wouldn't do to leave the body in case there were fingerprints or a stray thread from the murderer's clothing. Plus, it wouldn't fit with the townspeople's romantic ideas about the legend—the curse. How much better to connect it to Washington Irving's tale of Ichabod Crane, especially since Bobby had just played Ichabod on stage."

"And," Rita said, "what better way to implicate Sandro, who played Brom Bones. The townspeople would instantly make the connection. 'Sandro and Bobby were rivals for Kate's affections,' they would think, 'so Sandro must have made Bobby disappear, just like Brom Bones was always rumored to have caused Ichabod Crane's disappearance. Of course, in both cases, no one can prove anything...' "

The widow smiled ruefully. "And that is just what they did say. Poor Sandro. The moment he graduated high school, he left town, never to return. I heard he joined the Marines and went to Vietnam."

"He was a strong guy, then?"

"Oh, yes, very! Strong as an ox, and very athletic. The quarterback of the high school football team."

Rita thought of the pictures she'd seen of Bobby. He'd been tall, reed-thin, kind of gangly and awkward. He'd never have had a chance fighting back against Sandro. If, that is, Sandro had been his killer.

"And what about the other men who raced off after Kate?" Rita ticked each one off on her fingers. "Her dad, Senator Van Tassel. Her brother Hank. Vito Napoletano." She winced as she said Vito's name, feeling as though she were accusing her own son, even though she knew this was ridiculous. "Did any of them have dealings with Bobby besides the obvious?"

The widow pursed her thin fish lips. "The senator knew Bobby quite well. Bobby volunteered for his campaign, see."

"Why?"

"What do you mean, why? To get some political experience. Bobby was student body president and had ambitions to run for governor someday."

"Not to impress the father of the girl he had a crush on?"

Rita was something of an expert in teenaged love, having lived through its trials and tribulations for each of her three children, and she rather thought this was the stronger motivating factor.

"I told you," the widow said, her dark eyes flashing. "Bobby and Kate were not an item."

"But what if you're wrong?"

"I'm not wrong. Not about this. And as for Kate's brother, Hank—well, of course, he knew Bobby, mostly through Kate. But he also worked for his dad's Senate campaign, so I'd expect that way, too. And Vito? I can't see there'd be any connection besides school and the play."

The widow lifted her bony little shoulders in a shrug and sighed. "Well, dear, it will be up to you to sort this all out."

"And you," Rita said. "You're my biggest asset in the case. You knew these people in their youth. I won't be able to solve it without you."

"Ah"—the widow winked—"but I may not be around to help you."

Rita shook her head. "Now, Emma, don't go starting that again. You're healthy as a horse. You'll probably outlive us all."

"Oh, Lord," the widow deadpanned. "I hope not."

The widow rested a pale hand on Rita's arm. Rita looked down at the knotted veins, brilliantly blue and pulsing, at the life force of this woman of surprising vitality and strength.

"Remember," Rita said, "Regardless of what *you* may call it, *I* am hosting a celebration of life party, not a funeral. You need to be alive to hear all of the nice little things people say about you."

The widow cracked a smile and giggled, displaying her crooked yellow teeth. "Oh, yes!" She clasped her bird-boned hands together. "How I'll enjoy that! And the food! You remembered my instructions, right?"

"Full fat, loads of sugar and calories. We'll be serving spinach-artichoke dip with full-fat Parmesan cheese from the creamery, pumpkin ravioli swimming in a sage brown butter sauce, Italian meatballs drowning in a rich red gravy, an enormous antipasti tray piled high with fatty meats and cheeses, oysters Rockefeller, fried calamari, and for dessert"—Rita's eyes twinkled—"an apple crisp, a cranberry-pecan tart, a very decadent pumpkin cheesecake"—at the mention of "cheese," Luciano and Cesare suddenly sprang to attention, their furry ears rotating up and out like antennas searching for a signal—"a chocolate-cherry flourless chocolate cake and, of course, tiramisu."

"Marvelous!" The widow clapped her hands. "I do always love your tiramisu. And since it's my funeral, I'll treat myself to seconds—even thirds."

"You know, you never told me how many RSVP'd. I have no idea how much food to make."

"Ah." The widow reached into her black satchel, pulled out a crinkled sheet of notebook paper, and smoothed it out. The sunlight streamed through the paper, illuminating a long list of names in the widow's exquisite curlicued penmanship, heavily annotated in red pen. She ran a bony finger down the list, her lips moving silently. "Forty, maybe forty-five. That takes into account the likely no-shows, although"—she cackled—"I can be quite persuasive when it counts."

Rita's jaw dropped. The widow was a recluse with very few friends and no living family members other than one eccentric and highly agoraphobic octogenarian niece. Everyone she'd ever loved was here, in this cemetery.

Who could these forty-five people be? Seized by curiosity, Rita leaned closer, peering over the widow's bony shoulder and trying to make out the individual names scrawled across the sheet of paper.

But just when she got in range of her bifocals, the widow abruptly folded the list with one sharp crease, then another, and stowed it away in her satchel. The satchel snapped shut with a loud click, which startled Luciano and Cesare.

"Uh-uh-uh," the widow said, wagging her finger at Rita. "We wouldn't want to ruin the surprise now, would we?"

Chapter Twelve

Rita spent most of the following week preparing the world's most decadent funeral feast—and managing the love triangles in her life.

On Monday, she drove down to the Italian grocery store in Poughkeepsie and stocked up on prosciutto, salami, sopressata, and enormous glass jars of garlic-stuffed Sicilian olives flecked with pepperoncino, Jerusalem artichoke hearts marinated in extra-virgin olive oil, roasted red peppers, and San Marzano tomatoes nurtured in the volcanic soil of Mount Etna and air-dried to a tangy sweetness on the sunbaked plains of Sicily.

"Hosting a party?" the clerk asked as he rang her up. The bill came to an eye-watering two hundred and eighty-seven dollars.

"A funeral."

"*Che peccato!*"

"Oh, don't be sorry." Rita put her bags in the cart and waved good-bye to the astonished clerk. "The guest of honor is still alive. She wants to hear the eulogy, you see."

After a quick stop at the Culinary Institute of America for a half-dozen French baguettes, she drove down winding country roads to the creamery, where the day's sheep-milking demonstration was in full swing. She'd seen the show dozens of times, though, so she slipped past the tourists and into the shop, where she ordered whole wheels of aged Parmesan, Manchego, and pecorino, plus burrata made from buffalo milk.

"I hope no one's lactose-intolerant," the farmer's wife joked as she helped Rita cram twenty pounds of cheese into her trunk.

On Tuesday, Rita sliced up the baguettes, now a day old and slightly firm, brushed them with olive oil and garlic, and transformed them into *crostini* for the bruschetta that was to grace the widow's funeral feast, all while trying her best to dissuade her sister from pursuing Orlando any further.

"Face it," she said into the phone for the umpteenth time, "he's taken. I saw it with my own two eyes. He and Penny Albanese are an item."

"Really? Then why the secrecy? They're both single."

"Perhaps because her husband died just six months ago. It wouldn't be seemly."

"It wouldn't because it isn't. What if they've been knocking boots for more than six months? And then, what if she decided she wanted more than an occasional furtive roll in the hay? What if Penny wanted to be with Orlando so much she offed her husband?"

"Rose, the man died of cancer."

"Oh, yeah? How do you know? Did you personally inspect the death certificate?"

Rita sighed. Larry Albanese had battled stage four pancreatic cancer for years. Every time he appeared in public, he was white as a sheet and frail as an old lady. She didn't see how you could fake that.

But her sister would not be dissuaded. "Maybe she was in the cahoots with the doctor. Remember that case in Florida? The one where the doctor diagnosed all these healthy people with cancer just so he could make a buck?"

Rita nodded ever so slightly, loth to admit she did.

"So she gets a doctor at that fancy new cancer center in Albany to say Larry's got cancer, he fries his insides with all those cancer drugs, and eventually he dies."

"But you forget that when Larry was diagnosed, Orlando was happily in love with Greta."

"Yeah," Rose said darkly, "and look how that turned out."

"But Greta," Rita said, "wasn't killed by Penny, was she?"

Rose grunted, which Rita knew was as close as she was going to get to an acknowledgement that Rita might be right. "Even if—if—you're right, that doesn't mean that Penny is not a danger to Orlando. You yourself said that she's a Montelusa. She could be a moll for the mob, trying to weasel her way in there just to get the winery back in the family. How did you say they are related again?"

Rita rifled through the photocopies she'd made at the county courthouse, leaving a trail of oily fingerprints on each page. "Penny's the daughter of Caterina Montelusa and Tony Ferrara, which makes her"—Rita thumbed through a few more dog-eared pages—"the granddaughter of Guido Montelusa, the niece of Sandro Montelusa, the grand-niece of Pietro Montelusa—"

"The mob kingpin?"

"The very same. And that also makes Penny the grand-niece of Anita Montelusa, who became Anita Gambone when she married Joey."

"Who is the number one suspect in the murder of her husband Joey, who owned the farm with the tunnel where Bobby's skeleton was found. So maybe Anita told Penny about how she killed her husband and stashed his body in the tunnel. You know, like a deathbed confession. And that gave Penny the idea."

"But Penny was hardly out of diapers when Bobby disappeared."

"Really? I guess she hasn't aged well."

Rita begged to differ, but she wisely held her tongue.

Rose said, "Just because Penny didn't kill anyone doesn't mean that she doesn't know who *did*."

Rita had been wondering the very same thing. She thought of all the times she'd made an impolitic remark over the dinner table, only to have the unfortunate remark repeated at the most inopportune time, like the time Vinnie told Aunt Carmela that it must have been nice to receive such a fancy car as a divorce present.

"Well, all the more reason to get close to Orlando. To find out what Penny knows. Hey, check your phone. I just texted you a couple of selfies in two different outfit options for my hot date."

Rita sighed and checked her text messages. Both outfits were red dresses that left little to the imagination.

"What do you think?" Rose asked. "Which one says 'forget all about Penny, she's a gold-digger and a mobster' and I'm much more fun, younger—"

Rita coughed.

"—at heart, at least, sexier and more financially stable?"

"I don't think any dress can say all that." Rita squinted at the second photo. "But these both say 'I'm desperate.' I'd wear the first one, preferably with a turtleneck underneath." Rita sighed. "Why don't you just give it a rest and let me go to *Aida?*"

"No way. I held up my end of the bargain. You hold up yours."

"But you can't just bully Orlando into dating you. He has to decide who is right for him."

Rose barked out a laugh. "Hah! Talk about the pot calling the kettle black. You don't trust Sal to pick out his own brand of toothpaste. And if Orlando is so good at making his own decisions, how come he got married to a gold-digging shrew, got dumped and taken to the cleaners by said gold-digging shrew, then got engaged to a pathological liar who got bumped off when her old life finally caught up with her, and is now secretly dating yet another gold-digging shrew, this one with mob ties and possible knowledge of not one, but two, murders? Orlando," she said emphatically, "doesn't know what's good for him. But I do. So now, it's just a matter of making him see that."

When her sister put it that way, Rita found it hard to argue.

On Wednesday, Rita rolled sheets of dough through her pasta maker until they were "*così sottile per leggere un giornale giù*"—thin enough to read a newspaper through, as her *nonna* used to say—while giving her twin a crash course in opera.

"*Aida*," Rita said as she arranged tiny scoops of pumpkin puree on the sheet of pasta, "is like Romeo and Juliet, only instead of Montagues and Capulets, they're ancient Egyptians and Ethiopians. And it's twice as long."

"I hated *Romeo and Juliet*," her sister groaned.

Rita rolled another thin sheet on top of the first one and pressed down, then began to cut away little squares of ravioli with a pizza wheel. She smiled sweetly. "It's Orlando's favorite."

On Thursday, Rita blended pumpkin puree from her garden into a rich, tangy mascarpone from the creamery, then baked it into a homemade gingersnap crust; chopped pecans and cranberries for the tart, staining her fingers a deep reddish-purple; and whisked together the decadent ingredients for her chocolate cake. Her kitchen smelled divine, like a spicy drinking chocolate: the rich aroma of Valhrona chocolate mingled with ginger and cranberries.

Whistling "*O Patria Mia*" from *Aida*, Rita revved up her espresso machine, set out two giant rectangular pans, and began dunking the ladyfingers in the espresso.

The front door swung open and slammed shut. She heard light, quick footsteps, the squeak of wet sneakers.

"Vincenzo Salvatore Calabrese! *Togliti le scarpe!*" Rita shouted without bothering to peek into the hallway. She knew exactly who'd be uncouth enough to tromp through the house in wet shoes. There was probably a trail of muddy footprints stretching down the hall already. Vinnie, she thought, should never rob a bank. He'd leave a trail right to his hideaway and be caught red-handed within an hour. The easiest case I ever solved, Detective Benedetto would boast.

Rita shuddered. He'd probably left a trail of footprints on Jake Johnson's porch too.

"Sorry, Ma." Vinnie peeked sheepishly through the swinging door to the kitchen, removed his muddy sneakers and tossed them in the corner, then padded across the linoleum floor in his stocking feet. He tossed a few treats to Luciano and Cesare, who were lurking in their customary spot by the refrigerator, then sidled up next to Rita and began dunking ladyfingers in the espresso and arranging them in the pan without having to be asked.

He really was a sweet boy. But gullible too—far too gullible.

"Your food's gonna be great. I'm looking forward to it."

Rita snatched a ladyfinger out of his hand and shot him a supercilious look. "None of this food," she said, "is for you. I'm catering the widow's funeral—er, celebration of life party."

"Yeah, I know, Ma. That's what I meant. I'm gonna eat it at the party."

Rita could hardly believe her ears. All this time she'd been trying to cajole the guest list out of the widow, and here she had one of the guests living under her roof!

Vinnie took in her dropped jaw and shrugged. "I got an invite at rehearsal. All the cast and crew did."

Rita tallied up all the speaking parts and the backstage crew. That had to account for half of the guest list. She found it strange that Rose hadn't mentioned getting an invitation. But then, she figured, maybe Rose had no intention of going. She and the widow were not close.

Rita took the mascarpone out of the refrigerator and plunked it into a mixing bowl. "Well," she said brightly, "I guess we can go together."

"Together?" Vinnie had turned pale. He ran a hand through his spiky dark hair. "That would be great, Ma, but you see, I promised to give a ride to An—"

Rita looked up at him sharply, and Vinnie gulped.

"A friend," he finished lamely.

"Ana Rivera?"

"Well, now that you mention it, yeah, my friend happens to be Ana."

"You seem to be spending a lot of time with Ana lately."

"Well she's in the play. I thought you'd be pleased. She's all studious and responsible. A good influence, you know?"

"She's also seventeen," Rita said. "And her mother owns a gun."

Chapter Thirteen

The mood at the widow's party was definitely more celebratory than funereal. Rita stood by the buffet table in the widow's old-fashioned burgundy-wallpapered dining room, warming herself by the roaring fire. Her eyes darted around the room, taking in the eclectic mix of guests. She recognized several members of the Acorn Hollow Historical Society, all ladies of a certain age who oozed old money and good, old-fashioned, prim-and-proper breeding. They nibbled on her antipasti, took abstemious little spoonfuls of carrot-ginger soup, and proudly swapped photos of their grandchildren. The cast and crew of *The Legend of Acorn Hollow* were over in the living room, huddled around a long, low table crammed with framed family photos, most black and white. Orlando Rinaldi and Penny Albanese were among them, almost touching but not quite. Rita noticed that Vinnie's hand rested on the small of Ana's back, but when he caught his mother staring, he retracted his hand quite suddenly, as if he'd been scalded, and shoved it in his pocket. Apparently, tonight was not the night he was going to come clean to his mother.

Both Ana and Penny seemed to be pointing at a large color photo in the center of the display, then at some yellowed newspaper clippings, and finally up at a framed hand-drawn map on the wall. Rita decided to investigate. With a plate of meatballs and fried calamari in hand, Rita squeezed through the crowd until she was standing right behind Ana and Vinnie.

"There you are!" she trilled loudly, causing Vinnie to jump. His skin looked unusually pale in the dim light of the widow's parlor; his dark eyes were wide and his hair, already gelled into stiff little peaks, seemed to stand even further on end.

"Hey, Ma," he stammered, "I didn't realize you were behind me."

"Evidently not."

Rita let her words linger for a moment, then pointedly looked at Vinnie's hand, which he abruptly shoved in his pocket again.

Ana managed to play it cool. "Hello, Rita," she said warmly, pulling her in and blowing air kisses on Rita's cheeks. "Your food is terrific. Everyone's talking about it." Her smile turned tentative, almost nervous. "I was wondering, actually, if you could give me some cooking lessons. I'd love to learn how to make a killer cannoli."

"You must read The Dude," Rita said stiffly.

"The Dude?" Ana lifted an eyebrow quizzically, but she did not fool Rita. Ana knew exactly what Rita meant.

"Well, that's the advice he gave to that young lady. To show her boyfriend's 'grizzly mamma'"—Rita said "grizzly mamma" ever so slowly and bared her teeth as she did so—"that she would take care of her son, raise three Mass-attending, *nonna*-worshipping, Italian-speaking grandchildren, and learn to make a killer cannoli."

Rita savored a bite of tiramisu, then set down her fork with a clatter. She clapped Vinnie, then Ana, on the shoulder. "The Dude must have seen the movie *Grizzly Man*. Did you see that? This back-to-nature hippie goes to live in the Alaskan wilderness, thinking he can befriend grizzly bears. What a poor deluded soul! He got torn from limb to limb." She licked the last bit of cream off her fork. "Absolutely devoured. All they found was his camera."

Ana opened her mouth as if to speak, but for once no words came out. Vinnie turned green.

"So," Rita said brightly, ignoring their horrified expressions and pointing at the display, "what's all this?"

"Oh"—Ana shook her head vigorously, as if trying to dispel images of herself being torn limb to limb—"it's a tribute—a shrine, really—to Bobby Bruickhuisen."

"Yeah," Vinnie said, "I guess the widow was kinda a grizzly aunt. I mean, she's got his trophies, his yearbooks, his class ring, his acceptance letter to Yale…"

Rita stood on her tiptoes, craned her neck, and peered over Vinnie's shoulder. Trophies for baseball, lacrosse, and debate glinted in the firelight. There was a blue ribbon for first place in the county's art fair, and a framed certificate indicating Bobby placed third in the state French competition. An old yearbook was open to the page where Bobby celebrated his election as class president.

"And here's a cast photo," Ana murmured, nudging Rita. "Look how the three of them—Sandro, Vito, and Bobby—are all gazing adoringly at Kate Van Tassel."

Rita squinted at the caption, then counted four from the left in the very back row. "Lydia Van Zandt's in the picture, too—Kate's erstwhile best friend, the one who spilled the beans about her pregnancy. She's looking at Kate, too."

"And she doesn't look too happy." Ana grimaced. "She's here, you know."

Ana pointed at a tall, slender woman about Rita's age, with an immaculately coiffed head of frosted blond hair. She wore a long-sleeved black velvet dress, a double strand of pearls, and black pumps. She would have been beautiful were it not for her beady little eyes, which roamed about the room, and her horsey long nose. So this was Lydia Van Zandt.

"And that," Ana said, discretely tilting her head in the direction of a tall, spare gentleman with thick gray hair and horn-rimmed spectacles, "is Hank Van Tassel, Kate's brother. I overheard him tell someone he's a political consultant and has three grown children."

"You are good," Rita said admiringly. "It must be those young ears."

Rita wasn't all that surprised to see Hank Van Tassel. After all, the widow had been great friends with his mother. But she could not understand what could have prompted the widow to invite Lydia, on whom she'd rained down invective just a few days earlier. She turned back to the shrine. Her gaze roamed up the wall to an enormous photo. At first, she struggled to make sense of it: a bright blue line slicing through a dark background like some sort of modernist masterpiece. Bu there was something hauntingly familiar about it.

With a start, Rita realized this was *her* photo. It was the one she'd taken of the fragment of Bobby's scarf stuck in the wall of the Gambone fallout shelter—magnified and slightly pixilated. She was just turning to examine an adjacent bulletin board when she heard a woman shout "*Zio!*"

Rita spun around in time to see Penny Albanese, arms outstretched, pushing her way through the crowd towards a stocky man with a salt-and-pepper crewcut, a long craggy nose, and a protruding brow accentuated by brows thick as caterpillars.

Beside her, Ana murmured, "Doesn't that mean 'uncle'?"

Rita nodded.

"So that's...?"

"Penny's uncle, Sandro Montelusa."

"Well, that's quite a reunion," Ana remarked as they watched Sandro and Penny embrace. "They must not have seen each other in years." She dunked a ring of calamari in some cocktail sauce. "You know, I can see why they cast Sandro as Brom Bones. Even now, he still exudes that Neanderthal vibe, that hint of danger."

"Yeah," Vinnie said, "like 'if you mess with my girl, Katrina, I'll run you right off the road.'"

Rita frowned. "Are we talking about Brom Bones and Katrina Van Tassel in the original legend or Sandro Montelusa and Kate Van Tassel?"

Ana shrugged. "Maybe both. Sometimes art imitates life." Then she sighed. "Poor Ichabod. Poor Bobby."

"The poor widow," Vinnie murmured. He nudged Rita and pointed up at the bulletin board. The light in the parlor was dim; Rita could just make out some sort of hand-drawn map crisscrossed with angry red lines and dotted with push pins. "They're color-coded, see? Blue is for Kate's dad's movements that night, red is for Bobby, orange—"

Rita didn't get to hear who orange denoted because just then Sandro stammered in a deep, stentorian voice, "V-V-Vito!"

He staggered backwards and turned suddenly pale, as if he'd seen a ghost.

Rita's jaw dropped. She looked back at the bulletin board, then Sandro and Vito. Suddenly, it all clicked. Sandro. Vito. Lydia. Hank.

The widow had assembled all of the living suspects in the disappearance of her nephew.

Rita whirled around and locked eyes with Emma, who was surrounded by a gaggle of well-wishers. The widow raised her glass in a silent toast. The crystal glinted in the firelight; the red wine within seemed to glow.

A shiver went down Rita's spine as Emma winked at her and mouthed the words, "To Bobby."

Chapter Fourteen

Rita lurked by the widow's shrine, nursing a cup of steaming hot mulled wine, mopping up the last of the spinach-artichoke dip on her plate with a slice of focaccia, and then slurping down two oysters Rockefeller. Really, she thought with satisfaction, she'd outdone herself. The focaccia was still warm from the oven, salty and generously flecked with rosemary, springy to the touch yet just slightly crunchy on top. The spinach-artichoke dip was rich and creamy, loaded with Parmesan cheese, definitely full fat, full flavor. The smooth, slightly slippery flesh of the oysters was perfectly complemented by the crunchiness of the toasted breadcrumbs; the brininess of the sea offset the pungent garlic and herbs and the rich buttery finish.

And adding to her enjoyment was the fact that she was perfectly placed to observe all four suspects.

When Lydia wandered into her orbit, pausing to pick up the framed photograph of her old friend Kate Van Tassel, Rita boomed "Such a pretty girl, wasn't she?" and Lydia nearly jumped out of her skin.

"What? Oh—oh, yes," she twittered. The photo slipped through her fingers and came crashing onto the

117

table, sending the other photos falling like dominoes. Hastily re-arranging them, Lydia started to babble, "It's just surprising to see her picture after all these years. We were so close and then..." She trailed off for a moment, swallowed hard, and then shook her head as if to dislodge some painful memory. "You know how it is with girls. You have some little misunderstanding and suddenly you're no longer as close...and then life happens and pretty soon you drift apart."

She pursed her lips, and the firelight illuminated a thin sheen of tears, which Lydia hastily blinked back. "You always think that one day you'll catch up again and it will be like old times."

Rita nodded sympathetically. "I hear she died in an accident."

Lydia took a big gulp of wine. "Up near the Canadian border. A deer jumped out of the woods and she swerved, but there was a patch of black ice.... She was driving a brand-new Mercedes with her beautiful little boy in the back seat." Lydia shook her head. "Before what happened to Bobby, I thought she was the luckiest girl on earth. After Bobby disappeared, it seemed like she became one of the unluckiest. But you never really know what's going on with a person, do you? Below the surface?" She stared into the depths of her glass and swilled the ice around. "We're like icebergs, you know?"

Rita wondered just how much Lydia had had to drink, and whether this inebriated hack philosopher mode was her usual state or just a temporary condition brought on by the unusual circumstances. Lydia's loquaciousness was an unexpected boon, but Rita also found their strangely intimate interaction unnerving.

"That's what my ex used to say, anyway," Lydia went on. "He was a frustrated polar explorer stuck being a psychotherapist, so everything became a metaphor about ice. I got so sick of hearing about ice that I spent a whole week in a sauna after I left him." She snapped her fingers. "I just up and went to Finland—yes, near the Arctic Circle and yes, I realize that's ironic—and locked myself in a sauna, sweating out all of my hatred and resentment. I lost ten pounds just like that." She narrowed her eyes and peered at Rita. "I bet you went to school with us, too, didn't you? You probably did the smart thing and married one of these local boys, not some navel-gazing Manhattanite. A real man."

Rita noticed that, as Lydia said this, her gaze drifted over to Sandro, who was still talking to Penny and Orlando. Rita could tell just what Lydia was thinking: this was the one that got away. The one Kate stole.

"I was a few years behind you in school."

"Really?"

Lydia gave Rita the once-over and looked doubtful, which made Rita scowl. She bared her teeth for a moment in an involuntary "grizzly mamma" growl, then tried to make it seem like a grin.

"And what about Kate?" Rita asked even though she knew the answer. "Did she marry a local?"

"Actually"—Lydia lowered her voice as if confiding a deep, dark secret and gave Rita an unflattering glimpse of the teenaged gossipmonger she'd once been—"I heard she ended up married to Vito."

"Was Vito the father of her baby?"

Lydia looked across the room to Vito, who was huddled with Vinnie by the fireplace. "If he was, the baby didn't take after him at all. Blue eyes, blond hair. Like a little Viking."

Rita picked up a framed photo of Bobby and took in the sandy hair and bright blue eyes. "Could it have been Bobby?"

"Maybe. It could have been anyone, really. There wasn't a man or boy in Morris County that wasn't chasing after Kate. It was like the rest of us didn't even exist." Lydia must have realized how petty that sounded, because she hastily added, "But that wasn't Lydia's fault. And she wasn't just pretty, either. She was fun, vivacious—smart, too."

"Ah, but I hear you were a spelling bee champion—after, that is, Lydia had to pull out."

"Yes, I was the alternate."

The word "alternate" seemed to stick in her throat.

Lydia raised her empty glass. "I need to get another drink." She sounded almost apologetic about taking her leave. "I don't think we'll ever know who little Tommy's father was. All I know is that she told me 'it happened at camp.'"

"Camp?"

Lydia shrugged. "Some overnight camp for rich kids in the Adirondacks. Networking for the future gods of Wall Street and the women who'd bear their perfect children. Horseback riding, private tennis lessons, golf. Kate had such a charmed life—until she didn't."

****

When the last of the meatballs and calamari had been devoured, and the towering platters of antipasti had been reduced to a faint streak of creamy burrata, Rita knew it was time for dessert. She sailed through the swinging door to the kitchen, slid two enormous trays of tiramisu out of the widow's bulbous white refrigerator, and deftly sprinkled each one with a thin layer of deep, dark, velvety cocoa powder.

Then she dove back into the refrigerator to retrieve her other masterpieces: her brilliantly-hued cranberry-pecan tart with its perfectly fluted crust; flourless chocolate cake topped with a layer of homemade sour cherry preserves and then smothered in the world's richest, most decadent chocolate ganache; and lusciously creamy pumpkin cheesecake. She balanced them on the widow's grooved, metal washboard—since kitchens this old apparently did not have proper countertops—next to her golden-brown apple crisp, which was best at room temperature.

Rita was just working out exactly how she was going to transport this all when the problem solved itself in the form of a trim, athletic, and vaguely familiar-looking woman who strode through the door and boomed in a commanding voice, "There you are!"

Before Rita could mutter that the woman was very much mistaken—however unkind the years and three children had been to her, she was certainly *not* the centenarian guest of honor—the woman whipped out a handheld camera and began snapping close-ups of each dessert.

"I've heard all about you," the woman said, wagging a finger even as she kept snapping away. "Champion pie-baker, champion pasta-maker...."

Rita still couldn't quite place the woman, but she beamed with pride nonetheless.

"Oh, yes—your reputation precedes you." The woman zoomed in for a closeup of the apple crisp. "The crumb on that one—I can tell it will be perfect. And the sheen on that ganache!" She turned her camera on the flourless chocolate cake. "Real butter, I can tell, and the chocolate, I'd say it's Valhrona, sixty-seven percent dark."

"Seventy-two," Rita corrected her.

The woman sighed—swooned, nearly—and finally put down her camera. "Even better." She turned her megawatt, blindingly white smile on Rita and held out a perfectly manicured hand. "Isabella Montelusa. Pleased to meet you."

Now, the penny dropped. Isabella was more petite than she appeared on TV, and she looked slightly older in the harsh fluorescent light of the widow's kitchen, but her copper-colored curls were just as shiny and bouncy and her dark eyes just as lively. She looked elegant but occasion-appropriate in a black cashmere sweater set and a gray pencil skirt. Like Lydia, she was swathed in pearls.

"I really must have you as a guest on my show," Isabella said, taking a tiramisu and cheesecake and shooing Rita through the swinging door ahead of her. Isabella crooked her finger at a middle-aged woman and her teenaged son and exhorted them to bring the other desserts along. Clearly, Isabella was used to being in charge. "My audience," she said without missing a beat, "absolutely swoons over Italian desserts, and you are just in our target demographic. What about a holiday special on Italian Christmas cookies? Or maybe you could make panettone? Everyone wants to get their hands on an authentic panettone recipe from a real Italian *nonna*. We could even film at your house..."

Under any normal circumstances, Rita would have hung on Isabella's every word, in thrall to her vision to launch Rita to her completely justified and long overdue fifteen minutes of fame. But Rita's attention was elsewhere as she snaked her way through the cozy dining room en route to the buffet. Her eyes were trained on the widow, who had been backed into a corner by Vito. His thin shoulders were thrust forward; he was pointing out something on a sheet of paper. It was an ordinary white sheet of paper with black type; its many creases suggested it had been folded and unfolded many times. But whatever was written on it was clearly extraordinary because the widow's mouth fell open. Then she shook her head sadly and pinched the bridge of her nose. When she finally looked up, she brought her lace handkerchief to her eyes. Then she folded the paper, stuck it in the pocket of her skirt, and beckoned for Vito to follow her into the adjoining enclosed back porch where, Rita surmised, they would be alone.

"Hank!" Isabella suddenly bellowed.

Rita forced herself to tear her eyes away from the porch door—it was such a pity that despite what she'd told her three kids, she didn't *actually* have laser vision—and to focus on Kate Van Tassel's brother instead.

"Hank Van Tassel, may I present Rita Calabrese, Acorn Hollow's best chef, the woman responsible for this magnificent spread"—she took the flourless chocolate cake out of Rita's hands and arranged it fussily on the table—"and the next very special guest on my show."

Rita opened her mouth to protest that she had not actually agreed to be on the show, but Isabella already had one hand raised to forestall such a protest.

"And Rita, may I present Hank Van Tassel, a dear family friend and the man single-handedly responsible for launching my father's political career."

Rita raised an eyebrow. That was an interesting connection. She had known Guido Montelusa, Sandro's father, had been a giant in New York politics, a governor in the seventies and later a political king-maker. But she hadn't known that Hank Van Tassel had been involved in Guido's campaigns.

Hank smiled modestly. "I'm just the fundraising guy, Isabella. You know that. There's no career, and there's no campaign, without a compelling candidate."

"Hank's also on the board of the Guido Montelusa Foundation," Isabella said, patting Hank's arm. "He's helping me keep my father's legacy alive."

"It's nice to meet you, Hank," Rita said warmly. "Emma often speaks fondly of her friendship with your mother."

"Oh, I wouldn't miss it for the world." Hank chuckled. "I think my mother would return to haunt me if I didn't come to her best friend's funeral, er, that is—"

"Celebration of life party," Rita supplied.

"Exactly." He laughed. "I guess Emma hasn't changed—she always did things her own way."

Rita turned to Isabella with a slight frown. "I must say that while I'm delighted you're here, I can't quite figure out how you're connected to Emma. I don't recall her mentioning you."

"Oh, I'm just a plus one, I'm afraid. Ever since his wife went into a nursing home, I've been accompanying my brother Sandro to the occasional function. He just hates going alone."

Her gaze drifted over to her brother, who was still chatting amiably with Penny and Orlando.

"He doesn't look so lonely tonight," Rita observed. "It looks like the reunion of a long-lost uncle and niece."

"Yes," Isabella murmured, helping herself to a thin sliver of the flourless chocolate cake. "He doesn't get back to Acorn Hollow as often as he should."

Glad she didn't have some TV producer telling her to watch her figure, Rita helped herself to a giant slab of the chocolate cake and a big square of tiramisu. She saw Isabella twitch ever so slightly with jealousy.

"I can understand why." Rita lowered her voice to a hushed tone and wagged her chin in the direction of the widow's macabre display. "I understand he was considered by many to be the number one suspect in Bobby Bruickhuisen's disappearance."

Isabella's famous smile collapsed into a thin, frigid little line. "The only reason people think that," she sniffed, "is that Sandro was dating Kate Van Tassel and she was apparently pregnant"—Isabella's lips curled in disgust—"by another boy."

"Bobby—or Vito?"

"It hardly matters. Not my brother, anyway. But Sandro wouldn't have touched a hair on Bobby's head—

or anyone's head. He was the soft-headed one in the family. He cried for days when our dad flushed our dead goldfish down the toilet."

Isabella's trademark grin returned. "*Acqua passata*, as our parent's generation would have said. Small-town gossips had their fun. Sandro moved on, became a decorated Vietnam veteran, started a successful trucking business, married, had three kids. Two are doctors; one's a lawyer. It all worked out for the best."

"But not for Bobby."

"No. Not for Bobby." Isabella glanced over at the widow's macabre display and shook her head. "Poor Emma. She just can't let it go."

Hank cast a nervous glance at the display, checked his watch, and then extracted a small pill bottle from his pocket.

"Too much of this divine tiramisu?" Isabella clucked sympathetically. "Indigestion?"

Hank laughed. "I wish. Unfortunately, a beta blocker for my high blood pressure and angina. My doctor tells me to retire and just relax, but that's not in my vocabulary so I take these instead."

He popped one into his mouth, then washed it down with a swig of mulled wine.

"So Sandro," Rita asked, returning to the subject at hand and gesturing towards the widow, "was close to Emma?"

"Oh"—a shadow briefly crossed Isabella's face—"I wouldn't say they were close, but they knew each other through Mrs. Van Tassel, Kate's mom. Since Emma was always at the Van Tassels, and Sandro was often there visiting Kate, they must have often crossed paths."

"That could be, I suppose." Rita took a bite of her deliciously decadent flourless chocolate cake, then slowly licked the blood-red cherry preserves off her fork. "And here I was thinking that the widow had engineered all this"—Rita waved her hand over the buffet table, at the bizarre display on Bobby's disappearance, and the crowd spilling out of the dining room—"to bring together the four living suspects in the disappearance of Bobby Bruickhuisen."

"Four?" Hank choked.

He had been attempting to screw the lid of his pill bottle back on—no easy task without a hard surface nearby—and now, suddenly, the lid flew off. As he lurched forward, he twisted his wrist, sending a torrent of little blue pills raining down on the widow's floral carpeting.

Rita leaned down to help him pick up the stray pills, and Isabella did the same.

"Four," Rita said as she placed a handful of pills into his palm. "You—"

"Me?" His face was as pale as the creamy layer in Rita's tiramisu.

"Well, sure," Rita said. "You were Kate's brother. You had to protect her honor, that sort of thing."

"Hardly," he said, straightening up and taking a handful of pills proffered by Isabella. He screwed the lid back on and cleared his throat noisily. "This isn't Saudi Arabia."

Rita shrugged and ticked off the remaining suspects on her fingers. "Then there's Sandro..."

Now it was Isabella's turn to scoff.

"And," Rita went on, "Vito and Lydia."

"My wife?" Hank said. "Surely, you must be joking."

It took a moment for Rita to process what he had just said. "Oh—I didn't realize you and Lydia were married. I heard she married a scientist...a polar explorer, wasn't it?"

"That was her first marriage. It didn't work out. Then Lyddie and I reconnected when she returned for her high school reunion...."

Rita finished his sentence for him. "...and the rest is history."

History, Rita thought, that Lydia had neglected to mention. She'd had thought Lydia might have mentioned that she had followed her own advice and married a local boy the second time around. But something told her that the local boy Lydia had had in mind had been Sandro, not Hank.

"Well, of the remaining three," Hank said, "I'd put my money on Vito. Always was a bit of a screw-up and he had a bit of a chip on his shoulder. No dad, maid's kid—you know the type."

"Oh?" Rita said, hoping Hank would elaborate. "I'm not sure I do."

To her chagrin, he failed to take the bait.

"Most likely," he said, "it was just some maniac, some psycho with a *Legend of Sleepy Hollow* fixation."

"So you think this 'psycho' was just passing through town and just happened to choose as his victim a boy who only hours earlier had been accused of deflowering a powerful senator's young daughter in a dramatic and very public confrontation?"

Hank winced. She could tell that when she put it that way, even he thought it sounded preposterous.

"And then," Rita said, turning the screw a little further, "the killer—this 'psycho'—is so obsessed with *The Legend of Sleepy Hollow* that he re-enacts the story down to the victim's abandoned vehicle by the old stone bridge, leaves Acorn Hollow, and never comes back to repeat this crime that so filled his heart with glee?"

Hank nodded halfheartedly. Isabella shrugged.

"Well, it's a theory," Rita said in a tone that meant it wasn't a very good one. "Whoever it was certainly had a flair for the theatrical. Burying him in the old fallout shelter at the Gambone farm, thereby linking him to Joey Gambone's earlier disappearance, which was also linked to the old stone bridge?" She chuckled. "Now that was a stroke of evil genius."

She looked over at Isabella, and noticed that a deep crease had formed across her forehead.

"That tunnel from the fallout shelter," Rita said as if it were suddenly occurring to her, "connects to the Rinaldis' winery. That was once your family's estate, wasn't it?"

"Why yes," Isabella said. "I have so many fond memories of growing up there." Two little frown lines appeared at the inner creases of her heavily plucked eyebrows. "But a tunnel? I certainly don't remember that. It must be ancient—maybe used as part of the Underground Railroad."

"It could be that old, I suppose," Rita said, "but it certainly was used much more recently. It's lined with concrete. Perhaps your father upgraded it."

"My father?" Isabella fingered her pearls and then her fingers fluttered to her hair, smoothing back a wayward tendril. "Oh, no, I don't think so. Lydia's father, perhaps. He owned the estate after my father."

"Is that so?" Rita said as though Orlando Rinaldi had never mentioned this to her.

"My father-in-law never mentioned any tunnel to me. It seems very unlikely." Hank laughed, but it came out forced, the kind of laugh his politician clients chortled out when asked an inconvenient question on TV. "Old Van Zandt was so frugal he wouldn't eat out if it was a minute past five and he couldn't get the early-bird special. He'd hardly splurge on a tunnel."

Rita looked from Isabella to Hank and back again. Their cold, pinched expressions told her she would get no more out of them, so Rita excused herself and make a beeline for the restroom. The line for the downstairs bathroom was long, so she joined the shorter queue for the upstairs one, a cramped, old-fashioned lavatory with nineteen-fifties floral wallpaper and a checkerboard tiled floor. When she came back down the stairs, she spotted Vinnie and Ana warming themselves by the fireplace, engaged in an earnest discussion with Vito.

Rita went to size up yet another suspect in the disappearance of Bobby Bruickhuisen.

"But how exactly did Kate react when Lydia announced Kate was pregnant?" Ana was saying when Rita came up behind them. "Did she look at Lydia? Or at her dad? Or Bobby? Or did she just bolt for the door? I still feel like I'm not doing her justice, and the widow's memory is only so good."

Vito fiddled with the clock on the mantle. Rita was surprised to see it was already nearly midnight. "I think she looked at Lydia," Vito said. "Kind of horrified-like.

Betrayed. And then she looked at all of us—me, Bobby, and Sandro—covered her face with her hands, and ran out."

"Looked at you—how?" Ana asked. "Like she was asking for understanding or pleading for forgiveness?"

"I don't know. I felt like she was saying with her eyes, 'You'll still be my friend, won't you?' I'm not sure what she was trying to communicate to Bobby and Sandro—or if she even knew. And then, she was gone, off like a shot."

"And what did you do," Vinnie said earnestly, "when she looked at you? Our director keeps telling me to brood, but I think my performance is kinda one-note, you know? Like I just get to brood and brood, but I was wondering if..."

Rita never got to hear what her budding thespian of a son was wondering because just then, she felt a tap on her shoulder.

"Yes?" She spun around, annoyed at being interrupted in mid-eavesdrop, and was surprised to see Isabella. "Oh—if it's about scheduling a time to tape your show, you can just give me your card and I'll call your office on Monday. I'm sure we can work something out."

"Oh, no, it's not that." Isabella lowered her gaze and touched Rita's arm. "It's just...could we have a word in the kitchen?"

Rita nodded and followed Isabella through the swinging door. Isabella slumped against the sink. One manicured hand tapped the grooved metal surface, the other massaged her left temple as if warding off a migraine. In a small, quavering voice, she said, "I think I know who killed Bobby."

"*You do?*"

Rita had been wrong—this was definitely worth being interrupted.

Isabella leaned in very close. She smelled of hairspray and expensive perfume, and her breath was hot in Rita's ear. "I didn't want to say anything in front of Hank."

"Yes?"

"I think—I'm fairly sure, that is," Isabella whispered, "it was Senator Van Tassel. Once, late at night on the campaign trail—my father's campaign, that is—Hank got very, very drunk. It was four days after his father's funeral. He was very emotional. And he told me—"

Just then, there was the tinkling of glass. "Ahem!" On the other side of the door, the widow's rich, plummy voice cut through the chatter. She was clanging her fork against her water glass, as if about to launch into a wedding toast. "Attention, please!"

Conversation ground to a halt. Rita cocked her head in Isabella's direction, smiled apologetically, and motioned that she would return momentarily. Then she slipped through the door. Rita felt compelled to hear what the widow had to say, if for no other reason than to be able to faithfully recount this historic event for the readers of the *Morris County Gazette*. Isabella must have been intrigued as well, because she followed closely behind.

"I want to thank you all so much for coming tonight, for making this a funeral"—she winked and nodded in Rita's direction—"a celebration of life party, if you will, that I will always remember."

"For the next ten or twenty years!" hooted a young man that Rita did not recognize.

"The widow will outlive us all!" someone else shouted, raising a glass.

The widow laughed good-naturedly, and a snowy-white tendril came loose from her tightly coiled bun. "Sadly, or perhaps fortunately," she said, tucking the tendril back in place, "I think not. All good things—and among these good things I include my life among all of you—must end."

"No," she said over a few murmurs of protest, "our good Doctor Stein tells me I have but a few months left. Cancer, he says, the great equalizer. If you've still got your marbles and your ticker's pretty good—well, that's what will still get you in the end. But to quote one of the few self-help gurus who makes any sense, it's not the years in your life, but the life in your years. And I've still got some living to do." She thrust a gnarled, veiny hand in the direction of her macabre display. In the firelight, it cast a long, eerie shadow, her elongated fingertips seeming to stroke the frayed edge of Bobby's scarf.

"And some unfinished business," she added, setting her lips in a thin, determined line. "That's right," she said grimly, "tomorrow morning, I'm going to march right into the Acorn Hollow Police Station and tell Detective Benedetto that my nephew's killer was right here"—she pointed a bony finger around the room accusatorily—"with us tonight. And then I will tell the good detective who he—or she—is, and justice will be served."

Rita frowned. Clearly, the widow did not share Isabella's suspicions about the senator. So whom did the widow suspect? Cagey, fidgety Vito, who played the part of Kate's wounded widower so well? Lydia, who still oozed resentment out of every booze-sozzled pore? Sandro, whose sister was doing her best to throw suspicion away from him? Or Hank, who had looked so startled when Rita had insinuated that he was a suspect?

The widow's gaze gave nothing away.

The widow suddenly let loose a merry cackle. "But until then," she said, breaking into a snaggle-toothed grin, "eat, drink, and be merry!"

Chapter Fifteen

The widow's announcement sucked the air right out of the room, turning the mood from festive to somber, from a celebration of life party to a funeral. One by one, the guests made their excuses and drifted off, until Rita and the widow were left quite alone.

The widow hobbled upstairs to get ready for bed, while Rita took the dirty plates to the kitchen, filled the sink with warm, sudsy water, and put the tea kettle on to boil.

As she scrubbed away streaks of chocolate and smears of pumpkin-infused mascarpone, Rita could not stop thinking about Isabella's outlandish story: that Hank Van Tassel, while deep in his cups, had confided that his father had once handed him a large sack, told him not to peek inside, and asked him to bury it deep in the cornfield. But curiosity had gotten the better of Hank. He'd opened the sack, only to have Bobby's possessions come tumbling out. Hank had never trusted his father again.

The tea kettle began to whistle. Rita turned off the stove and poured the hot water into a mug that said

"Don't Mess With Me – I Didn't Get This Old By Being Stupid."

"Well, that's the understatement of the century!" Rita murmured as she dunked a bag of chamomile into the hot water and the tea began to steep.

She carried the mug upstairs to the widow's bedroom, a cozy little space tucked beneath the eaves. The walls were painted a cheery yellow; the dormer windows looked out over the widow's roses and, beyond that, to a quiet little lane of Victorian painted ladies.

The widow lay on an antique single bed, propped up by a floral reading pillow. Rita tried to hide her astonishment at the widow's bedtime attire. Rita had never seen Emma wear anything but widow's weeds, long, stiff-necked black dresses, the sort of mourning clothes that had last been in style when the Titanic sank. She always accessorized with a tiny splash of red—a brooch, perhaps, a ruby-red choker, or a crimson sash. The black widow, the townspeople joked, never realizing just how close they were to the mark. But now the widow was clad in flannel pajamas, a garish red and green plaid, the sort she might have ordered from an L.L. Bean catalog just the other week.

On the vanity beside her was a framed photo of her first (and favorite) husband in front of his long-gone pharmacy and a framed photo of Bobby and his family. Rita set down the mug on the vanity, next to a glass of water and a small plastic pill bottle, and picked up the second photo. The fifty-something woman in the latter photo bore, unsurprisingly, a striking resemblance to the widow; her light-colored hair was braided and piled high on her head, her eyes were small and beady; and she had the same willowy, bony frame. But unlike the widow, this woman wore a pinched expression, one of loss and resignation, as if she already had a presentment that her child would be wrested away from her. The man next to her was tall and hollow-cheeked, with a prominent brow and big, dark bushy eyebrows. His long, muscular arms were draped around his family; it was meant to look protective, but Rita found it menacing. Bobby looked earnest but faintly ridiculous in a suit far too big and baggy. There was a fair-haired teenaged girl in the photo as well, roughly Bobby's age. She had that fresh, all-American-girl-next-door look, like a young Doris Day.

The widow craned her skinny neck to see what Rita was looking at. "That's Judy," she said with a sigh, "my niece. She and Bobby were very close. Poor girl. She was hot to trot, as our mother used to say – that was the nicer way to put it. Other people said she'd tested out the backseat of every Oldsmobile in town. A couple months after that picture was taken, they had her lobotomized and sent to a mental institution—just like that Kennedy girl."

"How cruel."

The widow shrugged her bony shoulders. "It was a cruel era. Crueler than we remember, at least."

Rita tapped the middle-aged man in the photo. "And didn't you end up later marrying him..."

Rita trailed off, grasping for the right euphemism.

"...after he killed my sister?" The widow laughed. "I sure did. It was worth it though when he, well, you know." Emma drew a pale, bony finger across her throat in a sharp, slicing motion, and Rita shuddered.

Since Rita did not want to know any more about the demise of husband number two, she abruptly changed the subject. "So he was at the party too? He was the Van Tassels' farmhand at the time, right?"

Emma nodded. "We weren't married then, of course. He was there with my sister."

The widow reached over and stroked the photo of her first husband fondly, then grasped the mug and brought it to her thin fish lips. She took a sip, then settled back into her reading pillow. "Wasn't that delightful!" she exclaimed with glee, clasping a bird-boned little hand to her chest. "I felt like the belle of the ball. Everyone said such nice little things."

Rita sat down on the edge of the bed. She took the widow's hand in hers and said gently, "And you accused one of them of being a murderer."

"Well, because one of them *is* a murderer," the widow said indignantly. She took a swig of tea. "It's not rude if it's true."

"But is it true?" Rita pressed her. "Isabella tells me that Hank, while very drunk, told her he suspected his late father."

The widow harrumphed and waived a hand dismissively. "The senator? Trust me, he didn't have it in him. He loved Bobby. I could see him forcing Bobby into a shotgun wedding with his daughter. But kill him? No way."

"Well," Rita said, taking the mug from her and setting it down, "even if it's true one of your guests tonight was a murderer, that doesn't make accusing him or her very smart. Haven't you read any Agatha Christie novels? Someone always says they know who the murderer is and then, before they can go to the police—"

"They wind up dead." The widow nodded sagely. She reached over, picked up her water glass, popped two pills in her mouth, and took a gulp. Settling back into her pillows, she remarked with a wan smile, "Yes, that is often the case—in fiction, at least."

Rita glanced nervously at the window, which had been flung open to let in the cool, crisp night air. At this hour, there was unlikely to be anyone about, but even so, she felt the need to lean in closer to the widow and lower her voice. "So who was it?"

"Who—what?"

"Who killed Bobby? Who are you going to turn in to the police tomorrow?"

The widow laughed merrily, displaying her crooked tea-stained teeth. "I believe it's called bluffing, Rita. And now it's time for the others to show their hand."

"You were bluffing?" Rita repeated, scarcely able to believe her ears. She remembered how the widow's voice, normally so cultured and plummy, had turned icy and imperial as her accusations sent shockwaves around the room. Emma had emanated a rock-ribbed certainty. Perhaps, Rita thought, Emma should not have been relegated to a behind-the-scenes role with the Acorn Hollow Players. The widow was a far better actress than anyone could have imagined.

Rita shuddered, and not only because of the cool breeze. "I'm calling Sal," she said firmly, "and telling him I'm going to spend the night. Until you've been to the police station and completed your little charade, I'm not letting you out of my sight."

"That's very kind of you, dear, but hardly seems necessary." The widow sank beneath her lavender duvet with a smile and murmured drowsily, "But if you insist...."

Rita crept out of the room, closed the door gently behind her, and tiptoed down the stairs. Even before she reaching the landing, she heard the widow's little mouse snores floating down the stairwell. Poor thing, Rita thought. She must be exhausted.

Rita went back to the kitchen, finished washing up, and left Sal a voicemail. Then she curled up on the widow's stiff-backed floral couch in the parlor, pulled a blanket over her, and shut her eyes. She was just drifting off to sleep when she heard a series of stomps, a loud, sickening splat, and a shout. She woke with a jolt, her heart pounding in her chest. Rita sprang to her knees, leaned over the back of the sofa, and peeked between the blinds. She saw taillights speeding down the street and heard a loud, angry rumble of an engine and the screeching of brakes. Teenagers, she thought—they have no idea how to drive.

She snatched her bifocals off the coffee table, put them on, and pressed her nose through the slats of the blinds, against the glass, which was smooth and cold to the touch. There was something on the porch which shouldn't have been there at all: a wet, pulpy mess spread over the concrete stoop, the stringy, tangerine-hued innards spread in every direction like the tentacles of a giant squid. In the center was a half-melted lump of wax, its flame snuffed out.

That was all that remained of the widow's prized jack-o'lantern, a sly fellow every bit as flinty-eyed and snaggle-toothed as its owner. The widow had painstakingly carved it, arthritic fingers be damned, from a pumpkin so bumpy and gnarled it resembled a burl and so large it required six strapping members of the Acorn Hollow High football team to roll it up her walkway.

It was just a bunch of teenaged ne'er-do-wells, Rita told herself, out for an evening of pumpkin smashing. It was cruel and senseless—but hardly the work of a would-be murderer. Hardly a threat to the widow, other than her pride.

But then Rita noticed something else. Just beyond the stoop lay a ghostly white grid sunk in amongst the overgrown grass. It was the trellis that had marched up the side of the widow's ivy-clad walls, reaching to just beneath Emma's bedroom window.

The window that was wide open.

And on the other side of the open window was a frail, elderly woman who had just threatened to expose a murderer.

"Emma!" Rita called, bounding up the stairs as fast as her thick ankles could carry her. "Emma? Are you all right? Can you hear me?"

There was no reply but, then, perhaps that was not surprising. The widow was probably fast asleep.

"Emma!" Rita called out again, the floorboards creaking under her weight. She hurried down the hallway and flung open the door. "Em—"

The words died in her throat. The widow's eyes were wide open; her skin was ghastly pale. But she did not acknowledge Rita at all. She did not move. She did not speak. She did not twitch a single muscle.

Rita rushed to her bedside and placed two fingers on the widow's scrawny, veiny neck, mottled like the full moon, jowly like a turkey wattle. At first, she felt nothing. But then she felt the faintest of flutters.

Reaching for the phone on the widow's bedside table, she dialed 9-1-1 to request an ambulance and then immediately hung up and called Detective Benedetto.

"Let me guess," he joked by way of a sleepy greeting. "There's been another murder."

"*Attempted* murder. She's still got a pulse."

"She—*who?*"

The jocular, slightly grumpy, and quite drowsy tone was gone. The detective was suddenly alert; she could almost hear him sit up straighter and reach for a pen.

"Emma, of course."

"Someone murdered the widow *at her own funeral?*"

"Celebration of life party," Rita sniffed. "It was a lovely party, too, right up until Emma accused one of the guests of murdering her dear nephew—and don't ask me which guest, because she couldn't or wouldn't say—and the party broke up. And then she went up to bed and not half an hour later, someone came through the window and tried to kill her. And they nearly succeeded."

"If I didn't know any better, I'd almost think she was asking to be murdered."

Rita gazed into the widow's unblinking eyes, usually so sharp and piercing. As much to the widow as to the detective, she murmured, "Yes, I know. I was wondering the exact same thing."

Chapter Sixteen

While the EMTs attended to the widow and Detective Benedetto was busy examining the window screen, Rita crept over to the hamper in the corner of the room and began to surreptitiously sift through the mound of clothes: high-necked, long-sleeved gowns; prim, ankle-length wool skirts; turtlenecks and cardigans—all smelling faintly of lavender and old age, all jet-black. Rita was hoping to locate the black velvet suit the widow had been wearing that evening—the black velvet suit that presumably still contained the sheet of paper from Vito.

"Blood pressure eighty over fifty and dropping!" The blond EMT sounded thrilled to be responding to something other than a sprained ankle or nicked finger.

Rita frowned. That sounded dangerously low.

The blond looked over at the nightstand, snatched a pill bottle, and held it aloft. "How many of these did she take?"

Rita snapped to attention and shoved her hands in her pockets. "Two."

"Are you sure?" The EMT set the bottle down.

Rita nodded and moved closer. The nightstand was old, a relic from the nineteen thirties, and heavily scratched. There was a tiny pale pink splotch on the edge of the table. Rita squinted at the label on the pill bottle. Vitamin B12, it said. For a moment, she almost felt like laughing. At the comparatively tender young age of sixty-eight, she and Sal already took a full cocktail of drugs. But the widow, four decades or so older, took only generic vitamins.

"And did she ingest anything else?" his dark-haired colleague asked.

"Water, a few sips of chamomile tea...fried calamari, meatballs, a whole plate of very creamy spinach-artichoke dip, a gob of burrata, two big slabs of tiramisu...or was it three?"

The EMTs looked down at the widow's frail little body, then back up at Rita and frowned. "This tiny old lady? Did she always eat like that?"

"Oh, no! She usually eats like a bird. But this was a special occasion, you see. It was her funeral."

"Oh, so this was, like, a suicide attempt."

"Of course not!"

The EMTs shot her a dubious look and then turned their attention back to the patient. Rita crept back across the room and dove into the mound of clothing again, her hands sinking deeper, brushing against starchy, ruffled collars and itchy worsted wool. The widow's wardrobe seemed terribly uncomfortable; Rita had always assumed this was because the widow was from an era in which women were expected to suffer for fashion, but now she wondered if it was the widow's somewhat more modern take on a hairshirt, penance for what she'd done to her husbands—or what she'd failed to do for Bobby.

With one eye on Detective Benedetto, who was carefully extracting something from the window screen, Rita dove back into the hamper.

Rita's eyes narrowed and darted about the room. She'd come across nearly every imaginable kind of black clothing in the hamper—but not the widow's black velvet suit.

She spied the widow's closet, with its white accordion-style door just slightly ajar. Rita tiptoed across the plush carpeting and waited until the EMTs began lifting the widow onto a stretcher before slowly, silently prying the door further open.

Rita held her breath as she took in the velvet sheen on the widow's jacket and the slim skirt on the hanger beside it. She slipped a hand in the right skirt pocket, then the left. Her fingers brushed a well-worn, smooth sheet of paper, thickly folded, and with trembling fingers she extracted it and slid it into her own pocket.

Rita crept back across the room and peered over Detective Benedetto's shoulder. Now she could see what he had lifted from the window screen—a curly brown hair, now nestled in a clear plastic evidence bag. He was in the process of extracting a second item, a one-inch-long fragment of yarn. It was most unusual, flecked with all the colors of the rainbow.

"I'm right, aren't I?" she boomed, and Detective Benedetto jumped. "Someone snuck in through the window."

The detective spun around and let out an exasperated sigh. "I suppose it's no use to ask you to wait outside."

"None whatsoever."

"I could arrest you, you know—for interfering with a police investigation."

"Oh, don't be silly. There wouldn't be a police investigation if it weren't for me. I called you, remember?"

He grunted. "Well, I'm not sure there's much to investigate." He turned to face her and folded his arms over his chest. "We have a body—or, more accurately, a just barely breathing woman—with no bullet wounds, no stab wounds, no ligature marks, no abrasions, no bruises, not even a scratch. This woman is older than Methuselah and apparently dying of cancer—and yet you suspect foul play."

"Exactly."

"So how did they try to kill her then?"

"Suffocation," Rita suggested. "They snuck in through the window and smothered her with a pillow."

He shook his head. "No sign of that. No—most likely, we're looking at a stroke or some other natural cause and a completely unrelated attempted break-in."

The paramedics carried the widow out of the bedroom and slowly began to descend the stairs. Detective Benedetto clapped Rita on the shoulder. "I'm sorry, Rita. People get sick, people die. That's life, and it's not anybody's fault."

"And the fact that she had just threatened Bobby's killer with going to the police is—what? Just a big coincidence?"

He sighed. "I admit the timing is suspicious, but there are no signs of trauma, no signs of violence. Maybe she just got too emotional, too excited. It happens. No one's right all the time, Rita," he said gently. "Not even you."

She raised one eyebrow as if to say, prove it.

Detective Benedetto's lips curled into a close-lipped smile that was both sad and amused. He trudged down the stairs, with Rita in tow.

When they reached the widow's front door, he turned up his collar against the cold and rested his hand on the latch to the screen door. "The body in the fallout shelter? It's not Bobby."

Rita stopped dead in her tracks. "But there was that scarf. Emma made it—it was one of a kind."

"I'm not saying he was never in the shelter, or that someone didn't carry his scarf there. But that skeleton you found can't be Bobby. Forensics tells me the victim was five-eight at the most, no wisdom teeth, all the bones fused—meaning he was at least twenty-five years old."

"And Bobby," Rita said hollowly, "was an eighteen-year-old six-footer."

"With all his wisdom teeth, according to his mother. He was going to have them pulled the next week."

Rita's shoulders slumped. "Well, this is going to be quite the retraction. Any chance it could be Joey Gambone?"

"Off the record? Yeah, a pretty good one. He was five-seven, thirty-two years old. The dental records seem to match. But I wouldn't print that until the DNA confirms it, which could be quite a while. Cold cases like this aren't a priority." He half-laughed, half-grunted.

"Oh, and speaking of retractions, you're probably going to need to print another one." Detective Benedetto tapped his thick, stubby ring finger against his forehead. "There was a bullet embedded in Joey Gambone's right temple."

"So he wasn't poisoned by his wife?"

"Well, I suppose he could have been poisoned and *then* shot before the poison took effect. But that would really be a coincidence." He winked as he sailed out the door. "Which you don't believe in."

Chapter Seventeen

Rita locked the widow's front door behind her and then hurried past the ambulance with one hand shielding her eyes from the flashing red lights. She walked briskly down the street, slid into her Buick, and drove away, tires squealing. She needed to make a quick pitstop at home to retrieve the widow's emergency healthcare directive and still make it to the hospital in time for it to do any good.

By the time she arrived at the hospital, she was breathless and panting, the document clutched in one hand. By a stroke of luck, her daughter-in-law Susan was not only on duty that evening, but tending to the widow herself.

"Poor thing," Susan drawled as she walked Rita slowly down the corridor; to Rita's irritation, Susan, ever the Southern belle, would not be rushed, even if a medical emergency was unfolding. "She wanted a party, but it was just too much for her. She probably ate too much, drank too much, forgot to drink water and stay hydrated, stood too long. All of those things can cause a sudden drop in blood pressure, especially in folks her age."

They entered the room, and Rita froze for a moment. The widow looked so frail and tiny; an oxygen mask covered her face, and tubes were attached to each spindly limb. A symphony of electronic beeps filled the room.

"Are you sure it wasn't foul play?"

Susan's innocent blue eyes blinked at Rita. "With what?" she said, somehow drawing a simple question into at least ten syllables. "There are no ligature marks, no signs of smothering, no wounds."

Rita sighed. Susan was parroting Detective Benedetto's words, almost to a tee.

"Arsenic, then. Someone poisoned her wine."

Susan's perfectly tweezed eyebrows and smooth, white forehead puckered up into a frown. "Did she complain of abdominal pain?"

Rita shook her head.

"Was she vomiting?"

"No."

"Did she have muscle cramps? Were her fingers and toes tingling?"

"No."

"Then I don't think so." Susan squeezed Rita's hand. "It might have just been her time."

"She's not dead yet."

Susan smiled, pulled up a chair next to the widow, and patted the seat. "Set right down, Rita, and have yourself a good chat. I have some more rounds but I'll be back in fifteen minutes."

Rita sat down, reached out, and took the widow's hand in hers. She noticed a pink splotch on the widow's thumb and forefinger. With a rueful smile, Rita remembered just how much the widow had relished her desserts. She had thought her partial to Rita's tiramisu, but evidently Rita's cranberry pecan tart had been a hit as well.

She squeezed the widow's hand gently and muttered, "This was all your plan, wasn't it? To scare the living daylights out of Bobby's killer and flush him or her out."

The only response was a series of beeps. Rita thought the heart rate monitor showed a slight increase, and she wondered if this indicated some sort of response on the widow's part.

"Well," Rita said, "I can't very well solve the case if you just lie there all silent. You're going to have to come to and tell me who tried to kill you—and *how*. Now, I am going to name each of the suspects, one by one, and when I get to the one who tried to kill you, squeeze my hand. Can you do that for me? Vito... Sandro... Hank... Lydia."

But after each name that Rita called out, there was no discernable change in the widow's grip.

Rita sighed and removed her hand from the widow. As she did so, her hand brushed against her pocket, and she heard a distinctive crinkle.

The purloined paper.

Rita held her breath as she fished it out of her pocket and studied it in the harsh fluorescent lighting. "Likely relatives of Elizabeth Napoletano," she read.

For a moment, the name did not register. But then she remembered where she'd heard that last name: Vito. Vito Napoletano. But who was Elizabeth?

She scanned the list of a dozen names, gasping when she came to the last one.

Emma Schmalzgruben, she read, 24.5 percent match.

Rita snatched up her phone and did a few quick Google searches. As she skimmed through the results, which all seemed to agree that such a match suggested a grandparent-grandchild relationship, she heard the widow's words echoing through her head.

Suddenly, the pieces fell into place. Kate and Vito must have had a child of their own—Elizabeth Napoletano. And if Elizabeth was Emma's grandchild...the widow wasn't just Kate's mother's best friend.

She was Kate's biological mother.

Just thinking that, not even saying it aloud, felt like a sacrilege. The widow had always been so buttoned up, literally and figuratively. She was the last person Rita could imagine harboring a secret love child, flouting the mores of her era. But that would explain why the widow was so vehement that Kate and Bobby were not an item. Because unbeknownst to them—unbeknownst to everyone except the widow and Mrs. Van Tassel—Kate and Bobby were first cousins.

Rita bent down close to the widow and whispered, "You have a granddaughter, Emma."

She squeezed the widow's hand hard, much harder than she meant to. Rita felt tears welling up within her. Oh, what she would give to have a grandchild. But Marco and Susan were taking their sweet time about it.

Rita would be old and decrepit before she'd have grandchildren toddling about her kitchen, sneaking a cannoli while she pretended to be mad.

"If for no other reason than to meet her," Rita murmured, "you've got to wake up."

Rita drove home and then burned the midnight oil to put the finishing touches on her story about the dramatic end to the widow's celebration of life party. She slipped into bed beside Sal and slept until noon, when she was rudely awakened by a call from her editor.

"Rita!" boomed Sam. "What a story! The eerie, frozen-in-time parlor, the creepy shrine to the golden-boy nephew, the motley crew of assembled guests—you even managed to work in a celebrity sighting of Isabella Montelusa! Then the dramatic confrontation, the smashed pumpkin, the mysterious assailant creeping through the window...This story has it all! Well, except for the sizzle of an illicit affair, but one can't have everything."

Oh, Rita thought, but it does. But she was hardly going to tell Sam that Kate was the widow's love child, much less put it in print. Rita slipped on a robe and padded off down the stairs. Luciano and Cesare jumped to attention and followed her around the kitchen as she took out the baking supplies, a basket of cranberries fresh from the bog, and a bowl of freshly-shelled black walnuts.

"Yes, I loved, loved, *loved* your story, right up until"— here, Rita started to hear the click-click-click of Sam's tongue ring against her teeth, which was never a good sign—"I read your little postscript, like a poison pill ruining everything."

The clicks sped up until they echoed through the phone line, rat-a-tat-tat, like a burst of machine gun fire. Rita began chopping the cranberries and nuts in rhythm to the clicks.

"The body," Sam spat out, her normally deep, somewhat raspy voice rising, coming out almost strangled, "was. Not. Bobby. Even though—*even though*—we told the whole world just yesterday that it was."

Rita tossed some sugar into the chopped nuts and cranberries, wishing there was some way to pour some on her editor as well.

"A very easy mistake to make," Rita insisted as she mixed the dry ingredients for pancakes together. "Ana and I found a fragment of Bobby's one-of-a-kind scarf. What more of a clue does one need?"

"A clue," Sam said darkly, "that leads to the wrong conclusion—that besmirches the name of the *Morris County Gazette*—is not a clue at all. It's a stepping stone on the road to perdition."

Rita sighed. Sam certainly had a flair for the dramatic. She took out a small bowl, poured in some whole milk from the creamery, and then tossed in a few tablespoons of vinegar. Sour milk, she thought, and a sour editor. It was that kind of day.

"Now," Sam said as Rita flicked a gob of butter into the pan, "I'm sure you'd like to make this up to me."

Rita was not so sure of that at all. She spooned the batter into the pan, sprinkled in the nuts and cranberries, and waited for Sam's demands.

"The headless horsemen parade starts in twenty-five minutes, and I'd like you to cover it. Oh, and I need the story by six."

"Me?" Rita watched the steam rising from the frying pan, the butter sizzling rapidly. It mirrored how she felt. She wanted nothing more than to enjoy a leisurely breakfast of pancakes and lattes, walk her dogs, visit the widow, and then hop right back into bed for a well-deserved nap. Women her age should not be burning the midnight oil. "I thought Sandy was covering the parade."

"She was—but she's got a herniated disk from the pickleball tournament yesterday."

"What about Larry?"

"He's covering the sheep-milking contest in Chatham."

Rita crossed the room and hit the button on her espresso machine. "Susie?" she shouted above the roar, then put her phone down and stabbed the "speaker" button as she began to froth the milk.

"Hunting for the best fall foliage in the Berkshires."

Rita poured the foamy milk into the mug. As she reached for the sugar, she looked out into her yard and admired her sugar maple, whose leaves were a bright fire engine-red; beside it was a graceful, golden-leafed birch. There really was nowhere like the Hudson Valley for fall colors.

Rita opened her mouth, about to tick off a few more names of reporters and freelancers, but then she abruptly shut it as a tall, slim woman and a bespectacled man with thick gray hair came into view. They were walking on the sidewalk that ran alongside Rita's side yard.

Towards Main Street, Rita surmised—towards the parade.

Rita snatched her binoculars from the drawer and trained them on the couple. As soon as she saw that long horsey nose, she put them down again.

"Rita?" There was another click of the tongue ring. "Are you still there?"

Rita spooned a heap of raw brown sugar into the mug, stirred it, and watched it dissolve. There was something bothering her. Something that Sam had said.

"Rita? Rita?"

For a moment, she did not answer. Rita stared into the mug as if the answer lay in the depths of the swirling brown and frothy white liquid, like turgid floodwaters that would magically recede, revealing what was underneath.

What had Sam said?

Like a poison pill.

"You know, on second thought," Rita said, "perhaps I should go. Be a team player and all that. Oh, look at the time! I'd better run."

Rita hung up abruptly. She slid a perfectly golden-brown pancake on her plate, topped it with a dollop of cinnamon whipped butter, drizzled on some real Vermont maple syrup, and wolfed it down.

Then she raced upstairs, changed into corduroys and a cardigan, and grabbed a notebook and pen. As she ran towards the parade route, Rita frantically called Susan, who finally picked up on the fifth ring.

"Arsenic was the wrong poison!" Rita shouted, almost dropping the phone in her excitement. "You need to pump the widow's stomach and look for traces of medication for high blood pressure. A beta blocker, I think." Rita fumbled with her phone and did a quick Google search, scanning for a photos of little round blue pills. "Corgard, if I'm not mistaken."

"Corgard? Why would she take that? According to her medical records, she already had low blood pressure."

Rita sighed. Why couldn't Marco have married someone a bit smarter, a bit less naïve—someone a bit more like his mother?

"She didn't take it on purpose, dear," Rita said between gritted teeth, trying her best to sound pleasant. She tried to remind herself that Susan might very well give her grandchildren one day, and so it was absolutely necessary to stay on good terms. "Someone slipped it into her vitamin bottle."

"Ohhhhhh."

Oh, indeed. Rita rang off and a moment later, arrived at the corner of Pine and Main, where the horses were lined up. The jockeys were all shadowy figures half-hidden by long, billowing black capes. And balanced above each cape was a grotesquely grinning jack-o'lantern.

Mayor Carbunkle was pacing back and forth across the starting line, sweaty and florid as usual in a too-tight, three-piece black suit.

"Who's competing this year?" she asked.

"Now, Rita," he admonished her. "You know the rules. It's anonymous. Only the winner is announced."

Rita grunted her displeasure—Mayor Carbunkle was known to be a gossip, and there was no need for him to clam up *now*—and went to get some quotes from the spectators.

"I've got five dollars riding on number seven," a jolly young father told her, pointing at a jockey sporting a snaggle-toothed, slanty-eyed jack-o'lantern with alarmingly flared nostrils. "My strategy is this: pick the one with the scariest jack-o'lantern. It says something about the rider's personality, you know? And if his personality is anything like that"—he jabbed a thumb in the direction of number seven—"whoa, I wouldn't want to meet him in a dark alley at night. Know what I mean?"

Beside him, his big-boned, blond wife guffawed. "Strategy, my arse," she said. "He always picks seven. Says it's his lucky number. He even made me have seven kids. Said six was unlucky."

Rita shook her head in sympathy and moved on to a tow-headed teen, who said, "Number fifteen, definitely. He's real skinny, like a real jockey."

"Yeah," his sister said, "but his jack-o'lantern isn't even on straight. Seems pretty amateur to me."

"Which one are you rooting for?" Rita asked her.

"Eight," she said. "That's my dad. I saw his tattoo."

Hah! Rita thought. And Mayor Carbunkle thought I couldn't ferret out the identities of the competitors. Rita bet there wasn't a rider whose identity someone in the crowd didn't know.

"That's nice you want your dad to win," Rita said as she jotted down the girl's father's name.

"Yeah," the girl said. "Because then he'll be in a good mood and we'll all get to eat Rocky Road and stay up late."

Rita thanked the kids and hurried through the crowd, towards where Hank and Lydia were now standing. "So," she said brightly, causing them to jump, "I see you decided to stay in town for the race!"

Hank shot her one of his blandly pleasant smiles. "We thought we'd make a weekend of it. We get up here so rarely."

"Terrible about the widow, isn't it?" Rita said.

"About the widow...? Oh, yes, the cancer."

"Oh, no, I meant"—Rita lowered her voice—"the attempted murder last night."

"Last night?" Hank's voice was high, squeaky. "You mean after...?"

"She accused someone of murdering her nephew. Yes, that's exactly what I mean."

Lydia shook her head, like a parent scolding a child. "When you play with fire, you're apt to get burned."

"Lydia!" Hank shot a warning look at his wife. To Rita, he said, "That's dreadful, positively dreadful. Will she be all right?"

"Oh, I wouldn't rule the widow out. She's a survivor."

"I can just imagine her funeral," Lydia chortled. "Her real funeral, that is. She'll be lying in a coffin—open casket, very old-fashioned—and some neighbor will approach and then suddenly, like a jack-in-the-box, she'll spring up and accuse someone."

"Lydia!" Her husband blushed. Rita wondered if Lydia was still drunk from the night before.

"I'm sorry," Lydia huffed, "but I really resented all that finger-pointing last night. It dredged up terrible memories and you know how I get. You can't just go around accusing people of things with no proof."

Hank patted his wife on the arm. "She's just an old lady who's coming to the end of her life and wants more than anything to solve her nephew's murder. She's grasping at straws." Turning to Rita, he said, "Please tell Emma we wish her a speedy recovery—if that is, she comes to."

He started leading Lydia away.

Rita called out after them, "I never said she was in a coma."

Hank froze and spun back around. "She's not?"

"No—she is. I just didn't say that. I wondered how you knew."

"Oh—I must have heard it over breakfast at the B&B. You know, small towns—word travels fast."

"But a moment ago, you said you hadn't heard about the attempted murder."

"Oh...you know how it is. I must have heard some hushed conversation at the breakfast table that just sort of seeped into my subconscious. Perhaps that middle-aged woman with the big hair and the denim jumper. You remember her, Lyddie?"

His wife nodded. "She was reading the paper and talking quite loudly to her husband. With her mouth open, too! I tried not to look or listen."

"Mmmm," Rita said, sounding thoroughly unconvinced. "And did this loudmouthed woman also happen to mention *how* someone tried to kill Emma Schmalzgruben? Did that percolate into your subconscious?"

"I'm afraid not. But there's no need to tell us all the gory details. My wife is upset enough as it is—"

"Poison," Rita said. "That's the leading hypothesis."

She decided not to mention that this was merely *her* hypothesis, not necessarily the working theory of the Acorn Hollow Police Department.

"Like *Arsenic and Old Lace*," Lydia joked, "although the other way around. The guest poisons the old lady."

"Well, that points to Vito again, doesn't it?" Hank said. "I hear he's a pharmacist."

"Not necessarily. Most poisonings these days are with common medications taken in too high a dose...or by someone with no business taking them."

"That's very interesting," Hank said, "but we really have to go—"

"Your blood pressure medication, for instance," Rita said. "You have high blood pressure, so taking medication to lower it makes perfect sense. But if someone who already had low blood pressure, someone like the widow for instance, were given the pills—if they were, say, substituted for her vitamins..."

Suddenly, a shot rang out. "And they're off!" Mayor Carbunkle roared. There was a chorus of whinnies, claps, and yelps; people calling out their favorite jockeys; the calypso beat of hooves on pavement.

Rita spun around to snap a photo. Her back was turned only a few seconds, but when she turned back around, Hank and Lydia were nowhere to be seen. Rita pushed her way along the race route, scanning the horizon for a glimpse of Hank and Lydia; the horses were already far ahead. The townspeople stood on tiptoe, craning their necks.

"Come on, fifteen!" the tow-headed boy shouted.

"Seven!" the jolly young father bellowed. "Oh...stop riding like a girl, you pansy!"

"Oh, number eleven's off the bit!" someone to Rita's left shouted.

"Number nine, come on, nine...what's he doing? Is he seriously distracted by that kid's apple?"

"Number three can't even see...his pumpkin's spun all the way around..."

"Number fifteen's pulling ahead!"

"It's neck and neck with five, though...and five looks like he knows what's he's doing. Fifteen is holding on for dear life! Who's riding who?"

And so went the commentary from the crowd.

Rita was jotting down all of these colorful quotes when she felt a hand squeeze her shoulder.

"Oh!" Isabella wailed. "Isn't it terrible! What a wonderful celebration and then to have it end like that!"

"Ah, you read my article in the paper."

"Over breakfast at the Sunshine Café. Sneaking through the window like that. It's just so brazen, so bold!"

Rita winced. "Actually, we may need to print a retraction on that one. The window was open and there was an attempted break-in but it might not have been related to the attempt on the widow's life."

"No?" Isabella arched her eyebrows. "That sounds like a pretty big coincidence to me. What is the world coming to?" She shook her head sadly. "Well, what's done is done. But we've got to focus on what can be done for Emma now. How's she financially? Maybe you could come on my show and we could raise money to

162

pay for her medical bills. A bake-a-thon right here in Acorn Hollow. People could pledge so many dollars per hour of baking or we could raffle off your baked goods. Better yet, we raffle off an evening with you—you could come to their house and whip up a three-course Italian dinner—or maybe even custom-made pasta. Like say someone loves shih tzus – you could deliver a box of pasta in the shape of shih tzus..."

Rita could not even fathom how to respond to such a ridiculous suggestion. It was one thing to make pasta in the shape of butterflies (*farfalle*) or shells (*conchilie*). But she could not imagine how anyone could be dexterous enough to shape pasta in such a way as to distinguish between various dog breeds, using a mere half-inch section of pasta dough as one's canvas (how would, for example, one make a Labrador Retriever look oh-so-different from a Bernese Mountain dog?)...and she was both a champion pasta-maker and a dog lover!

So she was relieved to have Isabella drowned out by Ted Buscemi bellowing over the loudspeaker, his stentorian tones crescendoing in excitement. Ted announced all of the high school football and baseball games, so it was only natural that he'd be chosen as the commentator today. "And we're in the home stretch! Five and fifteen are neck and neck. Five is pulling away, no...now it's fifteen, if fifteen's horse doesn't throw him first...and across the finish line we have...fifteen!"

The crowd went wild. Rita watched as the victorious jockey slid off the horse (not very gracefully; clearly, he was not a seasoned rider) and made his way to the victory stand. He (she assumed it was a he) was slender but athletic, with muscular thighs and calves. No hair peeked out from under the jack-o'lantern, which was less terrifying than the others, with an impy grin and winking expression that sat slightly off-kilter on the rider's head.

"Now," Ted intoned, "do I have any guesses as to the identity of our winner?"

"The mayor's wife!" someone shouted.

"My wife!" someone else shouted to hooted laughter.

"My ex," a brunette yelled. "He looked just about like that when he hightailed it out of town."

Ted was milking it for all it was worth, so Rita took the opportunity to flag down Orlando and Penny, who were passing by, and let Orlando know that she could not accompany him to *Aida* that evening.

"I need to stay in Acorn Hollow," she said ruefully. "The widow's in the hospital, and I need to be on hand since I have her healthcare power of attorney."

There was no need to invent some gastrointestinal illness, although under the circumstances she wished there were.

To her surprise, Orlando did not look terribly disappointed. "Well," he said, "Penny has been wanting to learn more about the opera, so perhaps we could buy your ticket from you..."

"What a wonderful idea!" Rita trilled. "Great minds must think alike because I had almost the same idea."

"You did?"

"Yes—but not about Penny. You see, Rose has been wanting to learn more about the opera, too. Rose, Penny—it must be a fad among these budding thespians. After all, opera is the foundation for modern musical theater...."

Penny already had her arms crossed over her chest, as if anticipating the next words out of Rita's mouth.

"So," Rita said brightly, "I gave Rose my ticket and told her you'd pick her up at three."

"But," Orlando sputtered, "but I–I–"

Rita clapped him on the shoulder. "You're welcome. And just think–you two can practice your lines on the long drive down!" She winked. "I know you and Penny have been practicing a lot, so this will level the playing field."

Penny shot Rita a look that could kill and opened her mouth. But before she could get out a sharp retort, they were interrupted by an announcement over the loudspeaker.

"And the winner," Ted boomed, "jockey number fifteen, is none other than..."

Mayor Carbunkle, standing beside them on the podium, placed a doughy hand on the jack-o'lantern that bobbled on number fifteen's young, slim neck. He yanked off the pumpkin, and Rita gasped.

Despite the bits of pumpkin pulp in his hair, the jockey looked very familiar. Rita felt too weak to even raise her camera for a photo.

"...Vinnie Calabrese!"

Chapter Eighteen

In a state of shock, Rita repaired to the Sunshine Café for a restorative latte and giant slab of chocolate cake. She had never known Vinnie to ride horses—certainly, he'd never ridden them with Rita or Sal. They were not that sort of blue-blooded family. Where had he learned to ride—and what other secrets was he keeping from her?

Rita sat in a corner booth as dark as her mood, one eye on her laptop as she pecked at the keys in a desultory fashion, dutifully transcribing the spectators' colorful quotes, while the other cast a furtive glance around the room. She watched Fran Zefferrelli bustle between the tables in her old-fashioned frilly white apron; dashing Phil Baldassaro, Acorn Hollow's only attorney, stopping to chat with two obviously smitten older ladies from Rita's quilting circle; and the new high school principal lunching with the gym teacher. Ostensibly, nothing was amiss: Fran was waiting on tables (and making Rita money in the process, since Rita was her silent business partner), Phil was drumming up some estate planning work among the blue-haired set, and the principal and the gym teacher were discussing plans for the new gymnasium. But, Rita thought darkly, as she savored a forkful of thick, fudgy frosting, perhaps there was far more going on than met the eye. Perhaps she didn't know these people at all—or this town. Acorn Hollow, as she had learned of late, was a hotbed of secrets, old and new. Secret horseback riding lessons. Secret romances. And, if the DNA tests could be believed, secret love children.

An hour later, her cake devoured and three lattes downed, Rita filed her story. But instead of going home, she headed down into the musty archives of the *Morris County Gazette*. Squeezing between the towering file cabinets, she pulled out one musty yellowed newsprint after another, trying to reconstruct the six months leading up to Bobby Bruickhuisen's 1962 disappearance. She started by poring over each edition for any mention of the old Montelusa estate. She couldn't see the connection between Guido Montelusa and Bobby Bruickhuisen—other than the fact that Guido's son Sandro and Bobby were angling after the same girl, but the fact that Bobby's scarf was found in a tunnel leading to the Montelusa estate certainly seemed significant.

Next, she looked for any mention of any high school campaign activities involving Bobby or the suspects. She found several photos of Senator Van Tassel's campaign headquarters—with the names of the staff helpfully included in the caption. She came across a photo of the student council, all earnest, goody-two-shoes types with grins from ear to ear and Bobby, in a sports coat and tie, smack dab in the center. And finally, she found a photo of the cast and crew for *The Legend of Sleepy Hollow*. Most of the familiar names in the caption were just who she expected – Kate, Sandro, Vito, and Lydia. But she was pleasantly surprised to discover that the set designer for the production had been none other than Angela De Palma, who sang with Rita in the St. Vincent's Funeral Choir.

"Hullo, Rita," Angela shrieked in her ear-splitting soprano when she answered the phone. Rita had frequently feared for the stained-glass windows at St. Vincent's when Angela belted out "On Eagle's Wings," and now she feared for her hearing as well. Rita moved the receiver several inches from her ear. "Are you singing at Maeve Kowalski's funeral tomorrow? Poor dear, she hadn't a marble in her head by the time she passed. It was a blessing, really. Half the mourners are a bit off their rockers themselves. I'm thinking we need to sing something simple, really repetitive—"

"You're so right," Rita blurted out the second Angela took the teeniest of breaths. "But I'm not calling about Maeve's funeral, although I certainly plan to be there to give her a proper send-off. I'm calling about *The Legend of Acorn Hollow*, you see—"

"Oh, my grandson Tommy is divine in that, isn't he? He really reminds me of Sandro. I coached him, you know. Sandro's slightly lumbering jock walk, his deep oh-so-calming voice—he could have been a radio announcer! I had a little crush on Sandro, you know. I think we all did. I had his every little mannerism memorized." Angela clucked disapprovingly. "But I don't like the way this production seems to insinuate that Sandro was behind Bobby's disappearance. Sandro was just a big teddy bear."

"Oh?" Rita tried to sound casual. "Well, if Sandro wasn't the culprit, then who do you think was?"

"Well, frankly, Vito springs to mind first. He was in love with Kate, which was the worst-kept secret in Acorn Hollow, and he was a bit of a troublemaker, a little like your Vinnie. That was some inspired casting on Sylvester's part."

Rita scowled. Why did people insist on referring to Vinnie as a troublemaker? Between gritted teeth, she said, "And if not Vito?"

"Probably one of the Van Tassels. After all, where was Bobby's motorbike found? By the old stone bridge, right next to the Van Tassels' property. Who had reason to be upset by Kate's pregnancy? Her dad. He was very 'old school,' the strict Father-knows-best type. He watched Kate like a hawk—she had to be home by ten o'clock; all her skirts had to be below the knee."

Rita found it interesting that Angela's suspicions mirrored Isabella's. "So you and Kate were friends?"

"Not like her and Lydia but yes, I suppose you could say we were friends. Friendly, at least. Anyway, like I was saying, the senator ran on a real family-values platform. Can you imagine how a pregnant, unmarried teenaged daughter would torpedo his campaign?"

Rita certainly could. "But killing Bobby wouldn't have solved that problem. Senator Van Tassel would have needed him alive if there was to be a shotgun wedding."

"You've got me there, Rita." Angela sighed. "I wouldn't be any good at detecting."

"Well," Rita said graciously, "I wouldn't be any good at set design. And no one can hit the high notes quite like you, Angela."

With that dubious compliment, Rita rung off, a bit disappointed. Angela hadn't really told her anything she didn't know: the senator would not have been pleased about his daughter's pregnancy, Vito was in love with Kate, Sandro was sweet, Vito was a holy terror. Everyone, it seemed, was eager to point the finger at Vito.

With a sigh, Rita turned her attention to the Montelusas and their estate next. She located Guido Montelusa's 1996 obituary and was surprised to discover he had entered the race for Senate right after Senator Van Tassel dropped out on account of the scandal stemming from Kate's pregnancy and Bobby's disappearance. Beyond that, the most interesting part of the page-long obituary was that it included a long list of Guido Montelusa's most loyal servants. Alternating between the *Morris County Gazette* obituary archives and Google, Rita found that nearly all of Guido Montelusa's former servants were dead. Two had died in a mysterious house fire (was that suspicious?), one in a car accident, and one in a home invasion while visiting his daughter in Brooklyn (also potentially suspicious—could any of the servants have been blackmailing Guido?). The rest had died of natural causes—old age, mostly, which was not surprising given that it had been nearly sixty years since the events in question.

Of the four named servants still living, one had retired to Florida, one was reportedly living in seclusion in a monastery in Mexico (indicative of a guilty conscience?), and two were residents of the senior home in Mount Washington.

Rita slammed the file cabinet shut and headed straight to Mt. Washington, arriving at the senior home just in time for four-thirty dinner. Rita made a beeline for the two old codgers in golf shirts and khakis who were inspecting their chicken tortilla soup with undisguised revulsion.

"It's a conspiracy," the one in the blue golf shirt pretended to whisper, although his voice carried far and wide. Rita had a feeling that this was a well-rehearsed scene that they treated everyone to each day. "All this spicy food. They're trying to rile up my angina, so they can put me in the hospital and charge Medicare more for me." He carefully picked up each little green flake out of his soup and set it down on his tray. "Hah! I'll show them."

"You show 'em, Harry," the one in the red shirt urged him on. Rita had a feeling he said that every day too.

Rita came up behind them and said, "How'd you two like a free supply of homemade soup, any kind you'd like, as bland as you like. I can do Italian wedding soup, sweet potato, tomato, chicken noodle..."

They grinned at her. "Are you the new candy striper?"

"Hardly." She plopped down beside them and flashed her press pass. "Rita Calabrese, *Morris County Gazette*."

Harry had just the faintest glimmer of recognition in his eye. "Oh, you're that reporter lady." He brightened, and Rita naively thought he was going to rattle off one of her recent exposés or even maybe a few of her awards. But instead he exclaimed, "Hey, Frankie, I bet she knows The Dude!"

Rita fought the urge to roll her eyes. Did she ever.

"Yes," she said drily. "The Dude and I are colleagues. In fact, if you'd just answer a few questions for me, I'd be happy to get you an autograph."

"Would you? That'd be swell." He pushed away the soup and started poking and prodding his way through a bowl of tapioca pudding as if expecting to find razor blades lurking at the bottom. "So whaddaya wanna know?"

Rita told them all about her investigation into the disappearance of Bobby Bruickhuisen and the fact that his scarf was found in a tunnel that led to the Montelusa estate. "There are essentially four suspects—four living suspects, anyway—in the disappearance of Bobby Bruickhuisen: Lydia Van Zandt, Hank Van Tassel, Sandro Montelusa, and Vito Napoletano. Now I know you knew Sandro, but what about the others?"

"Lydia?" Harry screwed up his face. "Tall, blonde, horsey face, kinda pushy?"

Rita nodded.

"She used to hang around the vineyard some, claiming she was just 'taking a walk.' But she never fooled me. She always had one eye out for Sandro and then if she stumbled across him, she's say, 'Oh, Sandro, I had no idea you'd be here.' Yeah, right."

"Hank Van Tassel?" Frankie grunted. "Was he related to the senator?"

"His son."

"I dunno if I ever seen him," Frankie said, "but I saw his old man loads of times. He always had business with Guido, know what I mean?"

Rita raised an eyebrow. This was the first time she'd heard anyone insinuate that the senator and Guido's dealings had been anything other than above board.

"Vito?" Harry paused, let out a guffaw. He and Frankie exchanged a glance. "He was the 'maid's son.' Know what I mean?"

In this case, she wasn't sure she did. But she found it eerie how closely his words mirrored Hank's.

Seeing her puzzled expression, he broke into a grin. "Well, it weren't no Virgin birth, know what I mean?" He let out a coarse laugh. "And there weren't no Mr. Napoletano. And she worked all the time, didn't have no car—didn't really ever leave the Montelusa estate. And there was only one rooster in that hen house. You catch my drift?"

Well, Rita thought, the plot thickens: Vito and Sandro were half-brothers.

"Cain and Abel," Harry muttered, "were them two knuckleheads. The old man pretty much decided from day one that Sandro was going to be the golden boy, the heir—he'd never get his hands dirty."

"And Vito?"

"The errand boy. Did all the old man's dirty jobs. Little jobs, though. But Guido was grooming Vito for bigger things, trust me."

"And did Vito ever resist?"

"Not that I saw. He was a loyal soldier, know what I mean? But one time, when Guido's back was turned and he thought no one was looking, I saw this look"—he shuddered—"I dunno, it scared me. I thought that kid might kill his old man one day. He might just snap."

"But Guido died peacefully in his sleep," Rita said with a frown. "It was *Bobby* that disappeared."

Rita made one final stop on her way home, at the golf course where Greg Schmidt's wife told her he'd be playing eighteen holes. Greg had served as Bobby's "veep" on the student council, and Rita was delighted to discover he was just as loquacious as you'd expect a student government type to be.

"Terrible about Bobby, wasn't it?" he said, shaking his head as if it had happened just yesterday. He was a trim, silver-haired man with a military bearing and a politician's easy charm. It came as no surprise to learn he had retired as a general and then served three terms on the county council. Rita vaguely remembered his red and blue yard signs from several years ago. "And now his aunt? What an unlucky family! You don't think these incidents are related, do you?"

He must not have read her article in the *Morris County Gazette*.

"Well," Rita said, "she did accuse someone of murdering him right before she was attacked."

He took a driver out of his bag and eyed the fairway. "Hank Van Tassel?"

"Hank?" Rita was struck by the fact that, for a change, the first name that came to mind was not Vito. "Why do you say that?"

"Because of what happened the day Bobby disappeared." Catching a glimpse of Rita's thoughtful nod, he said, "Not Kate's pregnancy. The other thing."

Now he really had her attention. "What other thing?"

"Bobby caught Hank with his hand in the till. Stealing money from his dad's campaign. Hank wouldn't have wanted that to get back to his dad." Greg grimaced. "Old habits die hard. I heard a rumor at our class reunion that he did the same thing on another campaign later."

"Guido Montelusa's?"

"Could've been. I don't remember the particulars. But I guess it was pretty small-scale and it all got hushed up. No candidate wants to broadcast fraud in his campaign. His donations would dry right up."

He swung, and the club hit the ball with a satisfying thwack. It sailed high over the course, landed on the green, and then inched along until it popped into the hole. "Well, aren't you good luck!" His hazel eyes twinkled, and he gave her arm a little squeeze. "And I wish you good luck, too," he murmured, suddenly turning serious. "Bobby's gone without justice for far too long."

Chapter Nineteen

Rita slept in the next morning, went to eleven o'clock Mass, and then began preparing Sunday dinner for her family. Regrettably, on account of her daughter-in-law, it had to be vegetarian.

She thought of the velvety-soft sheep's milk ricotta, little round balls of buffalo's milk mozzarella nestled in a jar like pearls, the pungent, crumbling gorgonzola from the creamery in her fridge, and the tomato plants and pear trees groaning with heavy, ripe fruit in her garden. Rita decided they would start with an *insalata* of garden-fresh arugula and pears dotted with gorgonzola and candied pecans, followed by *gnocchi alla sorrentina*—pillowy, ricotta dumplings baked in a rich, garlicky tomato sauce and topped with a dollop of *mozzarella di bufala*—and finish their meals with a rich *affogato*.

Rita stopped in the kitchen just long enough to toss Luciano and Cesare a morsel of leftover *bistecca alla fiorentina*. Even her dogs, she thought with approval, were Italian gourmands who turned up their noses at lesser cuts of meat. She grabbed a large bowl, dashed out the back door, and dove straight into her patch of prized San Marzano tomatoes.

Rita cupped a San Marzano in her hands, felt its weight and heft, the sinuous curves of its oblong, almost pepper-like shape, its smooth, firm skin. As she plopped it into her bowl, the late afternoon sun gave a warm, fiery glow to its blood-red sheen.

Blood.

Her hand brushed against a small rock, hard and flinty, that lay in her soil. As she picked it up and hurled it across the lawn, she suddenly thought of Cain and Abel and then, Harry's words echoing in her head, Vito and Sandro. They were half-brothers, he had insinuated. Rivals.

In the Bible, Cain had killed Abel and then been cast out. But in this case, neither brother had been cast out. It was Bobby who'd been cast out, Bobby who had no brothers.

Rita gathered a few more tomatoes and then, with a sigh, moved on to the next plant. The fact that Vito and Sandro were brothers probably meant nothing at all.

Rita heard rustling in the grass and looked up to see her twin barreling across the yard and into the garden, a gleam in her eye, nearly trampling the basil in her haste to de-brief last night's "date" with Orlando.

"I have to agree with Sal," Rose announced without so much as a greeting as she reached down, plucked two tomatoes, and plopped them into Rita's bowl. "The opera really is tedious—all that weeping and wailing and gnashing of teeth and beating one's breast. And the way they draw out every syllable! It's like listening to your daughter-in-law drawl away, but in Italian. It takes twenty minutes for them to spit out a sentence, and by the time they come to the end of it, you've forgotten the beginning! And the audience—you never saw such a bunch of old dinosaurs! There won't be any opera in ten years—the audience will all be dead."

"I certainly intend to be around in ten years," Rita said archly as she ambled over to the pear tree.

Her twin followed, a dreamy look on her face, as she reached up and seized a lusciously ripe golden pear.

"So you were bored," Rita said, "and discovered that I was right after all: you and Orlando have nothing in common."

"Bored!" Rose scoffed. "How could I be bored? What was happening on stage was boring. But what was happening between me and Orlando? Pure magic. I had four hours to drink in that rugged, hyper-masculine profile, inhale his spicy, peppery scent—"

"That's just his cologne—"

"—watch his dark eyes flashing with passion—"

"—for opera—"

"—a passion," Rose insisted, "that will eventually be transferred to me."

Rita's hand closed around a fat, heavy pear. It was so soft and thin-skinned, its flesh so buttery, that the slightest pressure sent a rivulet of sticky juice down her fingers. She licked off the sweet juices and began heading back to the house, Rose trailing behind her.

"And as for things in common," Rose said as they went in the kitchen and began rinsing the produce, "we both love wine and Italian food."

"So do pretty much all the single women in Acorn Hollow, including Penny Albanese."

Rose took some arugula leaves, rinsed them in cold water, and began violently ripping them. "Penny! This is what I'd like to do to her totally fake platinum blond hair—"

Rita shot her sister an amused glance. Rose's expertly highlighted hair was blond too, even if more honey-colored than platinum, and was far from her natural color.

"—and this"—Rose took the ricotta out of the fridge, poured it out of the jar onto a paper towel, placed another paper towel on top and squeezed to release the moisture—"is what I'd like to do to her pasty-white, smug, smarmy face! Always watching me with those beady little eyes of hers"—Rose removed the top towel and poked two holes in the ricotta with her fingers, vaguely approximately eyes—"trying to ward off the competition."

Rose dumped the ricotta unceremoniously in a large bowl. Rita cracked two eggs into the ricotta. "Did Orlando mention her?"

"A few times. He just kind of snuck a mention of her here and there. He was all 'Penny this' and 'Penny that' And I was all 'oh, poor Penny, she must miss Larry so, she'll be on the rebound for quite some time,' and 'isn't it interesting that this is the *second* husband to die on her' and 'come to think of it, she was a Montelusa and there are so many unusual, even sinister, events swirling around them...after all, Penny's uncle Sandro was the prime suspect in the disappearance of Bobby Bruickhuisen, and now, fifty years later, Sandro just *happened* to be at a party where the host ended up in the hospital hours after saying she was going to rat on the killer in the morning!'"

Rita laughed as she stirred the ricotta and eggs together into a golden, creamy mass. "What did Orlando have to say to that?"

"He claimed that, right up until the widow's party—when Penny rushed up to Sandro shouting '*Zio! Zio!*'—he had no idea she was a Montelusa. Of course, he also said it didn't matter in the slightest, that he didn't judge someone by their family and, anyway, Sandro seemed like a nice guy."

Rita measured out a cupful of her special, imported, superfine semolina flour and tossed it in the bowl, then grated in some parmesan cheese. She was just grinding some fresh black pepper and sea salt into the dough when the front door creaked open and slammed shut. She heard quick, light footsteps pound up the stairs, then the upstairs shower. Vinnie was home from his shift at the nursery; Sal wouldn't be far behind.

Rita jutted her chin towards the ceiling. "Speaking of family secrets," she said, "how many more do you think Vin's got in store for me? First, I find out the boy can act, then I find out he's carrying on a clandestine romance with my teenaged co-worker, and now, apparently, he can ride!" She formed the dough into a ball and threw it down onto her butcher block, sending a cloud of fine flour dust skyward. "Did you know that?" she fumed. "That he could ride?"

Rose had always been the fun aunt, the one who let them eat junk food and watch horror films until the wee hours of the morning, then returned them home in the morning nearly comatose. It irritated Rita to no end that her children often confided in their aunt more than their own mother.

"No—oh, for heaven's sake, Rita! None of the riders could even see straight. Vinnie was just lucky, that's all. Vin's usually lucky—unlike that Johnson kid. It's like he lives under a black cloud. He seems to suffer some mishap every day."

Rita felt the hairs pricking up on the back of her neck. "Every day?" she repeated. "As in, something else has happened to Jake Johnson—other than the pumpkin falling on his head?"

"Didn't Vinnie tell you?"

Rita shook her head and felt herself growing hot, and not just because she was standing next to a vat of boiling water.

Tossing a handful of gnocchi into the pot, Rose wrinkled her nose. "At rehearsal yesterday, Jake—playing Bobby—was approaching the stone bridge on set, and Vinnie's ingenious headless horseman contraption was in hot pursuit. You remember that part, right?"

Rita nodded, feeling sick to her stomach.

"Well, suddenly," Rose said, "the wire frame for the headless horseman just exploded, sending these sharp wires, almost like spears, flying."

"Towards Jake," Rita said hollowly, "the only person on stage. Was he hurt?"

Rose shrugged. "Just a few nasty scratches. He'd just gotten a tetanus shot a few weeks ago, so at least that was taken care of. But it was a close call. It could have been bad."

Despite the steam rising from the pot of gnocchi, a shiver went down Rita's spine. "And then," Rita said softly, "the next day, Vinnie wins a race as a headless horseman, reminding everyone that it was his headless horseman that malfunctioned and nearly caused serious bodily harm to Jake Johnson, who is rumored to be his rival for Ana's affections."

To Rita's annoyance, her sister nodded sagely and said, "Life imitates art imitates life imitates art."

"No," Rita muttered. "An accident—a pure coincidence—is construed by suspicious minds as life imitating art imitating life—oh, I don't know how many times!" She heard the water upstairs shut off. Rita poked her head out of the kitchen and shouted up the stairs, "Vincenzo Salvatore Calabrese!"

The footsteps that had been padding around upstairs suddenly stopped. Her son knew he was in trouble. "Ma?"

"Come down here this instant, and explain to me what you know about these accidents that keep befalling Jake Johnson!"

Before he could answer, there was a knock at the door. "Mrs. Calabrese?"

Her heart sank. It was unmistakably Detective Benedetto's voice, and he sounded businesslike, even frosty. Very official. Normally, he called her Rita.

The knock came again. "Open up. I need to speak to Vinnie."

"Oh, you and me both," Rita muttered as she opened the door. Detective Benedetto was wearing his uniform, brandishing his badge, and carrying a small notebook. "You and me both."

Chapter Twenty

"Can't you see?" Rita fumed as she dunked the tomatoes in a vat of steaming hot water and watched the glossy crimson skins shrivel. She brushed away the skins to reveal the pulpy, pinkish-red centers, shot through with spidery yellow veins. "Someone is framing my son!"

Detective Benedetto and Vinnie sat at the kitchen table, while Rose busied herself with arranging the salads.

"Rita," the detective said, "I'm trying to interview Vinnie, not you. He was the one that was actually there, remember?" He polished off one of Rita's biscotti and brushed the crumbs away. "I didn't say he was guilty of anything, did I? But you have to admit, it looks pretty suspicious. There are rumors Vinnie and Jake are angling after the same girl, Vinnie's fingerprints are on the threatening notes—"

"*One* of the threatening notes!" Rita thundered. "And Ana Rivera, my eminently respectable colleague, witnessed the incident and already told you the only reason that his prints are on the note is because he wanted to help her with her story on the threatening notes."

"You seem quite well informed about what Ms. Rivera told me."

"I did not coach the witness in any way," Rita huffed, "if that is what you are insinuating."

"Oh, I'm not insinuating anything. Just investigating, keeping an open mind." Detective Benedetto chuckled. "So Vinnie's a chip off the old block now, is he? A sleuth?"

Rita glared at Vinnie, plunked another biscotti on Detective Benedetto's plate, and refilled his coffee. "Very amateur," she said. "A real sleuth wouldn't leave fingerprints."

"Hmmmm." Detective Benedetto did not seem convinced. "And this pumpkin that fell on Jake's head last week...I understand you rigged that up, correct?"

"Yeah." Vinnie was white as a sheet. "But anyone could have messed with it between the time I fixed it up and Roxanne pulled the rope."

"Is that so?" Detective Benedetto said mildly, taking another bite of biscotti. He pushed his pad of paper and a pen towards Vinnie. "I'll need the names of everyone who potentially had access to the ropes."

Vinnie reluctantly reached for the pen and began to scrawl a few names down the page. Rita sighed. He really did have atrocious handwriting.

"And this wire contraption that, er, exploded and basically shot daggers at Jake Johnson. Tell me how that worked."

Vinnie shrugged. "It was just a wire frame to hold the cape up, you know, like a mannequin. And there were tiny little fans attached to it to keep the cape billowing out just right." He ran a hand absentmindedly through his spiky black hair. "I don't know if the fans overheated or what, but it just—exploded."

"It did not just explode," Rita said tartly. "Someone made it explode. Someone other than you."

Detective Benedetto glared at Rita and cleared his throat noisily. "Vinnie, is there somewhere more private you and I could talk?"

"Uh, the basement, I guess."

Detective Benedetto sprang up, plate in hand, and began following Vinnie out of the room. Rita snatched the plate right out of his hands.

"Uh-uh-uh." Rita wagged a finger at him and shot him an icy look. "Biscotti is only provided when the interview takes place in the kitchen."

Rose chimed in. "We wouldn't want crumbs in the basement, would we? It might attract mice."

With a sigh, the detective surrendered his plate, and Vinnie and Detective Benedetto disappeared down the basement stairs.

Rose tossed a handful of candied pecans on a salad and cast Rita a sidelong glance. "Well, that didn't seem suspicious at all. The perp's mom interrupting every five seconds, hysterically screaming that, evidence be damned, her son is innocent."

"Because he is innocent," Rita insisted, turning her attention back to the *passata di pomodoro*, filling her food processor with thick tomato pulp, plenty of fresh basil and garlic, a generous sprinkle of sea salt, and a drizzle— more than a drizzle, really, more like a waterfall—of extra-virgin olive oil. She stabbed the button and the contents began to churn, fiery red and bubbling, like Mount Etna in full flow.

She felt anger welling up within her like magma, and worry too, and her stomach started to churn in rhythm to the bubbling, swirling *passata*. Someone was framing her dear, sweet, innocent, hopelessly naïve son.

And it was working.

Rita left the food processor running and crept closer to the stair landing, straining to hear just what they were saying. She could make out the distinctive timbre of their voices, Detective Benedetto's deep rumble and Vinnie's more tentative, softer tone, his inflection rising at the end of each sentence as if unsure of the answer. But the words themselves were indistinct. She slipped off her shoes on the landing and tiptoed onto the first step, holding her breath.

"You can't tell my ma, okay?" she heard Vinnie say. "But, I've been dating—"

Suddenly, the doorbell rang. Startled by the sudden interruption, Rita lost her balance and lurched forward, grabbing the banister just in time to avoid falling headlong down the stairs.

"Did you hear something?" Detective Benedetto's voice grew louder, as if he were moving towards the foot of the stairs.

"Just a mouse!" Rose shouted from the kitchen. She shut off the food processor. "See what I mean about the crumbs?"

Rita hopped back up onto the landing, slid on her shoes, and sprang out of sight.

"I'll get the doorbell!" Rita shouted loudly, for Vinnie and Detective Benedetto's benefit, then stomped down the hallway and flung open the door to find her son Marco and his wife Susan on the doorstep. As he crossed the threshold, Marco handed her a giant bouquet of roses and planted two *bacci* on her cheeks.

"We're early, I know," Susan drawled, giving Rita an awkward, bony half-hug and a single air kiss. Susan had never quite mastered Italian greetings. "But I just had to tell you the news!"

"The news?" Rita snuck a hopeful glance at Susan's midsection, but her belly still looked as flat as one of Rita's fettucine noodles.

Her daughter-in-law turned bright red. "Oh, no, it's not that kind of news. Not nice news at all—perfectly horrible news, in fact—but news you'll be glad to hear."

Her daughter-in-law certainly did have a way with words. Even in her honeyed voice, sweet and slow as molasses, she managed to make Rita sound like a downright dragon of a mother-in-law, an old crone who reveled in others' misfortunes.

"You hit the nail on the head, Rita." Susan seized Rita's hands and squeezed them. "We pumped the widow's stomach right after you called and you were right—she had Corgard in her system, but it wasn't on her list of medications."

"Thank you, dear. That's very helpful." She patted Susan's hand. "Anything else I should know about her medical conditions? Seeing, of course, that I have her healthcare power of attorney and must have all the information necessary to make any medical decisions."

Susan shook her head. "She was as healthy as a horse before—well...."

187

"The cancer."

"Cancer?" Susan wrinkled her little button nose. "No, I meant being poisoned. She doesn't have cancer. Who gave you that idea?"

"She did."

Rita smiled. Who, indeed. To her surprise, she did not mind being a pawn in the widow's deadly little chess match nearly as much as she would have thought. She hadn't been asked to cater a funeral or even a celebration of life party. She'd been asked to cater a very carefully choreographed charade to flush out a murderer—even if it meant tempting him or her to kill again. Even if it ended with the widow's actual funeral.

But Rita would not let that happen.

Chapter Twenty-One

The salad was crisp, the pears were ripe and luscious, and the *gnocchi alla sorrentina* was the perfect blend of supple, melt-in-your-mouth dumpling, rich tomato sauce, and decadent, gooey goodness.

But the focus of the dinner conversation was less on the food than on the attempted murder of the widow Schmalzgruben.

"Let me get this straight." Rita's daughter Gina stabbed the air with her fork, a lone *gnocchio* speared on its end. "The widow pretends to be dying—fakes having cancer"—Gina said the latter as if, in all this deception, this was the most despicable lie—"just to gather all the living suspects in the disappearance of her nephew Bobby in her parlor with the creepy shrine to Bobby."

"It's not creepy. It's touching. If you disappeared, *figlia*, I'd have a shrine for you too."

"Remind me not to disappear," Gina said with an eyeroll. "And then the widow accuses one of them of murdering Bobby—but she doesn't say which one—and threatens to go to the police in the morning. So presumably, whoever tried to kill the widow was trying to shut her up—and prevent her from telling the police he or she is guilty of Bobby's murder."

"So?" Rose looked expectantly at Rita. "Who looked guilty? Hank, Lydia, Sandro, or Vito?"

"Hank and Lydia looked apprehensive. But guilty? That's hard to say. Sandro...." Rita frowned. "I don't think I caught his expression. I think he was looking down or away, not towards me at all. And Vito, well, I can't recall seeing him at all. He's a rather short fellow. My view must have been blocked by someone tall."

"No, it wasn't."

All eyes turned towards Vinnie, who had mumbled this through a mouthful of pasta.

"Vinnie," Rita said sharply, "how many times have I told you not to chew with your mouth open?"

He swallowed, took a sip of wine, and grinned sheepishly. "A lot."

"A lot." With that admonition delivered, Rita smiled and said, "But you were saying something about Vito? About his whereabouts?"

"You don't remember seeing Vito because he wasn't there. He left a couple of minutes before the widow made her big announcement, while you were in the kitchen with the cooking-show lady."

"Isabella Montelusa." Sal said her name slowly, almost reverently, with round Italian vowels, and Rita scowled.

"Hey!" Sal threw up his hands. "I like her show, okay? I can't help it if she's good-looking, too."

Vinnie jerked his head in his father's direction. "Yeah—that's the lady. Isabella. Anyway, while you were in the kitchen, Vito just kinda teared up talking about

190

Kate. She was the love of his life, see? But she never loved him, he said, just married him out of desperation because she was knocked up and he was her good friend and she needed to get married in a hurry. Even after they were married, he said, she just kept pining for Bobby. And then he turned real sad and said, 'I gotta get outta here' or something like that, waved to the widow, and left."

"He waved to the widow?" Rita repeated. "Did she see that?"

"Yeah. She kinda nodded at him."

"And he was definitely out the door when she made her announcement?"

"Uh, yeah, Ma. That's what I already said."

Rita, Rose, and Gina exchanged a glance around the table. The men in the family would never succeed as sleuths. Neither would Susan, who was pushing her food around her plate as usual. Very little food ever seemed to go in her daughter-in-law's mouth, which presumably explained why she stayed whippet-thin.

"So unless," Rita said slowly, "someone called Vito and told him what the widow had said, he'd have had no idea that she was planning to go to the police in the morning."

"Meaning," Rose said triumphantly, "Vito had no reason to murder the widow."

In a flush of excitement, Rita leapt up from the table and announced it was time for dessert. She raced into the kitchen and arranged seven demitasse cups on seven saucers and filled each one with a dollop of vanilla gelato, her thoughts whirring in time to her espresso machine. Lydia and Hank had been so eager to pin the blame on Vito. Hank's words echoed in Rita's ears: *Always was a bit of a screw-up...he had a bit of a chip on his shoulder....That points to Vito again, doesn't it? I hear he's a pharmacist....*

But, Rita thought grimly, as she poured the inky liquid over the gelato, sending it bobbing to the top like an iceberg, Vito was perhaps the least likely culprit. And Sandro had turned white as a sheet when he'd first caught sight of Vito.

Which meant that either Sandro feared Vito because he suspected *Vito* to be a killer—or because Vito could point the finger at *Sandro* as the killer.

Rita was beginning to incline towards the latter view. She grunted in frustration as she arranged the cups and saucers on a tray. Why hadn't she sidled up to Sandro to conduct one of her famed interrogations-in-the-guise-of-small-talk?

She swung through the kitchen door and plunked the tray down on the sideboard. With a sigh, she began doling out the *affogati*. As she did so, the gelato began to melt and spread across the rippling, chocolate-hued surface. Blurred lines, Rita thought, as she watched the white seep into the dark brown. That's what this case was. Just when she thought she'd figured it out, another possibility popped up.

"So that leaves Lydia, Hank, and Sandro," Rose said, ticking off each one on a different finger. She gratefully accepted an *affogato* from Rita, dipped a tiny spoon into the gelato at the center, took a bite, and smiled. "Each of whom had excellent motives. Lydia was jealous because she was in love with Sandro, but Sandro was dating Kate. Sandro was jealous because he was in love with Kate, but suspected Bobby was the father of Kate's child. And Hank...Hank..."

Rose trailed off, a frown on her face. Rita realized she hadn't filled her sister in on her conversation with Greg Schmidt.

"...and Hank," Rita supplied, "was caught with his hand in the till by Bobby and was worried Bobby would spill the beans." She took a sip of espresso and felt a jolt of heat, caffeine, and bitterness, followed by a sensation of shockingly cold creaminess. Sometimes the simplest desserts were the best. "It could have been any one of them. I've tried to reconstruct the last twenty-four hours of Bobby's short life, I really have. But it's been so many years, and memories fade. And"—she made a face—"in any case, he didn't seem to have any close friends. He comes across more as a résumé than a real person. Smart, popular, well-liked...but not really well-known."

"Bobby must have been close to someone," Marco said. "A girlfriend, a sister."

Rita shot her eldest son a sad smile. "Well, by all accounts, Bobby was close to Kate, but she's long dead. And Emma said he was close to his sister Judy."

"Well, there you go. Is she still alive?"

"She's in a mental institution, has been for over sixty years. And part of her brain's missing. I doubt she knows her name."

"Not necessarily. The results of lobotomies can vary quite a bit. Many patients exhibit apathy, passivity, lethargy, attention deficit. Many become rather child-like. But that doesn't necessarily mean that they lose the ability to communicate or to recall old memories."

Rita smiled and took a sip of her *affogato*. Not for the first time, having a son with a medical degree had come in handy. Perhaps, she thought, it would be worth an hour-and-a-half drive to visit Judy.

Vinnie cleared his throat. "Uh, Aunt Rose, I was wondering when I could get my motorbike back. Mikey and me were thinking of going camping—"

Rita's ears pricked up. "But Mikey's got a truck. Isn't that more practical for camping?"

"Well, sure, but it's just that—that is, I mean..."

Vinnie was fiddling with his cup, stirring its contents with a small silver spoon, taking a rapid little sip, then setting it down on the saucer before picking it up again. His face was beet-red now. Rita had a sinking feeling in the pit of her stomach. Her baby was lying through his teeth and, true to form, making a hash of it. Not for the first time, part of her almost wished Vinnie were a more accomplished liar. She wanted to believe him, she really did. She wanted to live in blissful ignorance, then have a clear conscience when the chickens finally came home to roost.

But he made it impossible for her to pretend to believe him. Mikey had a truck. Mikey and Vinnie had no need of Vinnie's motorbike to go camping. And Mikey and Vinnie never went camping anyway. The subterfuge could only mean one thing: he and Ana had plans. Overnight plans. Plans that he would go to great lengths to hide from his mother.

Rose shot a helpless look at Rita. "Well, er, I promised to meet my new boyfriend for a motorcycle ride..."

"Oh." Vinnie fiddled with his cup some more. "Well, we're only going for a night. I could switch with you again when I get back."

Now Rose looked truly panicked. She was squirming, and Rita could almost see the gears turning in her mind, trying to work out why she could not accede to this seemingly reasonable request.

Taking pity on her twin, Rita reached out and patted Vinnie's hand. "That would be fine, *caro*."

"It would?" Vinnie and his aunt spoke in unison, Vinnie sounding guardedly optimistic, Rose suspicious and more than a little confused.

"*Certo!*" Rita exclaimed, which only served to deepen Rose's frown. "You've been very generous already, Vin, and I'm sure you and Mikey could use some male bonding time. It's going to be a dull weekend anyway, with me away."

"Away?" Sal's voice was strangled, panicked. He was no doubt thinking of how his elaborate Sunday meal would be replaced with a lukewarm takeout pizza.

"Yes, away. Marco *ha ragione*. Bobby's sister might be the linchpin in all of this. It's definitely worth paying her a visit. So I'm headed up there on Saturday." She patted Vinnie's hand. "With a friend of yours, actually."

His face fell, as if he knew exactly what she was about to say. Rita licked her lips, secure in the knowledge she'd won this round. "Ana."

Chapter Twenty-Two

"I had plans, you know," Ana grunted at Rita as she slid into the passenger seat of Rita's Buick, bleary-eyed. With no make-up and her hair in a messy bun, she looked younger than usual, more like a grumpy teenager than a starry-eyed young journalist.

"I know. An overnight date with my Vinnie."

Ana's mouth fell open, and for a moment no words came out. Rita handed her a giant Ziploc bag stuffed with chocolate-covered peanut butter biscotti (the most effective truth serum/bribe that Rita had yet devised) and turned out of the Riveras' driveway. "Biscotti?" She pointed at a thermos in the cupholder. "Latte? I made yours weak, without much sugar, just the way you like it."

Completely ignoring the proffered goodies, Ana blurted out, "You *knew?*"

"Eventually. After nearly everyone else in Acorn Hollow, it seems. Really, dear, if you want to be discrete, you shouldn't write in to The Dude. I read his column too, you know."

"I'm back to 'dear,'" Ana said acidly, "so I take it you don't approve." She extracted a biscotti and took a bite.

The crunch was almost deafening in the awkward silence that hung between them. "So, what's your objection this time?"

"This time?"

"Oh, Vinnie warned me. Gina too."

Rita raised an eyebrow. She hadn't realized that her daughter even knew about the budding romance between her little brother and Ana, much less that she was giving Ana advice.

"You always find something," Ana said, waving her biscotti accusatorily at Rita, "wrong with your sons' girlfriends or—now that Marco's married—their wives, even. Susan's too dim-witted, too Southern, too Baptist, too sickly-sweet, too vegetarian, too skinny—and she hasn't popped out even one Mass-attending, Italian-speaking, *nonna*-worshipping grandchild yet!"

Rita winced. There was a kernel of truth in what Ana said.

"Basically," Ana went on, "she's not like you, and you cannot imagine how any son of yours could possibly find happiness with anyone not like his mamma." Ana polished off the biscotti, folded her arms across her chest, and turned to face Rita. "Which is why I can't quite understand your objection in this case. I go to Mass every Sunday, I eat meat and pasta and Italian desserts with abandon, case in point"—she waved a second biscotti in the air—"I'm family-oriented and career-minded. Like you, I'm a journalist. Like you, I'm opinionated, pushy, smart, and determined. Like you, I appreciate how sweet and caring Vinnie is and yes, like you, I recognize he sometimes needs a little push. I know what Vinnie needs before he needs it. And I'm willing to learn Italian and learn how to make ravioli and cannoli and struffoli and panettone and whatever else I'm supposed to be able to make. So—what is it? Is it that I'm black? Dominican?"

"What?" Rita's head was spinning.

"Well, that's all I can think of," Ana huffed. "Either that, or it's just that no one will ever be good enough for your Vinnie."

Rita didn't know if she should laugh or cry. When she finally spoke, her voice came out high and strangled. "No, *cara*. It's not that I don't think you're good enough for Vinnie. I'm worried because you're only seventeen and Vinnie's older and he's always been a bit of a...wild child. I'm worried about *you*. And I'm worried about him, too, indirectly, because of what would happen to him if anything happened to you...."

Rita trailed off, feeling herself blushing. She snuck a glance at Ana, whose dark brows were knit close together and whose eyes had turned hard and flinty. A range of emotions seemed to wash over her delicate features—anger, but also confusion.

"For such a perceptive journalist," Ana said, "you're remarkably clueless when it comes to your own son. Yes, Vinnie may have pulled a few fire alarms and gone joyriding in a 'borrowed' car and even, apparently, felt up poor Mrs. DePalma in the library."

"In Vinnie's defense," Rita admitted sheepishly, "he was two. I may have glossed over that teeny detail."

Ana snorted. "My point exactly. That's who Vinnie *was*. That's not who he is. That's not who you raised him to be. You raised a true gentleman, Rita."

Rita wasn't quite sure what to say to that. It was hard to refute without impugning her own parenting skills. It was true that Vinnie was sweet, and he was very helpful. And he was at least finally working towards his associate's degree. But a gentleman? Rita did not think she'd ever heard that word and her son's name in the same sentence.

"And as for our overnight 'date' that you were so eager to prevent that you conspired with our editor to get me out of town..."

Rita fought the urge to take her hands off the steering wheel and cover her ears and hum. She absolutely did not want to hear any details.

"...I'll have you know," Ana said, "that it wasn't a date at all. Vinnie was going to drive me to my *abuela*'s house in Brooklyn, and he didn't want to take Rose's car in case it got scratched—or worse. I haven't seen her in months, and my mom works on weekends so I can't borrow her car. Plus, I have a Cinderella license and can't drive at night. Vinnie and I were going to enjoy my *abuela*'s plantains and *locrio de pollo*, play dominoes with some old ladies, and be asleep—in separate bedrooms—by ten o'clock." She took a sip of her latte and then raised the thermos to Rita as if giving a toast. "Quite a bad boy, your son."

Chapter Twenty-Three

Rita and Ana did not exchange another word for the next hour. Rita barely noticed the spectacular fall foliage that sped past, the brilliant scarlet and gold leaves that rained down each time a gust of wind howled down from the mountaintops. She was shaken to the core. A childless seventeen-year-old with no siblings and a Cinderella license had taught Rita a parenting lesson she would not soon forget.

The truth was she had underestimated Vinnie. She'd thought him incapable of change. Or maybe, deep down, she hadn't wanted him to change. Because if he didn't change, he was still her little boy; he would still need her.

But people changed. She'd changed after all. She'd launched a second act as a journalist, then a sleuth. She'd renegotiated her relationship with Sal and, a little grumbling aside, he'd adjusted.

And seemingly everyone but Rita had noticed that Vinnie had changed, too.

Well, Rita consoled herself, at least I never had Vinnie lobotomized. At least I'm not that horrible of a parent.

Rita pulled into the parking lot and took a deep breath as she peered up at the hospital through the windshield. It was a forbidding, fortress-like building, a Queen Anne-style turreted manse of charcoal-gray granite, like something out of a Gothic horror novel. Beside her, she heard Ana gasp and watched her stiffen. Wordlessly, they trudged towards the forbidding façade, heaved open the heavy oak doors, and crossed into a sterile, white realm—white walls, white linoleum floors, white furniture.

Ana and Rita signed the visitor guest log beneath the watchful gaze of an officious young woman and were then escorted to a pleasant, sunny enclosed back patio. Their escort wagged her chin in the direction of a wheelchair-bound woman with an orange tabby cat curled up on her lap.

"That's Judy."

Rita's heart sank. There was no sign of the beautiful young woman Judy had once been. The woman was thin, but not glamorously so. She was more like a scarecrow, all knobby knees, gangly limbs, and bony elbows. In that, Rita supposed, she resembled the widow, though Judy was much taller. Her long gray hair lay loose and scraggly around her neck. She wore a smile on her thin lips as she murmured to the cat, but her blue eyes were faded and vacant.

"Can she communicate?" Rita whispered.

"She can *talk*," the escort said. "It might not make much sense, though. Judy's in her own world, always has been since...well, you know. But at least she's a happy one. Not like some of them."

"Does she get many visitors?"

The escort shook her head no.

Rita and Ana approached Judy, but she did not look up. Rita called her name softly but got only a slight nod.

"What a beautiful cat," Ana murmured. "What's his name?"

"Bobby." Now Judy looked up, and her eyes took on a faint glimmer.

"Oh, like your brother," Rita said encouragingly. "What a lovely way to remember him. You must miss him."

"Oh, yes. But he does visit sometimes."

Rita raised an eyebrow, and the escort leaned in and whispered in her ear. "That's what I mean. She doesn't have a brother, and she's never had a visitor named Bobby. And the cat's name is Domino."

Judy paid no attention to their little side conversation. She clapped her hands with glee. "When Bobby comes, we play Uno. That's my favorite game. Will you play with me?"

Rita played three rounds of Uno, then left Ana to play a fourth. She lurked by the bathrooms and water fountain, which were in full view of the front desk, until the officious young woman left on her coffee break and a much more sympathetic-looking older woman was left quite alone.

"Poor dear," Rita clucked sympathetically in her direction. The woman was stirring four lumps of sugar and quite a generous glug of cream into a mug that said

"Sweet Tooth." According to the tag that wobbled up and down on her ample bosom, her name was Jane. "I came to see my long-lost cousin—Judy Bruickhuisen, perhaps you know her?—and I have to say I had no idea she was in such a sorry state."

Rita wondered if Jane would note the complete lack of family resemblance, but Jane just took a sip of coffee, grimaced, and added another lump of sugar. Nodding, she said, "Judy's one of our long-timers. It was cruel what they did to young women in those days. Take out their brains, for goodness sake, just because they liked boys too much for their own good. Their fathers would come to visit and they'd be leering at the staff—pinching their behinds, sometimes!—and then they'd have the nerve to turn around and say 'oh, there's nothing to be done about Elsie, I have no idea where she gets it!' And you'd just have to fight the urge to hit him over the head with a bedpan and shout 'She gets it from you, you idiot! You probably change beds twice as often as she ever did.' But it wasn't no use. They were men—they made the rules, even if the rules didn't make no sense."

Jane was not old enough to have been on staff when such things were commonplace, so Rita assumed she spoke from personal experience. Perhaps such a thing had happened to an older sister or an aunt.

"Men," Rita muttered. She took out an extra-large Ziploc bag of peanut butter biscotti and slid them across the table. "Here—some biscotti would go great with that."

Jane snatched one greedily, dunked it into her coffee, and brought it to her lips. She emitted a sound halfway between a grunt and a groan, which Rita interpreted as ecstasy. "Oh, my, you can bake!"

"My biscotti have placed first in Morris County's cookie bake-off seventeen years in a row."

"Morris County, you say...that's where Judy's from?" The woman frowned as though something did not quite add up. "I thought she was Canadian."

"Canadian—why?"

"Well, no one ever told me she was a Canuck, but I just assumed...her only visitor is from Canada. At least, I think he is. That's where the bills go."

"Really? That's good to know. I'd very much like to get in touch with this fellow. You see,"—Rita tried to steady her expression and make it look like she wasn't lying through her teeth— "my mother—Judy's aunt—just died without a will, and so I'm her sole heir. But I just know that if my mother had made a will, she would have surely provided for Judy. So I'd like to know if I should make a provision for Judy's care. But if someone's already paying the bill..."

Rita trailed off and looked at her expectantly.

Jane craned her neck to see down one hallway, then the other. When she was convinced the coast was clear, she winked at Rita and then typed a few strokes on her keyboard. "It's a strange name," she murmured, "not a proper man's name at all." She typed a few more strokes, then looked up at Rita with a triumphant gleam in her eye. "A Mr. Broussard," she said. "First name, Jean."

"Gene? Like Eugene?"

"No, like my best girlfriend Jean. But he says it funny."

"Does he sound French?"

Jane shrugged. "Only when he pronounces his name. But now that you say that, he does look kinda French. He wears that funny hat."

"A beret?"

"Yes—that's it. A beret. And he's always got funny-colored smudges on his fingers, like he's a painter or something."

Rita slid a second biscotti across the table, and Jane dunked it in her coffee. "Do you have a phone number? So I might get in touch, see how he wants to divide up the cost of Judy's care?"

Jane typed a few more keystrokes and frowned. "Sorry, hon. All I've got is a P.O. box in Quebec, Quebec." She laughed. "I guess like New York, New York, huh? Those Canadians—always imitating us."

Rita smiled politely as if sharing the joke. For a moment, she considered telling Jane that Quebec, Quebec was founded before the Dutch ever set foot in New Amsterdam—and decades before anyone thought to rechristen it New York. But then she decided against it. She thanked Jane, left her with a bag of biscotti, and went back to the sunroom, where she found Ana and Judy still playing Uno, and the orange tabby still curled up in Judy's lap. Judy was concentrating intensely, biting her lip as she agonized whether to play a red six or a blue two.

What a shame, Rita thought. From a young Doris Day to this.

Rita squeezed Ana gently on the arm. "Time to go," she said brightly. "You and I have just enough time to race back to Acorn Hollow and grab our passports before dinner."

Ana stared at her. "Why would I need my passport for dinner?"

"Because I have a hankering for authentic French food—in Quebec."

Chapter Twenty-Four

They arrived right before dusk, just the time, Rita thought, that one ought to arrive at such a magical spot. Behind them to the west, the sun was a bright orange fireball, sinking ever so slowly but defiantly on the horizon, turning the crenellated ramparts that snaked along the cliff above them from slate-gray to a warm, rosy-hued beige. Perched on the very pinnacle, like the topper on an elaborate wedding cake, was the Chateau Frontenac, a fairy-tale fantasy of turrets and towers. Its thousands of long, narrow windows, like slits in a medieval fortress, glinted in the late afternoon sun; its steeply pitched roof glowed a bright emerald green. On the other side of them lay the placid waters of the wide St. Lawrence and the ferries and pleasure boats that streamed across the golden waters to the far shore.

Rita and Ana parked by the port and set off on foot, eschewing the funicular in favor of trudging up the steep cobblestone streets of the old city—the *old*, old city, older even than the late seventeenth century *ville* above them—where the first French settlers had arrived, weary and seasick, kissed the ground, and erected a cross marking this land for God and country. Rita knew this because she had been to Quebec with Sal ten years prior, after an epic argument in which Rita demanded he take her to Paris, Sal had refused on account of the "snooty frogs," "prices high enough to make your eyes water," and "scary food" (snails, frogs' legs, and horsemeat), and a truce had only been established when the two parties had compromised on a trip to Quebec. Sal had liked the fact they could drive, that the menus were bilingual ("so they can't trick you"), and that they could make a detour to take in a hockey game in Montreal. Rita had loved the croissants, the baguettes, the mussels, the steak frites, the buskers, and the charming, old-world art and architecture.

Ana and Rita wandered past couples strolling hand in hand, a creperie, a fromagerie, a wine shop, an art gallery. When they came to a cozy old stone tavern with cheery red shutters and a tankard over the door, Rita nudged Ana inside. Squeezing around a creaky old wooden table, they tucked into a cast-iron skillet of mussels sizzling in white wine and olive oil and a cone of thin-cut, extra-crispy *pommes frites*, fried in duck fat and flecked with sea salt and herbs.

Rita mopped up every last bit of juice with hunks of crusty baguette and washed it all down with two glasses of the excellent house white wine. "I can't work on an empty stomach now, can I?" she said as she handed the waiter the credit card tied to her (very tiny) expense account at the *Morris County Gazette*. She was quite sure that, if her hunch paid off, her editor would hardly object.

When they left the restaurant, bellies full and spirits high, it was dark. The lamplights had been switched on;

buskers were on each corner, serenading with melancholy violins on one, astonishing with magic tricks on another. There were mimes and unicyclists, singers and circus performers. At the top of the very long wrought-iron staircase to the upper city, they came to the Place D'Armes, nestled against the walls, overlooking the far shore of the St. Lawrence, which now twinkled with lights, and in the shadow of the Basilique-Notre-Dame. Here was a wide-open space, an amphitheater of sorts. In the center, a man perched on a unicycle, juggling three flaming objects the shape and size of bowling pins. The fire arched over and above him; the crowd murmured and gasped. Beside her, Ana was spellbound. Rita smiled, glad that Ana felt what she had once felt—this intoxicating blend of the ancient and modern, of stolid tradition and wild spectacle. She could see why Quebec was the birthplace of Cirque du Soleil.

While Ana stood transfixed by the performance, Rita retreated to the art market that flanked the narrow Rue St. Anne just behind the amphitheater. As she admired the stunning impressionistic paintings of the Chateau Frontenac and the pointillist masterpieces of sailboats crossing the St. Lawrence, she struck up a conversation with each artist. "C'est magnifique," she murmured appreciatively, trying to remember what little French she had. "C'est beau."

She went from stall to stall until she came to a caricaturist, an older man in a jaunty red beret with clear blue eyes. He was focused intently on a beautiful young woman and her considerably more ordinary friend, who were posing for him on two battered camp chairs, bathed in a pool of intense yellow light. Rita positioned herself so she could look over his shoulder and watch the beautiful girl's long tresses swirl into being. Her head was overly large as in all caricatures, her eyes wide and long-lashed. He'd elongated her body, exaggerated her already ample curves and then, with a flourish, added a long curving tail, transforming her into a mermaid. With a few curving strokes more, the outlines of a fountain— the Victorian-era *Fountain de Tourny*, Rita guessed, with its elegant water jets and the Parliament building as a backdrop—began to emerge from the paper.

He worked with an intensity Rita had rarely ever observed, as if he were calling forth something that was already present on the page, even if obscured, as if he were simply revealing a reality that had been there all along. He had captured the girl's essence far better than any more anatomically correct photo ever could. The insouciant smile, the playfulness, the slight air of mystery—it was all captured in her mermaid form. Rita feared, though, for the girl's friend. What would he bring out in her? The large bulbous nose? It was the dominant feature on her face, but surely not one a paying customer would want exaggerated. Her slightly bugged-out eyes? Rita was almost afraid to find out.

She was relieved when he began to sketch her smile, a wide, gap-toothed grin.

"*Quest'ce aimez-vous faire?*" he asked the girl without taking the slightest pause in his work.

She wore a not very intelligent, deer-in-the-headlights expression.

"What do you like to do?" her beautiful friend translated in a posh British accent. "I think he means for fun."

"Oh!" The girl brightened. Her accent was not posh at all. "Dance! I go line dancing every Thursday at the Hair of the Dog. I'm always crashing into someone because I'm always mixing up my right and my left, and then we always turn and I get more confused. Like, is my right their left? And then..."

She went on far too long, never considering he might not speak English. He either did not understand the concept of "line dancing" or did not think it was suitable for such elegant surrounds, because he drew her with a fascinator instead, doing what appeared to be the Charleston, on the lip of the fountain right beside her friend the mermaid. He managed to capture her slightly vacuous, overeager-to-please expression but in such a way, Rita thought, that she would not notice.

He signed his name with a flourish, handed the girls their caricature, and accepted a wad of Canadian dollars with a Gallic little bow. Giggling, the girls scurried off.

The flame-throwers' act had just ended. Rita motioned Ana over and said to the man, "*Je voudrais un...un...*"

She did not know the word, so she pointed at one of his caricatures, then felt rather silly. Of course that's what she wanted. That's what everyone who came to his stall wanted.

Ana sat down beside her, and he adjusted the arm of the lamp so it was shining full on their faces. She saw a tiny frown cross his face as he looked from her to Ana and back again. "*Ta fille?*" he asked, though he sounded unconvinced. Ana's dark skin had clearly thrown him.

"*Aimee*," Rita said, squeezing Ana's hand. Yes, she thought, we are friends now. It was a pleasant, cheering thought.

The frown lines remained. The age difference apparently made a friendship seem just as unlikely as the difference in skin color had made a familial relationship. He shook his head slightly as if to say, Americans, they are an odd bunch.

He sketched them quickly, confidently, with the same intensity as before. But this time Rita could not see what was taking place on the other side of the canvas. So she watched him instead, observing his pale blue eyes, thin determined pursed lips, long aquiline nose, and the freckles and liver spots that were the rightful inheritance of a fair-skinned man who'd spent much of his life sketching in plein air.

"Madame watches me," he said in English without taking his eyes off her, "as much as I watch her."

His phrasing was charmingly French, but his English, she noticed, was unaccented.

"*Oui*," she said, the faintest of smiles on her lips.

He made a few more scribbles, then suddenly, triumphantly, ripped the paper off his pad and turned it for them to see. "*Et voilà!*"

Against the backdrop of the Chateau Frontenac, Ana was luminous, a pencil stuck through the bun in her hair, a notepad in hand. She had told him she was a reporter, apparently having decided to leave out the high school student part. Rita had a gleaming machete in one hand, a still-wiggling lobster in the other, and her black hair streamed off her head like a thousand writhing snakes that had just been jolted by lightning. She looked like a cross between the Mad Hatter and Julia Child.

Perhaps she should not have told him she was a chef. Or perhaps, she told herself, this was actually a highly flattering portrait from a French-Canadian perspective. A French chef, after all, would take a machete to a lobster—go to any lengths, really, to ensure the food was as fresh as possible.

"*Merci, Monsieur*"—Rita craned her neck and pretended to inspect the artist's mark on one of his creations—"*Jean Broussard.*"

Rita felt Ana tense beside her. Apparently, Ana had not questioned why Rita had chosen this particular caricaturist or, indeed, why Rita wanted a caricature at all.

Rita handed him several brightly-colored Canadian bills. For a brief moment, their hands touched. His palm was warm, his fingertips calloused from so many hours toiling at his craft. He started to palm the bills.

But instead of letting go, Rita squeezed his hand. "Or should I say," she murmured, "Monsieur Bobby Bruickhuisen?"

Ana gasped, and he froze. His hand went limp in Rita's grip, then turned clammy and cold. His blue eyes, which had been twinkling just a moment ago, turned gray. His jaw tightened. Rita could almost smell the fear emanating from him.

"But there's only one problem," she said. "You're supposed to be dead."

Chapter Twenty-Five

They repaired to Patisserie Paillard on Rue St. Jean. Tourists and locals crammed into long communal tables, huddling over streaming bowls of *chocolat chaud* and café au lait, dunking crusty baguettes into soup bowls, and leaving a trail of flaky pastry crumbs all over. Fresh-scrubbed, wholesome-looking girls greeted them in English and in French, presiding over the most beautiful display cases Rita had ever seen—row upon row of glistening éclairs and exquisite tarts, each a work of art in and of itself, but arranged into a mouthwatering mosaic of colors and textures, from the palest, most wafer-thin almonds to the ripest, most luscious raspberries to the smooth, glistening dark chocolate enrobing creations with names like *opera* and *trianon*.

Rita would never admit it out loud, but it put an Italian bakery to shame. Rita ordered a *poirier*, a glistening pillow of puff pastry cradling a poached pear on a bed of dark chocolate topped with slivered almonds, and a *trianon*, a dome of white, milk, and dark chocolate mousses encased in a thick layer of ganache. And to wash it all down, she ordered a *chocolate chaud*.

Bobby-turned-Jean (though he would always be Bobby to Rita) ordered a bowl of *soupe à l'oignon* and a baguette, and Ana ordered a chocolate-almond croissant and a café au lait.

"So," Rita said as they settled into a long, wooden communal table and she took a first heavenly bite of the *poirier*, "start from the beginning. How did a teenaged boy manage to fake his own death so convincingly that his aunt spent the next sixty years searching for his killer—and almost got herself murdered after insinuating that she knew the identity of the murderer?"

"*C'est pas possible!*" Bobby wobbled his earlobes, as if to make sure he had heard her right. "Do you mean to tell me Aunt Emma is still alive?"

"For the moment, yes. Though she is hanging on by a thread."

He sat back in his chair and let that sink in a moment. She could tell he was mentally calculating just how old his aunt would be.

"And while you're at it," Rita said, glaring at him, "you might tell me *why* you'd fake your own death and put your friends and relatives through so much pain."

Bobby hung his head and massaged his temples. He touched his wedding band, and Rita knew he was thinking about the life he'd made here, the comfortable existence that he did not want upended by his old life—a life, perhaps, that he'd rather forget.

"If it's easier," Rita said, "I'll tell you what I know and you can just fill in the blanks."

He nodded warily and took a sip of his soup.

"The baby was yours," Rita said, "conceived at camp."

He tilted his head, the barest hint of a nod.

"Kate kept up the pretense she was dating Sandro," Rita continued, "because she was afraid of how his father would react to his son being cuckolded."

"*Non*." Bobby wagged his index finger, and Rita was struck, once again, by just how *French* he had become, how far he had travelled from all-American boy to moody French-Canadian *artiste*. "She wasn't afraid. I was. Because I knew what Guido Montelusa was really like."

"How?" Rita said softly. "How did you know what he was really like?"

With a sigh, Bobby pushed away his soup bowl. He massaged his temples with charcoal-stained fingers, leaving dark smudges. Like ashes, Rita thought—like a trail of sin and atonement.

"It seems so long ago," he said softly, his eyes closing. "Like another lifetime. Like a nightmare." He lowered his voice another notch, so Rita and Ana had to lean forward and strain to hear him. "The worst day of my life began when Lydia told me Kate was pregnant. Lydia just whispered it in my ear during gym class when Kate threw up on the sidelines of our softball game. She looked so darn happy about it, too. Like she had finally beaten Kate."

"How'd you take it?" Ana asked.

"At first? I was furious. I thought it was Sandro's. I even stormed into the ladies' room when Kate was washing up. Accused her of betraying me with Sandro, which is ironic when you think about it—really, she was cheating on him with me, not the other way around. But she said the baby couldn't be Sandro's." He laughed. "Who would have thought? The son of a vicious mobster turned out to be a total Boy Scout. He wouldn't touch her with a ten-foot pole, treated her like the Virgin Mary."

Rita polished off her *poirier* with one last bite of flaky, buttery pastry and stuck her fork into the dark chocolate ganache dome of the *trianon*. As her fork emerged with a creamy swirl of white, milk, and dark chocolate cream, she was struck by how people's impressions, just like her dessert, could be variations on the same theme. Isabella had described Sandro that way too: as a Boy Scout, a soft-headed boy in a hard-hearted world. Neither Bobby nor Isabella saw this as a virtue.

He went on. "Kate and I argued during the four minutes between every period. I wanted to get married; she said we were too young and, anyway, her mother wouldn't approve."

Rita and Ana exchanged a glance. Now was not the time to tell him *why* her mother did not approve—why her mother would *never* have approved.

"So I took the decision—a terrible decision, I now realize—to tell her dad myself. I thought I was being brave, you know? Manning up. So I skipped last period and drove to campaign headquarters. I had my speech all ready. I'd written out part of it on my hand, but I was sweating so hard the ink was running down my hand, turning it black." He looked down at the black smudges on his hands and frowned at the irony. "And he wasn't there, of course! I was all ready to make my dramatic

217

speech, and *he wasn't there*. But Hank was—and I caught him taking money out of campaign safe."

"But how," Ana asked, "did you know he was taking the funds for personal use? I mean, he was the campaign chair, right? He could have just been taking petty cash to pay the printer for some more flyers or something."

He wagged his finger at her. "*Précisément!* But he didn't think of that—and I didn't either. Because he looked guilty. He wasn't just red-handed, he was red-faced, stammering. I just knew—and *he* knew *I* knew."

"So that was your second big shock of the day."

"*Oui.*" He shook his head ruefully. "And I was in for a third. Because, in my shock and surprise, I left my backpack there. I only realized this after dress rehearsal—a terrible rehearsal that went late since I flubbed nearly all of my lines—and so I had to go back to campaign headquarters again where"—he held up three fingers and tapped the middle finger—"I got my third shock of the day."

"Senator Van Tassel doing business with Guido Montelusa," Rita murmured.

Bobby nodded grimly. "They were in the back room. I could hear everything, but they couldn't see me, and I thought I could make my escape. But then my shoes gave me away. I had brand-new shoes, you see—I was so proud of these shoes. But they were new, and they squeaked. I ran for it, but I knew they saw me."

Rita licked a glob of dark chocolate mousse off her fork. "So Guido Montelusa, Senator Van Tassel, and Hank Van Tassel all wanted you dead."

He shrugged. "*Peut être.*"

Ana leaned forward and frowned. "And so, after the performance, after the cast party that ended with everyone running out into the night, you took your opportunity to make a run for it? You left your motorbike by the banks of the stream alongside a smashed pumpkin and fled to Canada, never to be seen or heard from again?"

"*Oui.*"

He shrugged again, but his eyes were evasive, clouded over. Rita could tell there was more to the story.

"But if that's true," Rita said, "how did your scarf—your very distinctive, one-of-a-kind, hand-knitted scarf—end up in Guido Montelusa's tunnel?"

Chapter Twenty-Six

There was an exceedingly long pause, during which Ana polished off her croissant and Rita scraped every last smudge of chocolate mousse off her plate.

"Well?" Rita demanded at last. "Did the Montelusas or the Van Tassels kidnap you and hold you for days, until you eventually escaped, staged your disappearance— very theatrically, by the way—and made your way to Canada under an assumed name?"

That last part particularly bothered Rita. She doubted many seventeen-year-olds would have the means or ingenuity to construct a whole new identity, as a Canadian no less.

He tilted his head slightly and regarded her carefully. His blue eyes narrowed as if he were performing some mental calculation. Then he pursed his lips and shook his head as if deciding against it. "*Non,*" he murmured in a voice so low she could almost have imagined it. He seemed to be saying it to himself, not to her. In a louder voice, he said, "I do not wish to dwell on the details. *Je suis ici*"—he smiled and waved his arms around their warm, convivial surroundings—"and Guido Montelusa and Senator Van Tassel are long in their graves."

"Sandro," Rita said pointedly, "is still alive."

"I already told you," he said. "Sandro's a Boy Scout. He wouldn't hurt a fly, and he certainly never hurt me. If anything, it's I who should have apologized to him."

Rita mentally crossed Sandro off her list, then immediately added him back on again. If Bobby still feared for his life, he would hardly implicate Sandro and risk his ire.

"We can help you, you know," Rita said.

"Help me?" He looked faintly amused. "Help me how?"

"Get justice," Ana sputtered, "for what was done to you!"

"Nothing was done to me," he said. "That's rather the point. I died, only to be reborn. I got the gift of a second act. Most people don't get *that*, do they?"

He glanced briefly at Ana and shook his head sadly as if to say, young people, they don't understand these things. Then he locked eyes with Rita, and they both nodded slowly. Yes, she knew. She was living her second act, and loving it. It was a gift—he was right about that.

"I want Bobby," he said, "to stay dead. Is that clear?"

"Very," Rita said, knowing full well this was a misleading answer. Just because his wishes were clear did not mean she intended to honor them.

"But what about your parents?" Ana cried. "And Kate? Didn't you spare a thought for what they were going through?"

"My father..." He shook his head. "He was not a good man."

Rita shot Ana a warning glance. From all the widow had said about him, she knew this to be true.

"As for my mother," he said, "I sent her a letter. She kept the secret to her grave, which sadly wasn't long after I disappeared. Six months, maybe."

He did not mention that she had died at the hands of his father. But then, Rita realized, there would be no way for him to know this. He had not been there, and he wasn't in contact with his Aunt Emma or anyone else who knew or at least suspected.

"And Kate?" Bobby said. "I thought about writing many times, and maybe I should have. But I couldn't see what good it would do. She'd already said she didn't want to get married. She wasn't going to come here. I couldn't go there. No, I decided it would be easier for her to move on, to marry someone else, perhaps, to find a good stepdad for her child—our child—if I just stayed dead."

"So," Rita said, "you never saw Kate again."

"*Alors*"—Bobby looked down and began stirring his spoon, as if the answers lay at the bottom of his *soupe à l'oignon*— "that's not quite true. I saw her once. Vito and Kate were married then, you see, and Kate—well, Kate wasn't happy...and she found out where I was."

Rita frowned. "Your mother told her?"

"My mother? Oh, yes—that must have been it." He sighed. "Isn't it amazing? When someone's gone, they suddenly become deified, all their faults fade, their virtues loom large. From a distance, they can't argue with you or leave dirty dishes in the sink or refuse to change a dirty diaper. But up close—well, a dose of reality is harsh medicine."

"So the reunion wasn't all rainbows and butterflies?"

"It was painful. We walked along the Terrasse Dufferin. It was the season of Winter Carnevale. We watched the icebergs bobbing down the St. Lawrence; drank caribou—it's this hot grog, very strong!; strolled through snow-covered streets, sucking on paddles of maple syrup quick-frozen on the snow. It was so beautiful; she was so beautiful, and so was her—our—little boy."

Rita noticed that he kept calling the child *hers*, then reverting to the pronoun *our*. He talked about all of these events as from a great distance, almost as if narrating something that had happened to someone else.

"But," he said, "it was not in the least romantic. It was as if someone had plucked two actors from some moody European art film and plunked them down on the set of a romantic comedy. We were no longer two teenagers—she was a mother, I'd narrowly escaped death. We walked past the Ice Palace and she said 'It's so beautiful, while it lasts. But in a few weeks, it will be a puddle and a memory.' That was her way of saying good-bye. She kissed me on the cheek, we walked back to her car, and she said, 'I belong with Vito. I know that now.' And I said, 'He's a good man.' And I honestly meant it. All those people who seemed so upstanding—Guido Montelusa, Senator Van Tassel, even Hank—had turned out not to be. And Vito, who seemed like such a troublemaker, had actually turned out to be a good friend, husband, and father."

Rita and Ana exchanged a glance. Rita knew just what Ana was thinking: should they tell Bobby that Kate never made it back to Vito? That her life—and their son's—had come to an end just hours later?

Rita took a gulp of *chocolate chaud* and wiggled her head slightly. To anyone else, it might look as though she were just slurping a ribbon of delectable melted chocolate sluicing down the side of the bowl. But Ana would realize she meant no, we will not tell him. He had not asked after Kate or even their son. He had a new home, new name, new family. Bobby Bruickhuisen was well and truly dead. Jean Broussard, the man who sat before them, had only met Kate once, fleetingly, on a walk of melancholy and regret. He had no sons—or if he did, they had names like Phillippe and Jean-Claude.

Rita and Ana stood up, and Bobby did too. They shook hands warmly. "*Bon soir*," he said softly before striding out the door and disappearing down a winding cobblestone lane.

Ana turned to Rita. "So, if neither Lydia nor Hank nor Vito nor Sandro killed Bobby—*if no one killed Bobby...*"

"Why would anyone try to hush the widow up? That's a very good question, indeed."

Chapter Twenty-Seven

The pale milky light of day was breaking over the eastern horizon as Rita pulled into her driveway. She tiptoed across the threshold, ruffled the fur of her slumbering pets (some guard dogs they made!), and then crept upstairs. Sinking beneath her fluffy duvet, she cast a fond gaze at her husband, who was snoring like a freight train, his salt and pepper mustache fluttering with each gust that escaped his fleshy lips, his barrel chest, clad in a stained old wifebeater, rising and falling in rhythm. She felt a sudden welling of emotion in her chest, gratitude for all their mostly happy years together, their lack of messy love triangles and secret love children. Sal had no secrets from her—at least, not ones she couldn't, and hadn't, unearthed. She already knew his biggest secret, his secret identity as the consiglieri to many a lovelorn teenager, suspicious housewife, or bewildered husband.

Sal must have stayed up late, drafting one reply after another to The Dude's ever-increasing volume of correspondence, because there was a sheaf of papers on the nightstand, Sal's reading glasses perched on top. Though she knew she should try to get some rest, Rita could not help but thumb through them, squinting to decipher Sal's chicken scratch in the dim light of dawn. There was a letter from a woman convinced that her husband was having an affair with their dog walker based on nothing more than their shared love of corgis and the extra generous tip her husband had given the dog walker at Christmas (The Dude's advice: switch to an ugly dog walker and spice things up with a corgi-print negligee), a college student wondering if she should marry her Saudi boyfriend and become a sheikh's wife or move to Manhattan and pursue her dream of becoming a Rockette ("given that dancing is illegal in Saudi Arabia, I'm going to go out on a limb and suggest you're not cut out for life behind a burqa," Sal had scrawled on top as his terse response), and a girl who was having a hard time moving on after the death of her pet iguana (Sal had just scribbled a giant question mark in red on the letter, apparently at a loss for words).

The fourth letter brought her up short.

"Dear Dude,

I was always the girl that everyone says is 'helpful' and 'nice,' the teacher's pet, etc. It used to be a good thing, but now it's got me in a whole lot of trouble. I like a boy who likes another girl. It's totally futile—she likes an older boy—so I thought I could get closer to him by offering to 'help' him with her. She's a reporter, so he thought he could get her attention if he was the victim of a series of attacks. At first, it seemed kind of harmless, but now he's planning ever more serious incidents and I'm worried that someone will actually get hurt. Plus, the police are now involved. I want to stop helping him, but now

he's threatening that if I do, he'll tell the police that this was all my idea.
Signed,
Wanting to Sing a Love Song, Not the Jailhouse Rock"

Rita ran her fingers over the sloping handwriting that spread in blue ink over the lined notebook paper. There were brown smudges on the corners—chocolate, she surmised.

Sal had scratched out a response on the reverse.

"Dear Wanting to Sing a Love Song,
I hate to break it to you but (a) you have terrible taste in men and (b) if you don't squeal like a pig headed for the slaughterhouse, you're going to be singing the Jailhouse Rock (and Heartbreak Hotel) very soon. It's time to cut your losses, lovebird, and make a date with Detective Benedetto. But first, fess up to your parents and get yourself a good lawyer. I hope you're a trust fund baby, because they don't come cheap.
Good luck!
The Dude"

Rita jolted upright in bed. She could draw only one conclusion from this letter: Jake Johnson, that little weasel, was framing her son by sending threatening letters to *himself*, and his accomplice was a smitten, eager-to-please, brown-nosing chocoholic with a better-than-average teenaged vocabulary (Jake's crush was "futile," not "hopeless") and an appreciation for Elvis songs.

Rita rummaged through the pile until she found the envelope with the same sloping handwriting and royal-blue ink. Stuck to the flap was a tiny piece of fuzz, fading from indigo to pink to pale yellow. *Where have I seen that before*, Rita wondered. Her mind raced through the past week; snippets of conversation played in her head, and brightly-colored images, fleeting impressions, flashed alongside. Bobby's blood-red beret, Judy's tabby cat's beautiful orange coat, the sterile white walls of the mental hospital, the glossy ebony shade of the dark chocolate enrobing Rita's exquisite *trianon* pastry at the *patisserie*.

But try as she might, that particular image stayed stubbornly out of reach, just on the edge of her consciousness. "Maybe if I sleep on it," she murmured drowsily, sinking down under the cover. Seconds later, she was fast asleep.

The sun was high in the sky when she was jolted awake by the *beep-beep-beep* of the garbage truck and the frantic yelps of Luciano and Cesare as they bolted out the front door to collect some tasty beef jerky bits from their softie of a garbage man, followed by the whirring of the coffee grinder and the opening strains of *The Isabella Montelusa Show* theme music. The heavenly scent of freshly-ground espresso wafted up the stairs.

Rita threw on corduroys and a cardigan and went down to the kitchen.

"Glad you and Ana got back safely," Sal murmured. "Was the food good?"

"Divine," Rita said. "And you'll never guess—"

"I'd love to hear all about it, *cara*,"—he gave her a quick peck on the cheek and handed her a perfectly-frothed, steaming-hot latte—"but maybe a bit later. It's my day off, so it's the only day I can watch Isabella's show, you know?"

And before she could say a word, he'd scampered through the swinging door and plopped himself onto the couch.

With a sigh, Rita went to sit by the window. As she admired the autumnal splendor right out her back door, she sipped her latte and munched a few biscotti, then clapped her hands and shouted, "*I guinzagli!*"

Her dogs (who, sadly, understood Italian much better than her human children) leapt up and grabbed their leashes with alacrity. A few minutes later, they trotted past the widow's painted lady, now dark and forlorn, through the cemetery gates, under the hickory tree, past her mother's grave (where she sprinkled a few drops of limoncello from Luciano's flask, then took a tipple herself), and then to the marble slabs bearing the names of the widow's three husbands.

A passing cloud cast a shadow on one of the tombstones and, for a moment, Rita could almost make out the L-shaped black form of the widow, sitting stiff and ramrod-straight on the gleaming white slab. Then, like a mirage in the desert, the form vanished as soon as it had appeared.

But she felt the widow's spirit still. Did that mean the widow had passed on, or that she had woken up?

Realizing she'd left her phone at home, Rita broke into a run, tugging at Luciano and Cesare's leashes, urging them on. "*Venite, ragazzi!*"

Fifteen minutes later, she arrived home, panting. Sal had not budged from his spot in front of the TV, transfixed as usual by Isabella, who was preparing her take on *braciole*.

"Did the hospital call?" Rita wheezed. It was a mile from the cemetery back home, and she had run nearly all the way.

"What? Oh—no. But Isabella did. Well, her assistant anyway." Sal's eyes remained glued to the TV. He whistled. "Look at how tightly she rolls the stuffing into the cabbage! Just like my *nonna* did. 'Cept my *nonna* didn't have nicely painted nails like that."

Sal jutted his chin towards the screen. Isabella's perfectly manicured pink nails were curving around a brilliantly green cabbage leaf.

Rita grunted. "Your *nonna* didn't have made-for-TV cleavage either."

As if to underscore her point, the camera zoomed in on Isabella's lovely, age-defying face, then slowly made its way back down to her hands.

"Aw, Rita, why you gotta be like that? Isabella's a terrific cook, and she's involved in all these charitable causes through the Guido Montelusa Foundation. Homeless vets, old folks, starving puppies, single moms—they do it all. And she wants you on her show, so she can't be that bad, right? All my friends are gonna be so jealous. I mean, did Isabella ask their old lady to be on her show? I don't think so." He turned back to the TV. "I left Isabella's assistant's number on the table."

Rita went to the kitchen and dialed Isabella's assistant's number.

"Could you do today, three p.m.?" The assistant had a thick Brooklyn accent and sounded bored, as if she'd already asked this a dozen times today.

"Today?"

"Well, there's been a cancellation, you see. We had a champion yodeler-slash-dumpling maker who was going to showcase the culinary traditions of the Italian Alps, but she came down with vocal nodes and can't yodel."

Rita was at a loss for what to say. "Oh...how terrible. That doesn't give me much time to prepare, but I suppose I could do that. What would you like me to make?"

"Oh, anything will be fine."

"Biscotti?"

"Did it last month."

"Chicken cacciatore?"

"No can do. That's one of Isabella's signature dishes."

Yes, Rita thought, but mine is better. But she supposed they couldn't risk having someone show up the star.

"Pumpkin cheesecake?"

"Ohhh, very seasonal, very *now*—that'll be great. Tell me what you'll need."

"Mascarpone, pumpkin puree, gingersnaps, real butter...."

As Rita rattled off the ingredients, she poured herself a glass of water, popped the lid off her pill case, and took a handful of brightly colored pills. Her daily cocktail, as she liked to think of it.

She stopped suddenly, staring at the pills, the wheels beginning to turn. "See you at three," she said hastily before ringing off and dialing Detective Benedetto's number.

"Now, Rita," he said, a hint of exasperation in his voice, "you know I can't discuss any police business with you, particularly the Jake Johnson case since Vinnie is a person of interest."

"My son," Rita spat out with a conviction that surprised even herself, "is a gentleman. He has nothing whatsoever to do with the Jake Johnson case. But you know who does? Jake Johnson."

"Are you saying that Jake's sending the notes to *himself?*"

"Precisely. But never mind that for the moment. I have other police business to discuss with you—and I'm quite sure you'll be delighted to discuss it with me."

She let that sink in a moment.

"Oh?" was his mild response. "And what would that be?"

"I found Bobby Bruickhuisen—"

"What—where?" Detective Benedetto sputtered, no longer sounding so mild-mannered. "You are not to disturb the site in any way. Do you hear, Rita? I'll get forensics—"

"There's no need. He's perfectly alive and well—not a spring chicken, of course, but then who is?"

"Did you say *'alive'?*"

"I ate a wonderfully flaky pear pastry with him in the most delightful little bakery in Quebec. Really, you must take Tricia there some time. The city is so romantic."

"But if he's not dead—"

"There was no crime. Well, no murder of Bobby Bruickhuisen at least. But his disappearance *is* related to the attempted murder of the widow. Now, I'll explain everything, detective, if you'll just round up the suspects in Bobby Bruickhuisen's disappearance—Sandro, Lydia, Hank, Vito. Say tomorrow, two o'clock, at the widow's bedside? I think that will really add the requisite drama, flush out the real culprit."

"But Rita—"

"Oh, look at the time! I've got to leave now if I'm going to get to Isabella's studio in Connecticut in time for the three o'clock taping. Tune in tomorrow at ten a.m. if you want to learn my secret recipe for pumpkin cheesecake."

"You're *cooking* at a time like this?"

"Baking," Rita corrected him. "Murder is no excuse to let one's culinary standards slip. And I am perfectly capable, detective, of solving a murder and whipping up a sublime pumpkin cheesecake in the same twenty-four period. Like any good grizzly mamma, I multi-task."

There was a beep on the line. "Oh, sorry, detective, but I've got another call coming in." She switched over. "Rita Calabrese, *Morris County Gazette*."

"Rita, it's Susan." Perhaps it was Rita's imagination, but her daughter-in-law's voice sounded even more syrupy sweet than usual. "The widow's woken up."

Chapter Twenty-Eight

"Bobby's alive?" Emma repeated. Her voice came out weak and raspy, she was paler than ever, and all kinds of tubes protruded from her.

But she was awake, breathing on her own, talking—truly, Rita thought, a miracle.

"I can't believe it. First, Thomas died of cancer. Then my niece Judy was taken away and lobotomized. Then my nephew Bobby disappeared. Not six months after his disappearance, my sister 'fell down the stairs.'" The widow raised her gnarled, veiny hands ever so slightly and made faint air quotes, casting a knowing glance at Rita. "Two years after that, Kate died in a horrible crash. For these past fifty-odd years, I thought I was all alone, the last of the line—well, except for Lucy, my other sister's daughter, but you've met her. That hardly counts as family."

Rita knew just what Emma meant. Lucy was a recluse. Rita had met her only once, and only because Rita had practically rammed down her front door to get information on the murder of the Acorn Hollow Squirrels' football coach. Lucy had not even come to the widow's funeral, although she had sent a bouquet of black roses.

"But now I discover"—the widow pressed Rita's hand feebly, and Rita responded with a gentle squeeze—"that I not only have a nephew again, but a granddaughter as well. No one thinks they'll learn *that* at their funeral. I knew Kate had a son, but I heard he died in the accident. With Kate and Vito moved away and determined to cut all ties to Acorn Hollow, and Kate's mother already passed away, I had no way of knowing that Kate and Vito had had a child of their own, and that she was safe and sound with Vito at home."

The widow shot Rita a wan smile, and Rita smiled back. "I think you win, Emma, for the most eventful funeral. And, apparently, for a much more eventful life than I would have thought."

"Oh, that." The widow, deathly pale as she was, seemed to blush ever so slightly. "A wartime fling with a German POW. There was a camp not too far away, and I was a translator—interrogator, more like. But none of this waterboarding nonsense, nothing terrible. Just asking the questions, lending a sympathetic ear, offering little rewards if they cooperated. Thomas had been called up, was serving in the Pacific. The years went by. I was so lonely. I befriended Friedrich, or maybe he befriended me. Stockholm syndrome, I suppose they call it. Nothing happened, of course, because I was still married and I loved Thomas. But it was hard, waiting, waiting, with so little news and when I did get a letter, half of it was blacked out by the censors. And then one day, I got a telegram that he had died."

The widow pursed her lips until they almost disappeared. "But he wasn't dead, of course. He was in a Japanese POW camp, and some other poor woman's Thomas was dead. But by the time I learned it had all been a mistake, I was pregnant with Friedrich's child." Emma twisted the top of her bedsheet into a tight little corkscrew. "What was I to do? I loved my husband, wanted him to come back, wanted him to think I'd been waiting faithfully for him while he'd been going through hell. I couldn't tell him I had another man's baby. And what kind of life would it be for my child, being the bastard child of the enemy? They'd call her a Nazi in school! So I did what I thought was best for everyone: I gave her to my best friend, who'd always wanted a daughter."

The widow made it sound very simple, very logical and straightforward. But Rita knew it had been anything but easy. Emma had given up not only her child, but her only *chance* at a child; Thomas and Emma had never been able to conceive. How painful it must have been for Emma to watch Kate grow up, so near and yet so far, to hear Kate call her best friend 'Mom,' to have to settle for the type of lukewarm hug children give their mother's friends. How terrible it must have been to hear the rumors about Bobby and Kate and to know, though she could not tell them, that their love could never be. And then the final blow, the cruelest of them all: Kate's sudden dramatic departure from Acorn Hollow, accompanied by the realization that perhaps the widow's choice hadn't been for the best after all. That her silence and her sacrifice hadn't prevented tragedy; it had fueled it. Because if Kate had known she was Bobby's first cousin, she would never have gotten involved with him, never ended up pregnant, never had to flee Acorn Hollow. And maybe no one would have had a reason to want the earth to swallow Bobby up and make him disappear.

"Did Senator Van Tassel know...Kate was your child?"

The widow shook her head so sharply that a snowy-white tendril popped out of her tight little bun. "I had a friend at the adoption agency who fudged a birth certificate for us. The senator was none the wiser."

Deftly, and so quickly that Rita almost thought she had imagined it, Emma's pale, veiny hand fluttered up to wipe at the corner of her eye. For one brief moment, something shimmered there and then, as if it had just been a mirage, it was gone. Emma shook her head, as if to banish all of that unpleasantness. She leaned back against her pillows and shot Rita a wan smile. "It turned out to be quite a celebration of life party, didn't it? I got the surprise of my life. And now I've got my nephew back, a granddaughter—a whole new lease on life! At this rate," she cackled, "I'm going to live to be a hundred and twenty!"

Rita laughed along with Emma. She would not be at all surprised if the widow lived that long.

"Some sleuth I turned out to be!" The widow slapped a bony knee through the sheet. "I set out to solve the mystery of who killed Bobby, and it turns out he's not even dead. So instead of solving a mystery, I created a whole new one: who tried to kill me?"

The widow sighed. "Which is a mystery we'll probably never solve. Susan tells me I was poisoned. I just wish I could remember someone tampering with my pills, but the truth is all I can remember is that silly O'Brien girl poking her head through the window in this wild rainbow-colored sweater. She thought she was going to give me a fright, but I sure gave her one!" The widow shot a snaggle-toothed grin in Rita's direction. She took surprisingly ghoulish delight in her near demise. "The poison was already taking effect—my vision was blurry; my face was contorted something awful. I probably looked like that Edvard Munch painting. You know, the one on the bridge with all those wavy lines—*The Scream?*"

Rita nodded.

"And then that silly O'Brien girl gasped and caught her sweater in the screen. The last thing I heard before everything went dark was a thud, so I assume that in the struggle to yank it out, she must have fallen. I hope," Emma said severely, peering at Rita over her eyeglasses, "she didn't trample my rosebushes in the process."

Rita busied herself with plumping up the widow's pillows, anxious to hide her smile. After all that had happened, she hadn't spared a thought for the widow's rosebushes. "I'm sure they will bounce back," she murmured. "You know, it was lucky actually. If it hadn't been for those kids, I never would have rushed upstairs to check on you."

Rita's mind flashed back to the smashed pumpkin, the trellis lying in the long grass, the open window, the cool breeze. The widow lying there, her rheumy brown eyes wide open and staring, her razor-thin lips parted to reveal two rows of crooked, tea-stained teeth. Rita remembered tiptoeing around Detective Benedetto as he worked, the piece of multi-colored yarn he had extracted from the screen. Yarn that was eerily similar to the multicolored fuzz that had stuck to the glue in the envelope addressed to The Dude.

"The O'Brien girl," Rita said, "wouldn't happen to work on the sets for *The Legend of Acorn Hollow*, would she?"

"Not the sets, no. But she's an extra—a partygoer in the scene where Lydia announces Kate is pregnant."

"Is she an Elvis fan? A real goody-two-shoes brown-noser type?"

"Hardly," the widow said sharply. "More like an empty-headed metalhead or whatever they call themselves. And I wouldn't expect her to be a teacher's pet. Sylvester couldn't stand her—she was always flubbing her line, forgetting the dance steps, talking when he was trying to direct. And as for a goody-two-shoes, look what she did to my pumpkin! And my trellis! And my roses!" Her beady little eyes roved over Rita's face. "Why do you ask?"

"Because someone who might have been wearing the same or a similar rainbow sweater and knows Elvis songs and has a good vocabulary and claims to be a teacher's pet just confessed to The Dude that she's helping Jake Johnson frame my Vinnie!"

The widow clapped her hands. "Well, that's marvelous!"

"It is?"

"For once, dear, I get to scoop you. There's another O'Brien girl—Priscilla. And she wears her mom's handknit sweaters, too. Priscilla's a senior, very studious, the polar opposite of her silly sister. She's the vice president of the senior class."

"Let me guess," Rita said, "she's some sort of engineering, math, and science whiz."

"First in the state science fair last year." There was a gleam in the widow's eye. "She's been coming to practices since Janice—that's the silly one—failed her driver's test three times and needs a ride home. At first, Priscilla just sat in the back of the auditorium doing her homework. But then she started taking an interest in the play, started helping out backstage with the props, costume changes, that sort of thing."

Rita checked her watch. "I've got just enough time," she murmured before hopping up, planting two *bacci* on the widow's cheeks, and racing out the door.

The widow's quavering voice echoed behind her, all down the corridor. "Time? Time for what?"

But Rita could not spare a moment to enlighten Emma. She hurtled down the corridor, out the front door, and through the parking lot. Sliding behind the front seat of her Buick, she gunned the motor and headed down Main Street until she came to a screeching halt in front of The Sunshine Café. Rita ran inside and sprinted around the restaurant, craning her neck into each booth.

When she finally found Phil Baldassaro, he was twinkling his famed blue eyes, which had held many a female juror in thrall, at two elderly members of the church decorating committee. "*Scusate*," she said apologetically to the ladies before turning to Phil. "I need you to negotiate an immunity deal."

Phil almost choked on his cinnamon bun. "*For you?*"

"No." Rita glared at him, miffed that he would think she would need such a thing. She checked her watch. "Look, I'm late for a taping of *The Isabella Montelusa Show*."

"Huh?"

"Tune in tomorrow at ten if you want to see me make my pumpkin cheesecake." She reached into her purse, ripped a page out of her notebook, and scribbled Priscilla O'Brien's name on it. "In the meantime,"—Rita pressed the paper into Phil's hand—"I suggest you find this young lady and let her know that I know everything—absolutely everything. And soon so will the police. So, she has a choice: either work with you on an immunity deal and wear a wire at tomorrow's performance of *The Legend of Acorn Hollow*—"

"A wire?" Phil sputtered. "Rita, this isn't The Bronx."

"—or go to juvenile detention." Rita patted him on the shoulder. "Don't worry. I'm quite sure Priscilla will explain everything. Once, that is, you explain to her that she's tangled with the wrong grizzly mamma." She bared her teeth at Phil, and he shrank back slightly. "*Capisci?*

Chapter Twenty-Nine

The taping of *The Isabella Montelusa Show* went off without a hitch. Upon arrival, Rita was whisked off to hair and makeup. She emerged half an hour later with her bushy black hair tamed and its perennial silver stripe gone, her eyebrows tweezed into a perfect arch that made her look interested yet not alarmed, and her nails painted in Isabella's trademark pale pink polish. They poured her into a scoop-necked black dress that made her look a good ten pounds thinner, then covered most of it with a cheery red apron emblazoned with the show's logo.

While she waited in the wings, Isabella introduced her as "the only guest I've ever met at a funeral. She's a proud Italian mamma, she's a reporter, she's a sleuth, and most importantly, she's renowned up and down the Hudson Valley for her authentic Italian desserts. Please welcome Rita Calabrese!"

Rita walked onstage to rapturous applause and followed Isabella over to the studio kitchen, where the ingredients were neatly laid out, already measured and poured into cute little stainless-steel bowls. It looked nothing like the chaos of Rita's kitchen at home.

"Technically," Rita said, feeling as though she needed to correct the record, "it was a celebration of life party, not a funeral. The guest of honor was still alive, although it almost turned into a funeral when someone tried to murder her."

A chorus of gasps spread through the audience. Isabella shot a glance at the producer, who has hovering in the wings and gesturing wildly. The producer must have also shouted something into Isabella's headset, because she jumped slightly and then tittered and chirped, "Well, the guest of honor at the funeral—er, celebration of life party—sure had a zest for life! And speaking of zest, one of the things I just loved about your cheesecake was the gingersnap crust. It's spicier than the traditional graham cracker crust, and it really brings out the cinnamon and clove notes in the pumpkin filling."

"And it's so simple to make!" Rita gushed. "You start by pulverizing gingersnap cookies into crumbs in your food processor."

Isabella tipped a stainless-steel bowl of gingersnaps into the food processor and stabbed the button. As it whirred loudly, she leaned in close and murmured in Rita's ear, "Sandro tells me there are new developments in the disappearance of Bobby Bruickhuisen."

Rita raised an eyebrow. Not two hours had passed since she had asked Detective Benedetto to call the suspects, and Sandro had already called his sister. "Yes, we're gathering the interested parties tomorrow for a briefing. You should come with him for moral support."

"Will he need it?"

Rita shrugged. "Detective Benedetto didn't preview the new developments with me."

Strictly speaking, that last statement was true. It was Rita who had shared the new developments with *him*.

Isabella took her finger off the button and instantly switched gears. Turning on her megawatt, pearly white smile and angling the contents of the food processor towards the audience, she said, "Perfect! Now, we add sugar, butter, and a pinch of salt until it resembles wet sand."

Isabella tossed the contents of each little stainless-steel bowl into the mixing bowl while the camera zoomed in. Once they had their "wet sand" mixture, Rita led Isabella through the process of pressing the mixture into a springform pan before baking it to set the crust.

"The crust is so important." Isabella wagged a knowing finger at the audience. "Some people think of it as an afterthought, just a cheese delivery mechanism. But it's really the foundation for the cheesecake, and its flavor profile is so important to the finished product."

"Just like in a murder investigation," Rita added. "What you often find is that beneath one crime lies another."

Isabella emitted one of her tinkling little laughs and her eyes darted offstage. Rita wondered what the producer had just barked in Isabella's ear. "I always learn so much from my guests. But now, tell us, where do you come down on the cream cheese versus mascarpone versus ricotta divide?"

"Ricotta's great for cannoli and cassata, but ricotta is just too low-fat to make a truly rich, decadent cheesecake. So I lean towards mascarpone, although I do add a little cream cheese for texture since it's a bit thicker. Cream cheese is just the poor man's mascarpone. Now for my cheesecake, I start by combining full-fat mascarpone with a little cream cheese, pureed pumpkin, Ceylon cinnamon, ground cloves, pure Madagascar vanilla, and some sugar and beat it until soft and fluffy."

Isabella tossed the ingredients in the stand mixer and turned it on. While the motor hummed, she said in a low voice, "So you think Bobby's disappearance was linked to the others?"

"In a way."

Isabella turned off the mixer, poured the creamy, tangerine-hued mixture into the pan, and slid it into the oven. "And then *voilà!*" Isabella whisked an already-prepared cheesecake, pale orange and topped with a perfect ring of whipped cream, out of the refrigerator. "After you bake and refrigerate it, you have a delicious cheesecake that looks like this!"

The audience oohed and aahed appreciatively.

Isabella cut two slices, plated them, and handed one plate to Rita. Savoring a small forkful, Isabella turned to the camera and said, "It's creamy and luscious and it positively screams Fall." She turned towards the audience. "Do we have any audience questions for Rita?"

A middle-aged redhead's hand shot up. "Yeah." She had a Boston accent and a harsh, no-nonsense delivery. "Who had the chutzpah to try to off the lady at her own funeral?"

Rita beamed. "Log on to the *Morris County Gazette* website tomorrow afternoon," she said, "and all will be revealed."

Chapter Thirty

They sat in a semi-circle around the widow's hospital bed: Lydia, with one leg crossed over the other, her fire engine-red talons clutching a water bottle; Hank, pushing his horn-rimmed glasses up his nose as his eyes darted nervously around the room; Vito, tapping his foot and running his fingers through his short, spiky salt-and-pepper hair; and Sandro, muscular arms crossed over his barrel chest, thick brows knitted together. Every now and then, Sandro cast a nervous glance at Vito. Isabella, ever the supportive sister, sat beside him. Rita occupied the last seat, by the door, and in the center of it all was the widow, rosy-cheeked and smiling, her hair arranged once more in a neat, snowy-white bun.

Detective Benedetto paced back and forth across their small semi-circle. "We are here today," he said, "because of new information in the disappearance of Bobby Bruickhuisen."

Lydia threw her head back and took a swig from her water bottle, which Rita strongly suspected contained gin. "Oh, so this is when you tell us which one of us offed him."

"No," Rita said. "This is when I tell you which one of you aided and abetted Bobby in making his escape and faking his death."

Isabella frowned so deeply her perfectly arched eyebrows nearly met. "Faking?"

"Faking," Rita said firmly. "But before we get to which of you helped Bobby fake his own death, we need to understand how and why. And to do that, we need to understand the legend of Acorn Hollow and the four separate crimes that have been linked to this legend." She held up a hand to tick them off one by one. "The original so-called *Legend of Sleepy Hollow*, which of course is a misnomer because we all know it took place right here; the 1936 disappearance of Joey Gambone; the 1962 disappearance of Bobby Bruickhuisen; and the recent attempted murder of"—she gestured towards the widow—"Emma Schmalzgruben, Bobby Bruickhuisen's aunt. All of these incidents took place around Halloween in and around Acorn Hollow and the first three of these involved a disappearance and the victim's vehicle being left by the old stone bridge beside a smashed pumpkin."

"But not the incident with the widow," Hank pointed out politely. He sounded calm and relaxed, as if he were discussing an anomaly in some polling data, not an attempted murder. "She didn't disappear."

The widow broke into a yellowed, snaggle-toothed grin. "And no one thought to drive my golf cart into the stream. Now that would have added a nice touch of drama!" Her grin then turned to a pout. "But my pumpkin did end up smashed."

Detective Benedetto frowned and looked up the ceiling. Rita knew just what he was thinking. The smashed pumpkin was a mere coincidence and had absolutely nothing to do with the attempted murder.

Rita said, "The first disappearance linked to a pumpkin and the old stone bridge is that of Ichabod Crane, who was vying with Brom Bones for the hand of the lovely Katrina Van Tassel, ancestor of the ill-starred Kate Van Tassel."

How ironic, Rita thought, that Katrina and Kate were not actually biological relatives. But Kate's parentage was not her story to tell, so she exchanged a brief glance with the widow and went on. "After a party at the Van Tassel farm—the very same farm where Bobby Bruickhuisen was last seen in 1962—Ichabod mounts his horse and heads home, only to find a headless horseman hard on his heels."

Lydia snorted. "Since Ichabod disappeared, how could anyone know that there was a headless horseman after him in his last moments? It's just an old wives' tale."

"That's what Washington Irving wrote, wasn't it?" Rita said. "It was an old Dutch wives' tale. But the Van Tassels believed it to be true and even told the story to the widow as a little girl. It really doesn't matter if it's true. What matters is that it linked three things in the popular imagination: a love triangle, a disappearance by the old stone bridge, and a headless horseman wearing a jack o'lantern—a jack o'lantern that later turns up smashed by the old stone bridge. So that when Joey Gambone disappears and his car is found by the old stone bridge, everyone thinks 'well, it's just history repeating itself; the legend continues.' And Joey Gambone was part of a love triangle, too, with his mistress Viviana Rossi, and his wife, Anita Gambone, maiden name Anita Montelusa."

All eyes turned on Isabella and Sandro. Fingering her pearls, Isabella shrugged and said, "We weren't close to *Zia* Anita, so I'm afraid we can't shed any light on that, though I doubt she was involved. My father didn't want us having anything to do with the more...unsavory members of the family. His brother Pietro was, well..."

"The mob boss?"

Isabella acknowledged the truth of this statement with a grimace. "He had the Montelusa talent for organization, but his talents were, shall we say, misspent. *Zia* Anita might have been all right, but she was the widow of Joey Gambone."

"Also," Rita said sympathetically, "not the best influence on children."

"In any case," Isabella said, "Joey disappeared before Sandro and I were born. I don't think we'll ever know what happened to him. My father had a theory that he'd gone back to Sicily, that there was less competition there. But my father used to say, 'We're Americans now, and we need to think like Americans. We're not tribal, not like our ancestors. We need to be public-minded, build the city on the hill. Oh, how he loved that phrase! 'City on the hill'—Reagan borrowed it from him, you know."

"Is that so?" The ghost of a smile played on the widow's lips. "And here I thought Reagan borrowed it from the Puritan John Winthrop's famous sermon. And of course, John Winthrop wasn't really original, either.

He got that from none other than Jesus. The Sermon on the Mount? Perhaps you've heard of it."

Isabella was momentarily flustered. Clearly, she was not used to being contradicted. "Well, wherever the phrase originally comes from, my father loved it. He named one of the Guido Montelusa Foundation scholarships after it. It's for young community activists looking for seed funding for a community project. I was just in Poughkeepsie last week to award one—"

"Yes," Rita sighed. "We know all about the foundation." She shook her head and tried to dispel its jingle from her head. She heard it whenever Sal turned on *The Isabella Montelusa Show*.

Detective Benedetto cleared his throat noisily. "As a matter of fact, I do know what happened to Joey Gambone."

All eyes swiveled towards the detective, who cast a slightly embarrassed glance in Rita's direction. "Thanks to our forensics team, I was able to solve my first murder. Every other murder since I joined the force," he added sheepishly, "has been solved by Rita."

"Although," Rita reminded him, "my Bernese mountain dogs did find Joey Gambone's body."

"Mmmm, yes—we'll be having an honorary K-9 induction ceremony for them next week. Anyway, where was I? Oh, yes—Joey Gambone's body was found by, er, Luciano and Cesare in an old fallout shelter on Joey Gambone's farm, suggesting that, contrary to eyewitness accounts, he never left the farm that night. He was shot at close range on the right temple, meaning the shooter was left-handed, and ballistics matched the bullet that was lodged in his cranium to a firearm owned by Frankie Della Ratta, the favorite left-handed hit man of Joey's brother-in-law, Pietro Montelusa."

"*Bravo*, detective." Rita was slightly chagrined to have her perfect murder-solving streak broken, but cheered by the thought that she was sure to get an exclusive for the *Morris County Gazette*.

"So I was right after all!" the widow cackled from her bed. "Anita Gambone and her brother were in cahoots. She got rid of her no-good philandering husband and inherited his ill-gotten gains, while her brother got rid of a rival. Though I guess it wasn't the rat poison that did him in."

"That looks to be about the size of it," Detective Benedetto said.

"So that explains what happened to Joey," Sandro said. "And Bobby?"

"Bobby," Rita said, "disappeared after the worst twenty-four hours of his life. First, Lydia tells him that Kate's pregnant, he proposes to Kate, and she rejects him. Then Bobby goes to her dad's campaign headquarters and catches her brother with his hand in the till."

"I was just getting a few bucks to buy the volunteers lunch," Hank mumbled. His eyes darted desperately around the room, and Rita's gaze followed. No one seemed convinced.

"And then," Rita went on, "Bobby comes back later and overhears Senator Van Tassel accepting a bribe from Guido Montelusa."

Isabella sprang up out of her seat. "That's a lie! A vicious, vicious lie. My father was as honest as they come."

She turned towards Sandro, evidently expecting him to back her up, but he merely frowned and said, "But how do you know this?"

"I got it straight from the horse's mouth: Bobby."

"Hardly a reliable source!" Isabella fumed. "You just admitted he faked his death."

"I might have thought that too, were it not for the fact that Bobby's very distinctive one-of-a-kind scarf—"

"—which I knitted," the widow proudly proclaimed, "and gave to him the day before he disappeared—"

"—was found in a secret tunnel leading away from Guido Montelusa's estate."

"Well, that's preposterous," Isabella scoffed. "Obviously, my father didn't kill Bobby. You yourself just said he's alive and well."

"Alive and well, yes, but that doesn't change the fact that he was in the tunnel before he made his escape. So the obvious question is, did the Montelusas kidnap him and hold him against his will—until, at the tender age of seventeen, he somehow managed to escape, flee to Canada, and assume a new Canadian identity? Or did a Montelusa harbor him in the tunnel and then help him escape? Or both?" Rita looked around their little circle and saw quite a few furrowed brows. "When I met Bobby," she said, "he was very cagey about how he ended up in Canada, but one thing struck me: it would have been very hard for a seventeen-year-old to pull off not only a disappearance, but a whole new identity, by himself. His motorbike, after all, was in a stream. He had no access to any other vehicles, no one reported their car stolen that week, and no one remembered a hitchhiker or a bus or train passenger matching his description. So how did he get to Canada?"

Hank shrugged. "Walk?"

"Nearly three hundred miles? Possible but not likely. And even if he could have done that, how would he have gotten a whole new identity? A new name, a Canadian passport? And then, Bobby himself inadvertently gave me a clue. He said Kate came to see him with their little boy. And when I asked who told her where to find him, he said his mother."

The widow suddenly stabbed a button, and her bed shot straight up to a ninety-degree angle. "His mother," she shouted, eyes blazing, "was dead less than six months after he disappeared!"

"Exactly." Rita snapped her fingers. "And the boy was already a toddler, so nearly two years had passed. While it's possible Bobby's mother had told Kate that Bobby was in Quebec before she died, it seems unlikely that Kate would wait a whole eighteen months to confront him. So who had actually told Kate of Bobby's whereabouts? And then it dawned on me: the only person who could know was Bobby's accomplice. The person who'd driven him across the border. The person who'd used his shadowy connections to get him a false passport.

"So who might this accomplice be? Someone with the wherewithal to create a new identity, someone with access to the Montelusas' tunnel, someone who knew Kate well enough to trust her with information about

Bobby's true whereabouts. Someone the Montelusas trusted, but someone who would ultimately betray them. Someone who was a Montelusa but not a Montelusa."

All but one person looked confused.

"Vito."

Chapter Thirty-One

"Vito," Rita repeated to an astonished room. "Guido Montelusa's illegitimate son."

Sandro's jaw dropped. "Vito and I are brothers?"

"Don't be ridiculous," Isabella snapped. "He was the maid's son, remember? And she had *quite* the reputation. She probably didn't know who the father was, and she wanted him to have a father figure to look up to—"

Sandro held up a hand in a silencing gesture. "Vito, is this true?"

Vito hung his head and stared at the floor. "My ma said I was. And he did too, kinda. He'd say, 'You've got the Montelusa nose' or 'the Montelusa chin,' or, worse, sometimes when he'd want me to do a favor, 'the Montelusa ruthless streak.' But for a while I was so grateful to have a dad at all, I just went along. It seemed normal, you know? 'Cuz you're supposed to do what your parents say. And for a while, I thought, you know, he's Guido Montelusa. He's a big deal, everyone loves him. He must be doing the right thing. It started with little jobs—delivering some kinda coded message to a shopkeeper like 'take the dog out for a walk at six' or

'Guido wants to know what to get your brother for his birthday.'"

"Why,"—Lydia rolled her eyes—"would the great Guido Montelusa care when someone walked his dog?"

"Well, obviously, he didn't," Vito said. "I was just a dumb kid. And later when I realized it meant something else, it just seemed like a game. Like some kinda inside joke among Guido's friends. Then after a while, I didn't just deliver and receive messages. There were packages. Like I'd go to the pharmacy and say 'Guido's got a toothache. Got anything for it?' and they'd hand me this package. Or he'd have me pick up a book he wanted to borrow. I'm pretty sure the book was hollow, but I knew—somehow, I knew without him ever saying it—not to look inside. Eventually it dawned on me that this Mr. Nice Guy thing was all an act but by then, I was in too deep. It felt like there was no way out."

"Why are you doing this?" Isabella cried. "He's making this all up. Can't you see?"

"We'll be the judge of that," Detective Benedetto said calmly. "But I warn you, Ms. Montelusa, another outburst from you and I'll have you escorted out of the room." He turned to Vito. "Go on. Tell us about the day Bobby disappeared."

"I was running errands for Guido after school, picking up deliveries"—he blushed—"er, payments, really, and dropping them off. So I was in and out of his study all day. And when I went in at one point, he was talking to his brother Pietro. He was saying 'that snot-nosed Bruickhuisen kid knows too much; he's got to be dealt with.' And Pietro was running through his list of guys who could do the job. Like, 'Carmine—he might be too much of a sissy to do a kid' and 'Tony—too dramatic, it's gotta look like an accident.' I knew my old man wasn't no saint, but ordering a hit on my classmate? That was low, even for him. So I said, 'You know what would be way better? If I dealt with it.' They started chuckling, but I said, 'No, I'm serious. I'm going to a party with him tonight. I'll follow him when he leaves, lie in wait, grab him, and then leave his motorbike and a smashed pumpkin by the old stone bridge.' Well, my old man thought he was real smart, a cut above the rest of those goombas, so he liked that literary touch. And Pietro just winked and said, 'Yeah, like what happened to my brother-in-law Joey. The headless horseman got him too.'"

Rita saw that Detective Benedetto furiously scribbled that last bit down. She wondered how much weight the police gave to a second-hand, posthumous almost-confession.

"So my old man clapped me on the shoulder and said, '*Grazie, figlio.*' It was the only time he called me son. He'd never looked prouder. But I was lying through my teeth. Man, I was so scared, I was practically shaking. I was holding onto the back of his chair, trying to steady my hands. But he believed me. So I went to the home of one of my old man's 'associates'"—here, Vito made air quotes—"who churned out all kinds of fake I.D.s, passports. He was the go-to guy when things got too hot for one of the *mafiosi* and they needed to lay low for a while. I went there a lot, so he didn't think anything of it when I said my old man needed an extra Canadian one, something French-sounding, kinda girly. I mean, I was saving Bobby's ass, but that didn't mean I liked the guy."

"Jean Broussard," Rita murmured.

"Yeah, Jean. Kinda girly, right? So I got the passport and headed to the party. I convinced Lydia she might have a chance with Sandro if she told everyone Kate was pregnant." He looked across the room at his half-brother. "'Cuz I knew it weren't Sandro's kid. Sandro was a real square. He couldn't have knocked her up."

"Worked like a charm," he marveled. Even now, there was a glimmer of pride in his maple-syrup brown eyes. The kid everyone had thought was stupid—"the maid's kid"—had managed to pull off the greatest magic trick Acorn Hollow had ever seen. "Everyone was rushing around, chasing after each other, chasing after Kate. But I chased after Bobby. Man, was he predictable! He went to their secret meeting spot—this place in the woods called the Poet's Corner. He thought no one else knew about it, but I did. Kate told me about it. I was 'the friend,' see, the one she never paid attention to—not in that way, anyway—but the one she told everything to. When I got there, Bobby was alone. Bobby had guessed wrong; Kate wasn't there at all. So I told him Guido had a hit out on him, that his only chance was to let me hide him."

"And so you took him," Rita said, "to the last place Guido would ever look for someone: Guido's own tunnel."

"Right. See, I grew up playing hide-and-seek in that tunnel. I knew every nook and cranny. And I knew Guido never used it anymore. I had driven Guido's delivery van to the party. So I put the motorbike in the back, drove Bobby to the old Gambone estate, and hid him in the tunnel. Then I drove the van back to the old stone bridge in Acorn Hollow, stopping in a farm field along the way to pick a half-rotten pumpkin. At the bridge, I tossed Bobby's motorbike onto the riverbank, smashed the pumpkin, and drove off."

"Thus ensuring the legend of Acorn Hollow would be perpetuated."

"Yeah. And then the next morning, I finagled my way into getting sent to run some errands for Guido around Troy. I ran the errands, drove Bobby to the border, handed him his new identity and a hundred dollars I filched from the old man, and wished him luck in his new life. Then I drove home, rolled back the odometer, and told my old man I had 'dealt with' Bobby and tied up the loose ends."

Detective Benedetto looked up from his notes. "Did you tell Guido that you killed Bobby?"

"Didn't have to. He assumed I did. That's how Guido worked. He never wanted to know the details, always wanted to keep his hands clean. He'd never order anyone to do anything, you know? Just make you understand that's what he wanted done. And what Guido wanted, Guido got."

"And it was you," the detective said, "who told Kate that Bobby was alive and well in Canada."

Vito nodded miserably. "She never got over him."

Hank stood up and pulled Lydia unsteadily to her feet. "Women," he said with a shake of the head and an awkward chuckle, "they never can appreciate a good man."

Rita wondered if Hank were talking about Kate and Vito, or Lydia and himself. Lydia must have been thinking the same thing, because she shot a sidelong glance at Sandro and licked her lips. Sandro frowned in return and then pointedly looked at the floor.

"You have my sympathy, Vito," Hank went on, "and my congratulations. What impeccable timing, what stagecraft! Very theatrical, too, with the pumpkin and the motorbike. Know your audience! That's the first rule in politics, I like to say, and clearly you did."

Lydia scowled at her husband. "He's not a politician, you dolt. He's not a client."

"Of course not," Hank said breezily. "But it's a remarkable story." He clasped Lydia's hand and nodded first at Rita, then Detective Benedetto. "In any case, Bobby's alive and well, thank goodness, and no crime's been committed. So, if you'll excuse us, it's been lovely seeing all of you, but Lydia and I have a long drive home."

"I strongly suggest you stay." Detective Benedetto sounded pleasant enough, but his gaze was steely. "Even if Bobby is alive and well, a crime has most certainly been committed."

The widow cleared her throat noisily, and all eyes turned towards her. "Someone," she said, her voice, still weak, tinged with an equal mixture of indignation and pride, "tried to kill me!"

Chapter Thirty-Two

"Oh, yes—that."

Lydia plopped down noisily on her chair and stared stonily at the widow. Rita shot Lydia an icy look in return.

"Well, you can't honestly think I had anything to do with it," Lydia huffed. "We'd never even met until her funeral."

"Celebration of life party."

"Sure." Lydia looked dubious. "If you say so."

"I can see," Hank said, "why you might have thought we'd have had something to do with the attempt on the widow's life when you thought Bobby had been killed. Because after all, Emma threatened to expose the killer. So it would make sense that Bobby's murderer would kill again to save his or her skin, so to speak. But if nobody murdered Bobby, then no one has a motive for murdering Emma."

"That's true," Rita conceded, "unless one of you *thought* someone else killed Bobby and you were trying to protect that person."

"What? Like Hank here thought I murdered Bobby?" Lydia smirked. "You forget that Bobby was far more useful to me alive than dead." Her gaze flitted to Sandro, who was studiously ignoring her. "With Bobby in the picture, there was always the chance Kate would dump Sandro and Sandro would come back to me."

"Back?" Sandro looked horrified. "We were never together."

Isabella spoke up next. "Well, then, maybe *Lydia* tried to kill the widow to protect *Hank*, who she thought killed Bobby so Bobby wouldn't tell the senator his own son was stealing from the campaign. After all, Lydia had access to Hank's pills. She could have snuck upstairs and slipped it in the widow's water glass on her nightstand— or in a bottle in her medicine cabinet."

"My wife," Hank said haughtily, his polite veneer stripped away, "is not a killer. She's a *vegetarian*, for goodness sake."

Rita could not see how this was relevant, but she smiled encouragingly, urging Hank to go on.

"And besides," Hank said, "it's a bit of a stretch to insinuate that just because I took a few dollars from the till I'd be willing to murder someone. Surely, my own wife would know that if Bobby had spilled the beans, I would have just begged my dad for forgiveness and repaid the campaign."

"You mean, your father would have repaid the campaign," Lydia said. "You had no money, and he would have done anything to avoid a scandal."

Hank shifted uncomfortably in his chair. "Mmmm, yes. But Vito here"—he pointed at Vito, who visibly shrank in his chair—"is a pharmacist. He has access to all kinds of drugs. He could have just popped one in the widow's wine."

"But she was poisoned," Rita said, "with the same medication you take, Hank."

"Which he undoubtedly had access to," Hank retorted. "It's a very common medication."

"And did you tell him you were taking it?"

"Well, no, but—"

"So he wouldn't have known," Rita said, "which medication to use to best frame you for the widow's murder."

"Well, maybe it was Sandro!" Lydia exclaimed with a sudden ferocity. Perhaps, Rita thought, she was peeved that their reunion had not turned out the way she had hoped.

Sandro looked up. "Me?"

"Well, sure. I mean, you had the best motive of any of us to kill Bobby. He knocked up your precious Kate."

There was real venom in Lydia's words.

"But I didn't kill Bobby," Sandro protested. "Haven't you been listening to anything anyone said? Rita found him in Canada. Vito drove him there."

"But maybe," Lydia said, "you *thought* Vito killed Bobby, and you acted to protect Vito in some sort of warped act of half-brother hero worship. Or out of guilt—because you were always the golden boy, and he was the 'maid's son.'"

"But until today, I didn't know he was my brother."

"So you say." Lydia pointed accusingly first at Sandro, then at Vito. "I saw how you too acted at the widow's party. You"—she waved a finger wildly at

Sandro—"looked like you'd seen a ghost—or a murderer. Maybe you thought Vito killed Bobby for you—or killed Bobby on your father's orders—and you were scared because you *knew* he was a killer. But then you decided to repay the favor and silence the widow."

"My brother," Vito said quietly, "would not do that."

Lydia shrugged. "Well, you're off the hook at least," she said to Vito. "You're the only person who knew Bobby was alive, so the widow's announcement couldn't have struck fear in your heart. If anyone accused you, you could just say 'ask him yourself: here's his address in Canada.'"

The widow clapped her bird-boned hands together. "So many people might have wanted to kill me!"

Rita thought she sounded nearly as giddy as she had the night of the party, when she'd felt like the belle of the ball. The widow seemed to want nothing more than to be in demand, even if as a murder victim.

"But only one of you actually did," the widow said with a wink, "and I'm sure Rita will tell us."

Chapter Thirty-Three

"Isabella."

There was a chorus of gasps around the room.

Isabella flinched. "Me? What motive could I possibly have? I'd never even met Emma Schmalzgruben before her celebration of life party."

"That's probably true," Rita agreed. "But when you arrived at the party and saw the shrine to Bobby, you recognized the photo of the tunnel. You knew it was on your father's estate. And you'd long suspected that your father had been behind Bobby's disappearance. After all, he had an excellent motive. Bobby had humiliated his son—his legitimate son, golden boy Sandro—by impregnating Kate. And Bobby had overheard your father bribing Senator Van Tassel, so he was a liability too. Getting him out of the way would kill two birds with one stone, so to speak. Maybe your father had even hinted as much to you. You were, everyone says, his favorite child, the apple of his eye. And not only were you the apple of his eye then, but you're the keeper of his legacy now—CEO of the Guido Montelusa Foundation. You never miss an opportunity to burnish your father's reputation.

266

"So you look at the shrine to Bobby, then you look around the room. You see who Bobby's Aunt Emma has assembled. And you realize that Emma has an ulterior motive and may be closing in on the truth. So you decide to act. When Hank spills his blood pressure medicine all over the floor, the perfect opportunity presents itself. You reach down to pick them up, but you palm a few in the process. Then later you head to the widow's upstairs bathroom, which isn't hard to do. There's a line for the downstairs bathroom, so plenty of guests are using the upstairs one. The bathroom has two doors: one leading into the hall, the other connecting to the widow's bedroom. You go in the bathroom, lock the door to the hall, then open the other door, and slip into the widow's bedroom. You notice the bottle of vitamins on the bedside table. They're pale pink, but Hank's pills are blue. So you take out your nail polish—your signature pale pink nail polish, which you always wear on your show"—Rita looked pointedly at Isabella's hand, and Isabella scowled—"and coat Hank's pills so the color almost matches. Then you put the pills in the bottle, leaving only the tiniest dot of polish on the table in your haste to slip away."

"Are there any witnesses?" Sandro asked.

"No," Rita cheerfully admitted.

"Well, then, you can hardly pin this on my sister. I mean, just because there was a tiny splotch of her shade of nail polish on the widow's nightstand..."

"...and on the widow's fingers," Rita added, "where she touched the pills. Only I didn't put two and two together at the time."

267

"Still." Sandro hunched his linebacker shoulders and his dark, furry brows drew together into one thick line. "Maybe the widow uses that shade of nail polish too. Maybe some other guest had that nail polish."

"Maybe," Isabella bristled, "someone snuck my nail polish out of my purse."

"That is all possible. When Detective Benedetto and I called everyone here today, I was only ninety-five percent sure it was Isabella. I knew Bobby was alive, and I knew Vito had rescued him, and I knew Vito had done so because Guido Montelusa wanted Bobby dead. Which means that the person who most wanted Emma dead was the person who knew the truth—that Guido was involved. And who would want to protect Guido? Isabella. And then there was the nail polish. And the fact she scooped up Hank's pills—the very pills that poisoned the widow. So she had motive, means, and opportunity, plus the telltale nail polish. It was all very circumstantial. But"—she wagged a finger in Isabella's direction—"then you did me a favor and slipped up."

"Oh?" One of Isabella's perfectly arched, heavily penciled eyebrows shot up.

Rita cocked her head at Detective Benedetto, who smiled. He had caught it too. "Detective?"

"At no point in the investigation," he said, "did anyone say that the poison was in the widow's pill bottle or bedside water glass. Hank, in fact, assumed incorrectly, as it turns out, that the poison was in her wine glass. But you said, and I quote"—here, he consulted his notes—" 'She could have snuck upstairs and slipped it in the widow's water glass on her nightstand—or a bottle in her medicine cabinet.'"

"Well, I was just giving examples!" Isabella said hotly. "And it was neither of those, actually. You just said it wasn't in the water glass or the medicine cabinet—it was in the pill bottle next to her water glass on her nightstand."

Lydia shrugged. "I don't know, Isabella. It sounds like a Freudian slip to me. Upstairs, water glass, pill bottle."

Rita winked. "I have a feeling the jury will agree with Lydia that it's too much of a coincidence. And if they don't? Well, there's always the physical evidence."

"Physical?" Isabella looked taken aback.

"I know. It surprised me, too," Rita said. "For someone so fastidious who emphasizes being so tidy in the kitchen, you were shockingly careless. You left a hair, Isabella. A hair that the wind blew into the screen in the open window, so I first assumed it belonged to the teenaged pumpkin smasher who scaled the widow's trellis later that night. The DNA hasn't come back yet, but it's a perfect match to your hair—down to the one-eighth inch of dark lowlight roots and then the coppery long shaft."

Rita heard the satisfying click of handcuffs, followed by the soothing tones of Detective Benedetto droning on about Isabella's Miranda rights.

But Rita had already moved on. She approached Vito, squeezed his arm, and whispered into his ear. "I want you to know Kate chose you in the end. Bobby told me that Kate told him she knew after seeing Bobby that she belonged with you."

Vito drew back, a veil of tears clouding his maple syrup-brown eyes. "Thank you," he mumbled. They were so close she could smell his breath, a mixture of garlic and peppermint. He took her hand and squeezed it, hard, as if he were a drowning man clinging to a life raft. "*Mille grazie, Rita. Mille grazie.*"

Someone nearby cleared his throat loudly. Rita looked up to see Detective Benedetto hovering over them. "I hope I'm not interrupting," he said gently.

"Oh, not at all," Rita said as Vito blushed. "I was just saying I hope Vito extends his stay in Acorn Hollow to attend tomorrow's performance of *The Legend of Acorn Hollow*. My Vinnie really does Vito justice."

"Mmmm." Detective Benedetto squirmed slightly at the mention of Vinnie's name, and Rita suddenly remembered her son was still a suspect in all of the misfortunes befalling Jake Johnson.

"And just like Vito, my Vinnie is as innocent as a lamb. Which," she huffed, "I will prove to you tomorrow night."

Epilogue

Rita sat in the front row of the auditorium, wedged between Sal and the widow. Emma had been released from the hospital the day before and appeared in the pink of health. She was seated with Vito and her long-lost granddaughter, grinning ear to ear. Rita's editor, Sam, sat behind them.

"Way to go, Rita." Sam clapped a hand on Rita's back. "Your story on the arrest of Isabella Montelusa crashed our website yesterday. We had people from as far away as Hawaii trying to access the site."

"That's my Rita." Sal's chest puffed up like one of Rita's overstuffed calzones. "A world-famous investigative reporter, known from coast to coast."

"Well," Rita said, attempting modesty, "it did help that Isabella gave me free air time on her show."

"Yeah," Sal said. "Isabella's eyes bulged out when you told that lady you were gonna name names on the *Morris County Gazette*'s website. That's when I knew Isabella was guilty as sin."

Rita harrumphed. Sal had done no such thing. Her husband had conveniently remembered his sudden piercing insight into Isabella's guilt only after she had been arrested.

"And you looked super hot, too," Sal said. "All my friends were already jealous you were on Isabella's show. But now they're jealous that you're hot, too."

Rita begged to differ. She'd been no 'hotter' that day than any other; all the credit went to Isabella's hair and makeup team, as she was quite sure Sal's friends were all perfectly aware. But she blushed at the compliment nonetheless. She turned around to wink at Sam. "If you thought yesterday's story was good, just wait until today's."

"Today's?" Sam looked puzzled. Rita knew what she was thinking. What story could there be? Sam had given Rita the day off.

The lights dimmed, and Rita turned back towards the stage, grinning from ear to ear. The show—the *real* show—was about to begin. From behind the black velvet curtain came the disembodied voice of a young man. "Is it all set?"

Rita looked to the far corner of the auditorium and spotted Detective Benedetto and another young police officer waiting just offstage. Detective Benedetto and Rita exchanged a glance.

Backstage, Priscilla must have nodded, because the young man said, "Good. So pull the lever just as I'm approaching the bridge so that the motorbike will catch fire—"

The audience erupted in a chorus of gasps.

"Wait"—Jake's voice cracked—"is this thing on?"

Detective Benedetto took that as his cue to burst through the side stage door.

"Priscilla," Jake cried, "how could you?"

Then Rita heard Detective Benedetto's deep, soothing baritone. "Jake Johnson, you are under arrest..."

Rita spun around and said to Sam, "I promised you a story, didn't I?"

The cast and crew had thought it only fitting that the afterparty be at the old Van Tassel estate. Rita catered, and Vinnie ingeniously rigged up a projection of a young Vito, Kate, Lydia, and Hank—even a young(er) version of the widow. The images flitted over the bare walls, across the chimney, and over the buffet table as the projections swung round and round. And so they mingled and nibbled and danced and congratulated each other—for it had been a truly marvelous performance, even with Jake Johnson's understudy thrust into the role of Bobby— amongst the ghosts of the past.

Rita took two plates of tiramisu to Vinnie and Ana. "*Bravo, figlio*," she murmured, her breath spurting out in little white puffs, crystallizing in the crisp autumn air.

Vinnie blushed and shuffled his feet. He had never been very good at accepting compliments. "Shouldn't I be saying that to you, Ma? I mean, you saved my hide for the millionth time. But Jake Johnson, huh?" He shoveled tiramisu into his mouth. "I never thought he'd send letters to himself."

"No," Rita sighed. "You wouldn't, Vin."

He was too naïve, too trusting. Rita found this irritating, exasperating—how could her own flesh and blood be so clueless?—but also strangely comforting. The world had quite enough of the hard-hearted and sharp-tongued and was sorely in need of a few gentle souls like Vinnie—provided, of course, that he had a grizzly mamma, or even perhaps a grizzly girlfriend (here, she cast a surreptitious glanced at Ana) to look out for him.

She looked over at Vito, still strong and barrel-chested, but now wrinkled and a bit stoop-shouldered, huddled in the corner with his brother. Making up, perhaps, for lost time. The specter of his younger, more innocent self flickered beside him. It was an odd sensation, to have this fleeting glimpse through time and space, to realize that even her children would someday grow old and die.

It goes so fast, Rita thought, as the images brightened, them dimmed. Like a blink of an eye, like the flicker of a candle. You're young, and then suddenly you're old.

A firefly zipped through young Lydia's ghostly figure and then slipped through the open hole that had once been a window, into the darkness. Rita followed it with her gaze, mesmerized, as it glowed brighter, bigger, until it took the form of a grinning jack o'lantern. But there was nothing malevolent in its visage. It was jolly, with a toothy grin, big, expressive eyes, and thick eyebrows raised in surprise.

Just then, Rita could have sworn, it turned and winked at her. And then the jack o'lantern bounced along, as if astride a galloping steed, until it faded away and disappeared right at the spot where she knew the old stone bridge to be.

"Vinnie, how did you—?"

The words died in her throat as she took in her son's puzzled expression, how his wispy eyebrows drew together in deep concern. Beside him, Ana looked just as worried.

"Do what, Ma? Oh, the projections? Well, I got some old photos and then—"

"No, the—" Rita couldn't bring herself to say the words so she just gestured out to the pitch-black expanse of woods and river. "Over there."

Vinnie followed her gaze and shook his head. "Are you feeling all right, Ma?"

"Maybe you're dehydrated." Ana handed her a water glass, and Rita took a grateful swig before handing it back to Ana.

Rita shook her head, eager to dispel all images of galloping jack o'lanterns, real or imagined. To Ana, she said, "When's your birthday, *cara?*"

"November nineteenth."

"Soon, then." Rita felt a rush of relief. In three weeks, Ana would no longer be a minor. "Why don't you come over for a family dinner to celebrate then? Invite your mother."

Ana and Vinnie exchanged a hopeful glance.

"So you...*approve* of my dating Vinnie?"

"Let's just say that a gentle soul like my Vinnie needs someone like you." Rita clapped them both on the back. "But not until you're eighteen. Until then, *figlio,* you're grounded."

Before Vinnie or Ana could utter a word in response, Sal came up behind Rita and swept her into his arms and onto the dance floor. "I didn't know you could ground a twenty-two-year-old."

"Oh, you can't. But Vinnie doesn't know that. That's his whole problem, isn't it? He's sweet and gullible, totally naïve. The rest of the world will use his gullibility against him, so it's up to me to use it in his favor."

Sal gave a grunt, but it was one of grudging admiration. He jutted his chin in the direction of Penny and Orlando, who were slow dancing, while Rose stewed in the corner, her gaze never leaving them. "That's never gonna happen, is it? Rose and Orlando, I mean."

Rita nestled into Sal's shoulder and pulled him closer. "Poor Rose."

They danced a few more songs, until Rita's feet ached and she saw that the seat next to the widow was now vacant, her granddaughter having gone to the refreshments table. Rita helped herself to a generous slice of her own flourless chocolate cake and plopped down beside Emma. "Is it just as you remember it?"

"Oh, yes!" The widow pointed at the flickering, spectral image of her past self. "Look how young I was. Only a few gray streaks. And the wallpaper—Vinnie recreated it just the way I remember it. The music, too." She inclined her head towards Vinnie's sound system and smiled. Elvis was crooning *Unchained Melody*. Rita smiled too. She recalled how her parents had forbidden her to watch Elvis on television. Elvis the Pelvis, her father had called him. You can't trust a man who moves like that, he had growled. Now the music just seemed quaint, almost wholesome.

"Of course, the food"—the widow winked and nudged Rita with a sharp, bony elbow—"is a lot better than it was then, thanks to you."

"Then why are you eating such a small slice? I thought you wanted full fat, loads of calories."

"That was when I thought I was dying."

"You mean, when you thought you could *goad* someone into killing you."

"Well, it almost worked, didn't it?" The widow regarded Rita with a gimlet eye. "But you can be sure of one thing: I don't plan on dying again soon."

Rita laughed. "Have you ever considered that *you're* the real legend? The living legend of Acorn Hollow?"

The widow waved her hand, and for a moment it seemed almost as though she were caressing the flickering images, the people that they were, the people who had no idea what that fateful night would hold, no idea who they would become. "We're all part of the legend—you, me, Lydia and Hank, Sandro and Vito and Isabella, and now Ana and Vinnie and Jake. Every generation takes the legend and makes it their own, adds to the legend, interprets it. Uses it to give voice to their darkest fears, to explain the inexplicable. Mark my words: As long as there is an Acorn Hollow, there will be a legend. But thanks to you"—the widow cast a fond glance at her newfound granddaughter, then at Vito and Sandro, acknowledged as brothers at last—"this generation's legend has a happy ending."

Ripped from the Pages of Rita Calabrese's
"Top Secret" Recipe Book...

Chicken Cacciatore

One of Sal's favorites, this is great for the meat lover in your life.

In Italy, this is called *pollo alla cacciatore* (chicken, hunter's style) and it comes in a variety of forms, but all are a hearty chicken and vegetable stew. In America, folks are apparently less imaginative and more rigid; woe betide the Italian cook who leaves out the tomatoes and peppers!

This is a delicious and relatively easy version.

3 chicken breasts, bone in and skin on, halved
2 tsp. coarse sea salt
2 tsp. oregano
¼ cup basil leaves, torn
1 tsp. thyme
1 tbsp. fresh rosemary, finely chopped
1 tsp. fresh ground black pepper
½ cup flour
3 tbsp. canola or vegetable oil
1 large red bell pepper, cut into long thin strips
1 sweet yellow onion, diced
4 garlic cloves, minced
¾ cup dry sherry
1 28-ounce can peeled diced San Marzano tomatoes
6 anchovy filets, chopped

Heat oil in deep skillet or wok on medium-high heat.

Mix the seasoning (salt, oregano, basil, thyme, rosemary, and black pepper) together. Add the flour and stir to combine.

Dredge each halved chicken breast in the seasoned flour, then pan fry until browned, about 5 minutes on each side, working in batches if necessary. Once browned on both sides, remove onto plate.

Add onions to the pan and sauté until translucent, a couple of minutes. Then add tomatoes, peppers , and anchovies, and cook about 5 minutes. Add the sherry and simmer until reduced by half, about 3 minutes.

Return the chicken breasts to the pan and turn to coat in the sauce. Simmer over medium-low heat until the chicken is cooked through, about 30 minutes.

Using tongs, transfer chicken onto individual plates, scooping up excess sauce from the pan and drizzling over the chicken.

Carrot-Ginger Soup

A wonderfully warming soup perfect for Fall!

1 lb. baby carrots
1 tbsp. olive oil
1 tbsp. garlic salt
2 tbsp. butter
1 sweet yellow onion, diced
½ tbsp. minced fresh ginger
2 cups chicken broth
2 cups water
Pinch cumin
Pinch salt
Pumpkin seeds, sunflower seeds, and/or chopped chives for garnish (optional)

Preheat the oven to 375 degrees. Place the carrots in a greased large glass baking dish, in a single layer. Toss with olive oil to coat, then sprinkle with garlic salt. Roast carrots, turning over once during roasting, until they are fork-tender and blistered, about 1 hour.

Melt the butter in a large soup pot. Add diced onions and stir until translucent. Add ginger, carrots, chicken broth, water, cumin, and salt.

Bring to a boil, reduce the heat to medium low, and cover. Simmer about 45 minutes, then turn off heat and let cool slightly.

Puree with a stick blender or puree in batches in a blender. Top with garnish as desired and serve hot.

Gnocchi alla Sorrentina

My go-to dish for the vegetarians in my life! It's a classic comfort dish oozing cheesy goodness.

This dish was supposedly invented by a sixteenth-century Sorrento tavern keeper who was experimenting with two then exotic New World foods, potatoes (an ingredient in the gnocchi) and tomatoes (which reached Italy from the Aztec Empire by way of Spain). In keeping with the spirit of culinary innovation, I've swapped ricotta gnocchi for the potato gnocchi; I think it goes better with the buffalo milk mozzarella.

For the gnocchi:

8 oz. full-fat ricotta, drained for several hours until excess moisture removed
¾ cup freshly grated Parmesan cheese
1 cup all-purpose flour, plus extra for dusting
1 egg
1 egg yolk
Pinch of nutmeg

For sauce:
2 tbsp. extra virgin olive oil
5 cloves garlic, lightly crushed
4 cups passata (tomato puree)
Pinch of salt
1 tsp. sugar
1 tbsp. balsamic vinegar
1 tsp. dried oregano

¼ cup basil leaves, torn

To assemble:
8 oz. mozzarella di bufala
½ cup grated Parmigiano-Reggiano cheese

To make the gnocchi, combine the gnocchi ingredients and knead a few times until you have a sticky soft dough. Turn onto a work surface lightly dusted with flour and pat into a thick disc. Cut into 8 pieces. Roll each piece into a log about half an inch in diameter, then cut into inch-long segments to form gnocchi. If desired, press each with a fork to make grooved.

Bring a large pot of salted water to a rolling boil. While waiting for it to boil, preheat the oven to 400 degrees and peel and smash the garlic cloves with the back of a large knife. In a second large pot on medium heat, coat with olive oil and add smashed garlic cloves. Do not let them brown. After 1-2 minutes, add passata to the pot. Add salt, sugar, oregano, and balsamic vinegar. Taste and adjust salt and sugar to cut acidity as necessary. Add torn basil leaves. Remove garlic cloves from the sauce.

When the salted water is boiling, add gnocchi.

Take a large glass baking dish and coat with olive oil, then add a ladle of the tomato sauce mixture and spread evenly. When the gnocchi float to the surface of the pot, use a slotted spoon to transfer half of the gnocchi to the baking dish. Top with half the mozzarella. Spoon more sauce on top. Then add the second half of the gnocchi, spoon more sauce on top, then add the other half of the mozzarella. Finish with a layer of sauce and sprinkle with a handful of Parmigiano-Reggiano cheese.

Bake for 20-25 minutes until cheese is slightly brown. Serve hot.

Cranberry Nut Pancakes

The white vinegar in this recipe "sours" the milk to mimic the tangy zip of buttermilk pancakes, not to mention their fluffy texture. For a taste of Fall, serve with real maple syrup and cinnamon whipped butter.

1 and 2/3 cups whole milk
4 tbsp. white vinegar
2 eggs
4 tbsp. butter, melted
2 cups flour
4 tbsp. granulated sugar, plus 2 tbsp. granulated sugar, separated
2 tsp. baking powder
1 tsp. baking soda
1 tsp. salt
¾ cup cranberries, chopped
¼ cup walnuts, chopped
Extra butter for the frying pan

In a large bowl, combine milk with vinegar and allow it to "sour" for 5 minutes. Then whisk eggs and melted butter into the wet ingredients.

In a separate large bowl, combine flour, 4 tbsp. sugar, baking powder, baking soda, and salt. Then mix the dry ingredients into the wet and stir to combine to a smooth batter.

In a third smaller bowl, combine cranberries, walnuts, and 2 tbsp. sugar.

Put two pads of butter in the frying pan. Once the pan sizzles if you put a drop of water in it, spoon batter into the pan and tilt the pan to spread into an even thickness. Once little bubbles form on the surface, sprinkle the cranberry mixture on top. With a spatula, gently lift up the bottom to monitor the bottom of the pancake; when it is golden brown, flip and cook on the other side.

Apple Crisp

An apple *crostata* would be more Italian, but there's nothing better than the combination of fresh-from-the-orchard apples and crunchy oats.

For the topping:

¾ cups flour
2/3 cup brown sugar, packed
Pinch of salt
6 tbsp. butter (3/4 stick)
1 cup steel-cut oats

For the filling:

5 cups McIntosh or other tart baking apples
1/2 cup granulated sugar
1 tsp. ground cinnamon

Preheat oven to 375 degrees. Grease 8" diameter round pie or cake pan. Peel, core, and quarter apples, then slice thinly. Add sugar and cinnamon to apples and mix to coat apples evenly. In a separate large bowl, mix flour, salt, and brown sugar, then cut in butter with a pastry blender until flour and sugar mixture is studded with tiny gold nuggets of butter. Add in oats and stir to combine. Spread apple mixture evenly in greased baking dish, then spread oat and flour mixture evenly on top. Bake 50-60 minutes until top is a deep golden brown. Serve warm with vanilla ice cream or gelato.

Pumpkin Cheesecake

The oldest known recipe for cheesecake (called "Savilium") was written down by the ancient Roman statesman and historian Cato. It was a mix of goats' milk ricotta, honey, eggs, and flour, cooked in a terracotta pot, and sprinkled with poppy seeds. Rather than considering it a dessert, Romans consumed it throughout the meal, perhaps as a palate cleanser.

The recipe travelled to Roman Britain and from there to the New World!

Modern-day Italians, particularly in and around Rome, continue this tradition of preparing cheesecake with goats' milk ricotta, the queen of all dessert cheeses and the key ingredient in both cannoli and cassata. (Though modern-day Romans leave out the flour and the poppy seeds!) Some Italian cooks add mascarpone, the cheese used in tiramisu, to impart a creamier texture, but I've gone a step further and omitted the ricotta altogether, adding a little cream cheese to the mascarpone to firm up the texture.

While pumpkins (*zucca*, more like squash) are popular ingredients in Italian cooking, Italians are purists about their cheesecakes, preferring the natural flavor of the cheese to dominate without added flavors other sometimes a mild hint of citrus. But the great thing about being Italian-American is that you can borrow from both culinary traditions, and so I happily incorporate other flavors—and in this one, the pumpkin flavor is strong!

For the crust:

2 cups gingersnaps
¼ cup white sugar
¼ tsp. salt
6 tbsp. melted butter

For the filling:

8 oz. cream cheese
16 oz. mascarpone cheese
1 cup white sugar
3 eggs
1 15 oz. can solid-pack pureed pumpkin
½ cup heavy whipping cream
2 tsp. vanilla
1 ½ tsp. cinnamon
¼ tsp. ground cloves

Preheat the oven to 325 degrees. Brush the inside of a 9-inch springform circular pan with 1 tsp. of melted butter.

Place the gingersnaps in a large Ziploc bag, close securely, and then pulverize into crumbs by crushing with a rolling pin. (Trust me, this is very satisfying! Alternatively, you can reduce to crumbs in a food processor.) Then mix the remaining crust ingredients, including the rest of the melted butter, into the crumbs until the mixture resembles wet sand. Press mixture into the bottom of the pan and ½" up the sides. Bake until the crust starts to brown slightly, 12-15 minutes. Remove pan from oven and allow to cool.

Beat the cream cheese and mascarpone until smooth. Then blend in the sugar and then the eggs one at a time. Next, stir in cream, pumpkin (removing any excess liquid first), vanilla, cinnamon, and cloves until thoroughly blended. Pour cheese mixture into the crust.

Place the cheesecake on a baking sheet on a middle rack in the oven. Place a pan of water on a rack below this, which will maintain humidity levels in the oven during baking to reduce the risk of cracks in your cheesecake. Bake until cheesecake center is firm even when the pan is jiggled, about 1 ½ hours. Turn off oven and leave door ajar to cool. When near room temperature, cool in the refrigerator. Serve topped with whip cream.

ABOUT THE AUTHOR

Maureen Klovers is the author of the Jeanne Pelletier mystery series set in Washington, D.C., as well as the memoir *In the Shadow of the Volcano: One Ex-Intelligence Official's Journey through Slums, Prisons, and Leper Colonies to the Heart of Latin America.* A confirmed Italophile, Maureen has studied Italian in Rome and enjoys testing Italian recipes (many of which make their way into Rita's cookbook!). She lives outside of Washington, D.C., with her husband, Kevin; her daughter, Kathleen; and their black Labrador Retriever, Nigel.

For more information on Maureen and her writing, or to schedule her for a book signing or book club event, please visit her Facebook author page.

AND IF YOU ENJOYED THIS BOOK...

Please post a review on amazon.com, goodreads.com, bookbub.com, or your own blog! Thank you!